D0332176

PRAISE FOR ANDREA CHRISTENSON

HANGIN' BY A MOMENT

This moving story of two broken characters overcoming trauma, finding their inner courage and strength, and falling in love along the way in the most charming small town imaginable blends all my favorite elements of a novel into a delicious, delightful concoction...perfect for your next summer indulgence!

— BETSY ST. AMANT, AUTHOR OF *THE KEY TO LOVE* & *TACOS FOR TWO*

CAN'T BUY ME LOVE

From a sassy meet cute, to hilarious shenanigans, this sweet romance will keep you turning the pages. If you love Hallmark movies, you won't want to miss this Cinderella tale.

— TARI FARIS, AUTHOR OF THE RESTORING HERITAGE SERIES

I love a small-town romance, especially when I get to travel back to one of my all-time favorite fictional small towns—Deep Haven, MN. If you're a fan of Susan May Warren's Deep Haven books, then you will enjoy seeing favorite characters pop up in *Can't Buy Me Love*. With this fresh take on the Cinderella fairytale and heart-warming romance, *Can't Buy Me Love* is a wonderful sweet read for a snowy afternoon.

— LISA JORDAN, AWARD-WINNING AUTHOR FOR
LOVE INSPIRED

A NOTE FROM SUSIE MAY

I love a great story about a second chance, but when Andrea came to me with a story about an ex-con, I thought...hmmm. Would readers go for a hero who's done prison time?

Maybe.

But then Andrea explained the story to me—and I got it. First, the theme is fantastic. Second chances for criminals...for sinners. For people like you and me. Done.

Secondly, Jack Stewart is an ex-con a gal could love. Former para-rescue trooper, jailed for something that he regrets, with a deep need to find a place to start over. (Deep Haven seems like the right place, doesn't it?) I fell in love with Jack from the moment he walked out of the prison doors, and I know you will too.

And then Andrea told me about the heroine...Colleen Decker. The spoiled, sassy teenager from *You Don't Know Me* (and Ella's friend from *Can't Buy Me Love*).

Colleen, who was in desperate need of a second chance with readers. Colleen, who is nursing a Dark Moment Story that I gave her in a previous novel. Yes, please, somebody help her!

Andrea to the rescue. She really flexed her rescue and adventure skills in this books, putting Jack and Colleen together on the Crisis Response Team. I was so impressed with her stepping up to the plate to create some authentic, thrilling scenes. And then there's Deep Haven in the fall, with pumpkins and hot cocoa and a broken but sweet and healing man who also needs rescue...

And finally, you'll see Annalise, Nathan, and the whole Decker family again. There's a moment in this book that brought me to real tears.

I love this story and I know you will too. There are second chances for everyone. Anyone.

Especially in Deep Haven.

Enjoy! (Hot cocoa and a warm blanket are optional.) Thank you for spending time in Deep Haven!

Warmly,

Susie May

To my family.
You make each moment worth hanging onto. Thank you for all the
laughter you bring into my life.

HANGIN' BY A MOMENT

SUSAN MAY WARREN
ANDREA CHRISTENSON

sunrise
PUBLISHING

CHAPTER 1

*I*t was a little thing. Stupid really.

Colleen Decker had already made it through six hours of her ER shift at Hennepin County Medical Center in Minneapolis without any problems. Sure, there had been that kid who'd kicked her, but she didn't blame him—it hurt to have gravel cleaned out of a road rash from a bicycle incident.

And then there'd been the psych patient who thought he was Genghis Khan and ran around the ER shouting about taking over the world before finally being subdued by a few of her larger nurse colleagues.

And don't even ask about the woman who came in with stage 4 lung cancer.

These patients didn't faze her. All in a day's work at HCMC.

No, it had to be something small. Embarrassing.

A flash of a frat boy's bicep tattoo, the crash of an instrument tray falling to the ground, and suddenly Colleen had jumped for the nearest space she could cram herself into.

Clearly, she hadn't licked the past. In fact, it had found her in this 12x12-foot storage closet. She curled herself into a smaller ball under the shelf full of cleaning products and rubbed her hands up and down her arms, the scrubs she wore making a swish with each pass.

"Get a grip." She spoke into the silence. A dim beam of light shone under the door, illuminating a stack of sheets, folded hospital tight. She closed her eyes. Concentrated on her breathing. "You have to go back out there."

Without warning, the door flew open. Colleen's head shot up. Julie Brage filled the open space, the light from the outer hallway shining around her.

"I've been looking everywhere for you." Julie crossed the few steps, crouched down, put her hands on Colleen's knees, and looked into her eyes. "It's okay to be freaked out."

"I'm not freaked out." Maybe if she repeated the mantra often enough, she would believe it. She reached up and adjusted her strawberry-blonde ponytail, pulling the elastic tighter around her hair.

Julie sighed. "Colleen, you have been missing from your unit for fifteen minutes, are sitting in the supply closet next to a wet mop, and you jumped a foot in the air when I came in. That says *freaked out.*"

"I just didn't expect anyone to find me here. That's all. I needed a minute to myself."

Julie speared her with a look.

Okay. Maybe more like fifteen minutes.

"I'm sorry. I know we're busy. I'll come right out and get back to work." As a nurse on the night shift, Colleen knew the importance of each team member. They couldn't afford for her to be absent. She stood to her feet. Brushed herself off. Took a deep breath.

"You'll do nothing of the kind." Julie stood as well, crossed her arms. "Are you in here because of Genghis Kahn? He's been moved to the psych unit."

"No."

"Colleen, I know you said you were fine after the incident

last night but you've been jumpy your whole shift, and then you left the unit without telling anyone you were taking a break."

"I'm sorry. It won't happen again." She took a step forward... or tried to, anyway. Julie refused to budge.

"This isn't about following procedure. I'm concerned about you." Julie gentled her tone, uncrossed her arms.

"You don't need to be. I've had a short break, and now I'm fine."

"Look. Anyone would be having a hard time adjusting after that trauma."

Don't get too close. The police officer's voice from the night before snaked through her mind. *This guy is a lot more dangerous than he looks. Don't let the good looks and charm fool you.*

"The whole thing is my fault anyway." Like a drum beat the words pulsed—*my fault, my fault.* If she'd followed procedure, it wouldn't have happened. She touched the Band-Aid on her neck.

"Are you kidding me? How is it your fault that a criminal held you at knifepoint?" Julie tossed her head, her light brown curls brushing her shoulders.

The events of her shift well before dawn Sunday morning washed in again. She saw herself leaning over the patient to give him a drink of water. Saw the doctor spilling the instrument pan.

"I should have listened to the officer. I got too close to the patient."

"How could you have known that he would find that scalpel and cut himself loose from the bindings holding him to the bed? You trusted your instincts to help someone who was hurting."

Please, just a sip of water. The criminal's voice in her head this time. *Help me out here. I can't do it myself. My cup's right over there.*

"Yeah, and my instincts were wrong." Just like always. "I should have stayed on my side of the room and let the officer and the doctor handle it." She closed her eyes and took a deep breath, the air in the closet pungent with bleach and orange-scented cleaner. When she opened her eyes, Julie was looking straight at her.

"Colleen, there is no way you could've known that things would go down that way."

True, she hadn't known that the gunshot victim in her ER room would take advantage of a Code Blue in the room next door. She also hadn't foreseen that he would be fast enough to pull her to his chest and hold the scalpel to her neck in a desperate attempt to escape. "I guess you're right."

"Of course I am." Julie put her hands on her hips and grinned at Colleen. "I'm always right. Listen, I came to find you because Nicole came in early and asked me to track you down. I think she's going to recommend you take a few days off."

"Thanks for the heads-up. I don't really think I need any time off." As long as no more criminals came in for treatment or pans of instruments crashed to the floor or tattooed men reminded her of events from years before...

Yeah. She'd be fine.

She relaxed her arms. Rolled her shoulders. "I'll go find Nicole right now." Colleen brushed past Julie and walked out of the closet.

Taking a left, she walked to the central hub of the ER. At the corner of the main desk stood Nicole Miller, the ER nurse supervisor.

"Ah, Colleen. There you are." The heavyset woman in navy scrubs turned toward her. "It seems I missed all the excitement last night."

Colleen tugged at the hem of her scrub top. "Oh, you know, just another routine day in the HCMC ER. It wouldn't feel right if there wasn't some excitement." She tried for a jaunty smile.

"I've read the report of the incident. Could you come into my office for a few minutes? There are some items I want to go over with you."

Colleen glanced at her watch, 5:30 a.m. Nicole really was in early. Usually she didn't grace their floor until after 7 a.m. on Mondays. She followed the older nurse into the semi-private space adjacent to the busy ER. Nicole left the door open, then sat down behind her desk and gestured for Colleen to have a seat.

"As I said, I read the report from last night." Nicole picked up a sheet of paper from the desk. "Was this your first time assisting in a room with a prisoner?"

Located near downtown Minneapolis, Minnesota, the Hennepin County Medical Center regularly treated gunshot victims. They also saw many patients who came in under armed guard. The night before hadn't been anything unusual.

No. The problem had been with Colleen.

"I've been in multiple situations where there was a police presence in the room, including violent criminals." She rubbed her damp palms across her scrubs.

"And are you aware of our protocol for those situations?"

Oh, she knew the protocol all right. Don't touch the patient. Wait for the police officer to give permission before approaching the gurney. Do what the doctor asks you to do, and *only* what the doctor asks you to do. "Yes, I know it."

Nicole jotted a few things on the paper she held. "Was there any particular reason you felt you could ignore it last night?"

"I don't know. He seemed so harmless." Even to her, the excuse sounded lame. She fought the urge to touch the Band-Aid on her neck—the one covering the small cut the scalpel had left behind.

"You thought the man, this Joseph Terranova, who came in strapped to a gurney, under armed guard, with a gunshot wound seemed harmless?" Putting down the document, Nicole sat back in her chair. Waited.

Colleen thought about arguing that he had a kind face and

5

really nice clothes. And wow, that sounded stupid even as she thought it. "Um. I don't know what to say."

"No, Colleen, *I* don't know what to say. Your actions endangered the whole ER. I'm just glad that officer was able to act quickly enough that no one was hurt."

A replay of the night before flew into Colleen's mind. The man's arm around her, scalpel at her throat. A glimpse of a tattoo where his shirtsleeve was rolled up. The police officer's hands outstretched in a "calm down" motion. The movie picked up speed and she saw another officer appear in the door, Taser in hand. Again, she felt the stiffening of the body behind her as the darts at the end of the wires hit their target. The scalpel dropped to the floor with a ping. A sharp pain bloomed on her neck.

Her breath sped up. She blinked several times and the images faded.

Nicole folded her hands. Laid them on the desk. Her gaze gentled. "I think you should take some time off."

"Are you firing me?"

"No. Not at all. I'm just wondering if it isn't a good idea for you to take a short leave of absence."

"I'm fine." If she kept saying it, maybe it would stick.

"That's not what the rest of the team is telling me. I heard you've been jumpy all night. You've been forgetting things. Making simple mistakes. There's no shame in taking time off. Working the ER, especially one like ours, is stressful. It can get to you after a while. Even if something like last night hadn't happened." Nicole unlaced her hands and shuffled a few papers on her desk. "I see that you are already taking a day off later this week."

"Yes, I'm going home for my grandma's anniversary party. She remarried eight years ago, and my parents are throwing them a party." Maybe now would be a good time to stop rambling. Nicole didn't care about her family history.

"Okay. Why don't you take the rest of the week off and all of next week as well? I really think it will do you some good."

The thought of home, of her mother's arms, and the memory of the smell of something delicious in her grandmother's oven flooded her. She bet the late September leaves were beautiful right now. Going home to Deep Haven for a while suddenly didn't seem such a terrible idea.

"You're right. Some time off wouldn't hurt. But I'll only go for a week. I'll be back before you have time to miss me."

"Fine, take a week. Call me next Monday and we'll see about you taking more time than that. I think you should at least consider taking a month or more."

Colleen caught her supervisor looking steadily at her. In her eye, a look of...pity? There was no reason for Nicole to pity her. She was all right. She would go home, eat some of her grandmother's pie, and be back in a week.

She was just fine. She'd prove it.

~

For the first time in a year, Winston "Win" Stewart would be on the other side of the razor wire with the Stillwater, MN, prison at his back.

An officer came to his cell and tossed him a duffel. Then he told him to pack. Win gathered up his few belongings, shoved them into the bag and paused, glancing around the 6x8 cell.

Oh, couldn't forget that—he plucked off the photo he'd hung on the wall the first day he'd arrived. In it, his father smiled at his stepmom, an arm slung around his half brother. The perfect family.

Good thing he wasn't in this one—he wouldn't want to ruin the image.

The inmates called out to him as he walked behind the officer toward the release office.

7

"Don't forget us, man."

"Never thought you should be in here anyway."

"Good luck on the other side!"

"You got a raw deal. Good thing they're springing you today."

He stood, waiting his turn for out-processing. Another officer handed him a bag that contained his wallet, cell phone, the contents of his pockets, and the clothes he'd been booked in. Win quickly changed out of his prison-issue clothes, thrusting on a pair of blue jeans and pulling a grey T-shirt over his head. He ran a hand through his dark blond hair to tame it, glancing for one last time into the mirror of the small dress-out room.

Iron-blue eyes stared back at him. He barely recognized the man in the mirror.

Win neatly re-folded the few other items of clothing he had and tucked them, his Bible, and a few other books into the duffel.

Once outside the prison gates, he took in a lungful of September air, trying to breathe in freedom.

Win looked around, knowing he wouldn't spot his dad's Lincoln Town Car, but hoping to see it all the same.

Good thing he'd arranged for his friend Boone Buckam to pick him up.

"Win! Over here!"

Holding a hand to shield his eyes from the Monday afternoon sunshine, Win spotted his buddy leaning next to a black pickup. Boone straightened, waved him over. Win's white knight was dressed in black slim jeans, a leather jacket, and shades perched on top of his dark blond hair.

"I appreciate you showing up." The two shook hands. Then Boone reached out with his other arm and Win found himself on the receiving end of a man hug. He hadn't known Boone was a hugger. They hadn't been allowed to even shake hands inside the prison. "It's nice to see you without the officers watching our every move."

For the past year, Boone had visited once a month or so. But the last two months, he hadn't come at all. Win had been surprised he'd offered to pick him up today.

"Good to see you in the sunshine, Win." Boone took the handle of the duffel and lightened his load. "Let me put this in the truck."

"Thanks. And I've been thinking—a new life needs a new name. It's not Win anymore. Call me Jack." It wasn't a totally new identity—Jack was his middle name. But Jack wanted to bury his past. Preferably deep where no one could find it.

"All right, Jack it is. Want a real meal?" Boone threw Jack's duffel into the back of his truck.

"After twelve months of prison food? You bet I do."

Jack sank into the front seat of Boone's truck with a sigh. Being outside the gates suddenly seemed…overwhelming. After a year of being locked in a cell, and the military dictating his moves before that, so much freedom ahead of him loomed like a cloud. It remained to be seen whether it brought a storm. He wasn't even sure where he was staying tonight. His dad's house could be an option, but his father hadn't been in contact much during his incarceration. All the same, Jack should let him know he'd been released.

"Mind if I plug in my phone?"

Boone turned the key and the truck roared to life. "I have a charging cord in the glove box."

Jack rummaged around in the small compartment, found the cord, and plugged it into the truck's cigarette lighter. After a few moments, his phone pinged on. He knew connecting with his dad was a long shot but maybe… he thumbed a text into his cell phone. *Dad, I'm out. Cell phone is still working. See you soon?*

No reply.

Jack and Boone made small talk as they drove to a casual

diner tucked beside the road along the cliff overlooking the St. Croix River. "This place has the best burgers. You'll love it."

Once they'd settled in their booth, Jack flipped open his menu. Hmm, pretty standard diner food. The next page listed their special offerings, including a Southwest barbecue burger and mac and cheese pancakes. Interesting.

"I love a good burger." He'd have to give those pancakes a try the next time he was out this way. Jack leaned back in his seat. "I haven't had a chance to say thank you yet."

Boone waved off the comment. "It was nothing."

"It was *not* nothing. I'd still be in prison if it wasn't for you." Boone's eyewitness testimony had cut his sentence down to just one year.

"Something about your whole case bothered me from the start. Don't forget, I was there. I saw the whole thing. You got a bad rap. The court overreacted because of your father. David Barelli's family never should have pressed charges." Their food arrived, each plate holding a burger the size of a softball and smelling rich and savory. Steaming, golden French fries piled over the rest of both plates, almost burying the small ketchup cup perched near the center. "Listen. You might be a felon, but you didn't kill anyone."

"Well, a felon's a felon. No one asks you what crime you were convicted of—everyone assumes it's murder."

"I still think the year you served more than paid for your so-called crime. And I'll tell that to anyone who asks."

"I appreciate it. I owe you one." More than one, really. If it weren't for Boone's intervention, Jack would have done at least twelve more years. "What have you been up to these days? It's been a while since you've visited. I thought maybe you'd forgotten me."

Boone hadn't lied. This place made great burgers. The savory beef melted in his mouth. He would've added a dash of pepper for a little heat, but otherwise it was delicious. The smoked cheddar cheese oozed perfectly and the tangy BBQ complemented the sweet, fried onions. He chased the bite with a few fries. He couldn't get food like this in prison, not even when he was the cook.

"I've actually relocated to a small town about five hours away, up on the North Shore. Deep Haven."

"Huh. I never thought you'd leave the city life. You did good work as a detective in Kellogg. I should know—I directly benefitted."

Boone wouldn't look him in the eye. "Yeah. Plans change. I went up there about two months ago for…a change of pace and ended up staying."

"Oh, so it's a girl."

The sheepish grin Boone shot him told Jack that he'd gotten it right in one guess.

Boone pointed a French fry at him. "I actually wanted to talk to you about Deep Haven. I think you should come back there with me. I've got a lead on a job for you, and even an apartment."

"I don't know, man. My dad is probably expecting me to come home to Kellogg."

"Is he even in the city these days?"

Jack's father was a congressman, campaigning for his fourth term in office. He divided his time between Washington DC and his home on Lake Kellogg. "He's around now, for the next week or so."

Still no text from his dad. Probably was afraid the photographers would catch him visiting his criminal son.

Jack took another bite of his burger. Gave himself a minute as he chewed and swallowed. "Tell me more about this job."

Boone dragged a few of his own fries through the ketchup on his plate. "To tell you the truth, it's not much. The VFW needs a new short-order cook. I remembered how much you enjoyed cooking, especially stuff like this." He gestured around the cafe with a ketchup-laden fry. "I thought you could do that for a while, but then I have another opportunity for you to consider."

Hmm. Hiding out in a small town while flipping burgers wouldn't have sounded appealing to Win. Win was more about action.

Saving the day.

Being the hero.

Jack wasn't Win anymore, though. Hadn't been since he'd been home from Iraq and his stint in Pararescue. He refused to allow his mind to wander to what had happened that first weekend back in Kellogg—the weekend that had sealed Win's fate. But really, he hadn't felt like "Win" since long before that.

He scooped the rest of his burger into his mouth.

"Deep Haven has started a Crisis Response Team." Boone put his hand up, silencing Jack before he'd even started to say anything. "Hear me out on this. They asked me to head it up. We recently acquired a medical chopper, and we have a local pilot. What we need next is a flight nurse. Someone to go with the patient transport. Someone trained in search and rescue as well as the medical pieces." Boone paused. Looked him in the eye. "I'd like that person to be you."

"Me?" Jack almost choked on his last bite. "No. I'm no hero."

"You'd be great at it. I know you have the certification from your time with the Air Force Pararescue. Your military service will have given you a steady hand in an emergency. I know you saw some action and made it through with a cool head. We can't just keep grabbing a nurse from the local hospital. They won't know how to deal with the extreme conditions we see out on these rescue situations. We need someone with grit."

Around them, the cafe hummed. Two tables over, a dish clattered to the floor. At the counter, a waitress rang up an order.

"How do you know all this?" It wasn't like Jack sat around

shooting the breeze about his time in the Air Force. Not after the way it had ended.

"When you were overseas, I saw your father around town from time to time. He liked to brag about his oldest son." At Jack's look, he added, "In a good way. A proud father. Also, I still have a few contacts in the military. Word gets around about the good ones."

Huh.

Jack's phone chimed with a text. He glanced at the screen. His dad.

Sorry I couldn't be there to pick you up. I trust Detective Buckam came as promised?

He thumbed in a reply. *Boone was there. He's feeding me lunch.*

The phone showed the flashing dots that indicated a reply was coming.

Glad you're being taken care of. Reporters camped outside. Do you have a place to lie low for a while?

So much for going home. He showed his phone to Boone.

"Looks like I'll be coming to Deep Haven after all. I guess it's my only option right now." Plus, he owed Boone, didn't he? He wouldn't be a free man if Boone hadn't stood up for him.

"I'd hoped you'd say that." Boone tipped the last of his drink back and signaled for the bill. "You're going to love it up there, I promise. It's a great place for a new start."

Five or so hours later, Jack could see what Boone meant.

They turned a corner and the skyline opened up, Lake Superior in all her shining glory as it flowed away and into the distance. The inland sea, as some called it, was calm with an early evening stillness, dotted with boats and framed by trees that wore their fall colors. In the Air Force, Jack had visited seashores on five different continents. From what he could see, Lake Superior lived up to its nickname.

The town was smaller than he'd pictured on the way up. Restaurants, an outdoor shop, and a few other businesses hugged the shoreline. The setting sun stained everything golden.

Boone pulled into a parking lot. "This is it. Home sweet home."

"This is a coffee shop." The two-story building in front of them stood next to a few others, its dark brown siding aged by the weather. A sign above the door read Java Cup.

"The owner, Kathy, rents out the room upstairs. She gave me the key this morning."

They got out of the car and Jack breathed in the crisp, fall air, trying once again to find some sense of freedom. He rolled his shoulders then grabbed his bag out of the back of Boone's truck and followed his friend up the stairs clinging to the side of the building.

Boone unlocked the door and tossed him the key. "I'll let you get settled in. You don't need a babysitter."

"Thanks."

"I'll come by tomorrow to help you get some wheels. We can stop at the VFW too, get that job worked out."

"I appreciate it."

Boone slapped him on the shoulder and disappeared down the stairs.

Jack stepped into the cool interior of his temporary home. A small kitchen and dining room, with two doors leading into what he assumed were a bathroom and bedroom. The room was dim, so he flipped on a light switch. A lamp in the corner blinked on, illuminating a sparsely decorated space. A table, a couple of chairs, a couch, and coffee table—they all looked hotel room standard, but comfortable. On the wall hung a single picture. A sunny, tropical island with palm trees caught mid-sway. Between the trees hung a brightly colored hammock. An idyllic spot to swing, a cold drink clutched in his hand. Without worries.

Maybe someday.

In another life.

Making his way into the bedroom, he scanned the space. A dresser stood against one wall. He crossed to it, opened the biggest drawer, and dumped all his clothes and other possessions into it.

There. Unpacked.

Now he just had to lie low and figure out how to start over.

CHAPTER 2

*C*oming home had been the right thing to do.

It almost felt like she'd never left, really.

Colleen ran her finger across the top of her dresser. Her old room was impeccable. She didn't expect her mom to tolerate dust, but she was always surprised to come home and find that her room was basically unchanged from how she'd left it in high school. Walking in felt like she was eighteen all over again. Never mind the fact she had graduated top of her class at the University of Minnesota and had been working in the HCMC ER for two years, seeing her Justin Bieber and One Direction posters on the wall took her straight back to senior year.

Her shoulders relaxed a little. When she'd arrived last night, her parents had been surprised but pleased. She'd put off their questions, only telling them that her boss had given her a few extra days off.

"This way I can help you get ready for the party," she'd told her mom after dumping her bag in her room and finding a spot on the sofa. Annalise Decker had never needed anyone to help. She was the perfect PTA mom, always volunteering for committees and hosting elaborate parties. Colleen's Grandma Helen's wedding anniversary party was sure to be amazing, with or without her assistance.

"I will be glad for the help." Her mom looked so much like an older version of Colleen, people often wondered if they were sisters. "Your grandma hasn't been as spry lately, so I'm doing most of the work myself. Plus, Frank fell last week. We told you that, right? He sprained his wrist and fractured his hip."

"I would never tell Grandma this, but having an eight-year anniversary party is a little strange, right?" Her grandmother's second marriage was actually somewhat scandalous. After many years of widowhood, she'd fallen in love with Annalise Decker's Witness Security agent, Frank Harrison.

Colleen had caught a look that passed between her mom and dad. "What? Am I missing something?"

"Mom always liked celebrating the little things. I guess she figured why wait for a big anniversary when she can celebrate her love anytime? After all, if we only celebrate the big things, we start to take the little things for granted." A graying version of her father had sat across from her. Colleen didn't remember him growing older. Not that he was any less handsome. He always carried himself with a slightly dignified air. She supposed it was because, as a real estate agent, he was always showcasing things. After a while, it rubbed off.

Not long after their conversation, she'd headed to bed, claiming a disrupted sleep schedule from working overnight shifts.

Now she looked at the clock sitting on the table next to her bed—9:43 a.m. Her best friend, Ella Bradley, was coming by in a few minutes to pick her up for coffee. Turning her back to the room of memories, Colleen ambled down to the living room to wait.

Her mom sat on the couch, flipping through a magazine. She glanced up at Colleen. "Oh, hi, honey. Come sit by me." She shifted over on the couch, leaving room for Colleen on the other end. "We didn't get much chance to talk last night. How are you doing, really?"

"I'm good, Mom. It feels like I haven't been home in a long time. Was it really last March?"

Her mom nodded. "That sounds right. We came down over the summer, but you haven't been back since helping Ella move in. How are things at your apartment? Are your neighbors still bothering you? Still playing loud music all night?"

"It's been quiet recently. Maybe they moved out. Oh! I got new throw pillows for my couch. I went with teal like you recommended."

"I'm sure they're beautiful. You've made a cute little nest for yourself down there." Her mother set the magazine on a table near the couch. "Any boys I should know about?"

"Mom, really?"

Her mom gave her a wide-eyed look. "What? A mom has a right to ask." She smiled. "That's fine. You don't have to tell me. I just hope you're not interested in any more wild boys like Tucker."

"Tucker wasn't a bad boy." Except, the memory of the time he'd snuck into her room late one night crept into her mind. And then there was the drinking... Okay, so he had been a little wild. It didn't help that his bad boy behavior was one of the things that had attracted her to him. But she was beyond that now. "No boys at all. Good or bad."

Her mother patted Colleen's hand. "I'm sure God will bring the right person into your life in His timing. Would you pass me my water? I left it right over there."

Please, just a sip of water... My cup's right over there.

Colleen's vision blurred. Her breath sped up—

"Colleen. Colleen, can you hear me?" Her mom's voice broke through the fog and a hand touched her shoulder.

Colleen closed her eyes. Opened them.

She stared at her knees until the tunnel in front of her eyes opened up and she could fully see again, though spots danced at the edges of her vision. Her heart rate slowed.

"I don't know what that was." Bracing her hands on her thighs, she concentrated on breathing in through her nose and out through her mouth. She didn't dare glance at her mom. Her concerned look would only undo Colleen's fragile peace.

Her mom squeezed her shoulder. "Honey, I think that was a panic attack."

"No, it couldn't be. I'm fine."

The doorbell rang and Colleen jerked.

Her mom raised an eyebrow.

"I'm *fine.*" She headed to the door, her mother trailing by a step or two.

"Fine. Have fun catching up with Ella. We'll talk about this later."

Colleen opened the door to her friend standing on the front porch. In her jeans, tall boots, and chunky short sleeve sweater, Ella looked like the princess of autumn. Her face lit in a smile at Colleen.

"Hiya, you!" Ella squealed and threw her arms around Colleen. "It's so good to see you."

Colleen laughed. Ella was always good medicine. "It's good to be seen."

Ella pulled back and grinned at her. "Ready for coffee?"

"Always." Colleen turned and kissed her mom's cheek. "Love you, Mom. See you later."

Her mom waved as they walked down the sidewalk toward town.

"I'm so glad you could come up to Deep Haven early. I have some trade shows I'll be traveling to over the next few weeks. I was afraid I would miss you when you came up for your grand-parents' party."

A light breeze blew off Lake Superior, rattling the trees in a neighbor's lawn. A leaf fluttered through the air and landed at

Colleen's feet. She picked it up. Half green and half sunset red, it was right in the middle of change.

"It'll be good for me to get out of the city for a while, I think." Colleen twirled the leaf between her thumb and forefinger as they continued walking. "I love my job there, and I love my place, but a slower pace for a week or so will be good."

"You sound like you're trying to convince yourself of that." Ella paused outside the Java Cup and looked squarely at her. "Is there something you aren't telling me?"

"No, it was just a long weekend. Same old ER craziness." Or at least she wanted to believe that.

"Well, if you're looking for a change of pace, I might have something for you."

Ella pushed open the door and Colleen trailed her into the coffee shop. A warm caramel scent infused the air with comfort, and the whirring of the cappuccino machine provided a pleasant white noise to the atmosphere. The specials board listed a maple cinnamon latte, and they both ordered a tall one before claiming a table in the corner.

"Okay, what's this change of pace you were talking about?"

Ella leaned forward, her blue eyes sparkling. "You know how Adrian bought a helicopter for the new Deep Haven Crisis Response Team?"

Her friend had told her all about the CRT over the summer. Ella's billionaire boyfriend factored heavily into those conversations. Not that Colleen minded—she was happy for her friend. Really. She wished she could find love like that. Someone who would cherish her and make her feel safe and loved for who she was inside. Kind of like the love her parents had. When their relationship was tested, they'd pulled through because that was what love did—it stayed true.

She focused back on what Ella was saying. "For now the CRT has a pilot, but they have to grab a nurse from the hospital in town anytime they fly out. I think even Rhino from the memory care center helps out. The EMTs aren't able to go right now, too much on their plate. What they really need is a flight nurse. Someone who is actually trained in trauma and can think on their feet." Ella took a sip of her coffee, her eyes glinting over the top of her cup. "You should apply for the job."

"Who, me? No. I don't think so." She sat back abruptly, nearly splashing her latte. "I have a great job in Minneapolis."

"I get it, I do. You work night shift in one of the busiest, most dangerous hospitals. So glamorous." Ella didn't exactly roll her eyes, but Colleen could tell she wanted to.

Hey, she did good work at HCMC. Her floor saved countless lives. And, okay, she supposed the adrenaline rush factored in too. "It's not just that. I'm trying to move forward with my life. Coming back home just seems..." Her One Direction poster flashed through her mind. "Besides, I don't know how to *rescue* people."

"I'm sure you could be trained to do all that. It can't be harder than the things you've already learned."

Colleen took a long drink of her latte. The cinnamon spice across her taste buds brought with it a sense of home. Her grandmother's kitchen always smelled like cinnamon.

A cool draft hit them as someone opened and shut the front door. A muscled man walked up to the counter and ordered a black coffee. As he raised his arm to adjust his ball cap, his short sleeve inched up. A black-and-red tattoo wound its way over his bicep before disappearing at his shoulder. Colleen saw a shadow of it at the base of his neck.

Heat flushed through her. *Not again.* A loud buzz sounded in her ears.

Ella was giving her a strange look. "Colleen, are you okay?"

Colleen gulped. Gave her head a small shake. "I'll be fine. Just give me a minute."

"You look green. Do you need to put your head between your knees?"

She gave her friend a weak smile. "No. Really."

The man at the counter received his order and left. The door swished open and shut again, and Colleen was grateful for the cool burst of air that brushed over her. Ella got up and grabbed a cup by the water pitcher Kathy always left out. She poured a full amount and brought it back to their table.

"Here, sip some of this."

Colleen complied with her friend's request. No, not request. Order. "Thanks. That helps."

"What was that? Are you sure you're okay?"

"Sorry, when I saw that guy's tattoo, it... It just brought up some bad memories."

"Now I *know* you need to take that job. If you're this edgy because of a stranger's tattoo, you need some time at a slower pace. There's no way you could finish a whole shift at HCMC without seeing a tattoo. At least up here, tattoos are mostly covered in flannel for like six months out of the year. C'mon. Finish your drink. We're going to go find Boone."

"Boone?"

"He's the one heading up the Crisis Response Team. He'll have all the info on what you need to do to be certified."

Stepping back out into the fall air, Colleen took a full breath. Sure, she'd hear what Boone had to say. What could it hurt?

After all, coming back to Deep Haven didn't mean she had to stay.

∼

Deep Haven was the perfect place to hide out.

Jack's drive through town this morning confirmed his suspicions. The sleepy little hamlet nestled on the North Shore of Lake Superior bristled with quaint streets and hometown charm. He saw an ice cream shop called Licks and Stuff, something labeled the Art Colony, and a funky little campground with a row of multicolored campers. Unfortunately that place looked abandoned.

Spotting a sign for World's Best Donuts, he filed the address away for future consumption. Around town it looked like there were enough tourists that Jack wouldn't stand out from the regulars, but not enough people that he needed to worry about being recognized. All he wanted now was to keep his head down.

Boone wasn't taking the hint though. He'd picked Jack up from his apartment over the Java Cup early that morning and they'd driven over to the used car lot where Jack had picked out a 2009 Chevy Silverado. Not too flashy, not too new, not too expensive—the truck fit perfectly.

Then he followed Boone to the VFW, housed in a nondescript building downtown. As they walked through the front door, he realized the interior had been updated, probably recently judging by the wood floors and the decor. They walked past the pool tables and pinball machines at the front and headed back to the kitchen.

The door swung open, and a leggy blonde stood in the doorway. "Hello, Boone. And you must be Jack. I'm Signe Netterlund. C'mon back and I'll show you your space."

She led them into a masterpiece of stainless steel. This kitchen was a cook's dream. A center island grill and fry station surrounded by prep areas, storage shelves, a large cooler, and a walk-in freezer. In a nod to history, the wall next to the door held photos of past staff.

He could see himself in this kitchen.

He'd be over at the grill while the other staff moved around him, plating orders and chopping veggies. He'd be able to see and direct everything from his post. A good kitchen had a choreography all its own, each team member part of the dance.

He turned slowly, taking it all in. A throat cleared behind

him. Oh. Must have been daydreaming longer than he'd thought.

Signe held out a menu. "Take a look."

He flipped it open, perused the dinner selections. Pretty standard fare. Sandwiches, burgers, fish fry. His mind started buzzing with ideas on how to jazz up the offerings. Maybe he would try adding brie to the turkey sandwich. And lingonberry ketchup.

He'd also love to add in the chicken recipe he'd been working on—Mama Creole's blackened grilled chicken. He could almost taste it now, the memory coming back to him over the two decades since he'd last eaten the dish. In a space like this, he'd have it perfected in no time.

"Can I keep this?" He'd take the menu back to his apartment and jot down some notes about changes he'd like to make.

"No problem." Signe shrugged. "Unless you need anything else, I think you're scheduled for tomorrow night?"

He nodded. "That works for me." He looked around one last time before heading through the swinging door with Boone.

Okay. Yes. This he could do. This job would be the perfect place for a fresh start.

"That takes care of one thing," Boone said to him as they walked to the parking lot. "Why don't you at least come take a look at the Crisis Response Team's headquarters?"

"Boone, I thought we talked about this. I'm not going there again."

"C'mon, Win—"

"Jack."

"Right. Listen, it'll only take a few minutes."

"I don't think so. I should head back to my apartment. Settle in." Liar. The idea of the CRT had spooled around in his mind for the better part of the night, as if it had loosened some unfinished thread.

"I'd like your opinion on something. Follow me." Boone spun on his heel and climbed into his truck.

His opinion. Well, it was nice to be respected. Needed, even. Fine. He got into his own truck and tailed Boone the short distance to the headquarters building a few blocks away. Huh, he could've walked that far.

Perched on the side of the road by the water, the building almost glowed. Its corrugated metal siding gave a nod to the steel blue waves of Lake Superior just beyond the lot. He parked next to a black Tahoe emblazoned with the CRT logo and got out to stand next to Boone.

"Here she is." Boone spread his arms wide. "Come inside. I think you'll be impressed."

Jack followed him inside the building, walked to the back. Stopped short. Stared. The room opened to a two-and-a-half-story atrium-slash-bay. Inside, a 40-foot climbing wall reminiscent of some he'd seen at military training facilities anchored one huge wall. An array of workout gear held a position under a twenty-foot picture window. Though the space needed some work—he could see areas without trim and other places that needed a few coats of paint—the overall effect was quite impressive.

He gave a low whistle. "You're right. This is really something."

"We've had some pretty generous donors. And one of our teammates, Ronnie Morales, has been writing a bunch of grant proposals for things we need. C'mon, let's take a closer look." Boone showed him around the room, telling him about the equipment as though showing off pictures of his newborn child. Jack occasionally made appreciative noises.

A second story held a few offices, a kitchen, locker rooms, and even a small bunk room.

Frankly, it was impressive—the kind of place that he would have liked to support. Even join.

Once upon a pre-prison life.

"This is my office." Boone ushered him in, gestured for him to have a seat. A clean desk sat in the middle of the room with a photo of Boone, arm slung around a pretty woman with dark hair, taking center stage. A stack of chairs occupied a corner of the otherwise stark space.

The longer Jack was at the CRT, the longer the shame of his recent past burned into him. He needed to leave, put behind him a life that no longer belonged to him.

Not to sit for a minute would be rude, but Jack still took a long look at the exit door before pulling a chair off a stack and settling in the corner.

Boone adjusted a pen cup on his desk. "Well? What do you think?"

"You have a nice setup here. You're right. I'm impressed."

"Like I said, generous donors. We're in the process of raising money for another rescue boat. We had a bad accident last year and lots of people got hurt. Also, every summer we have to rescue tourists who get in over their heads, literally, on one of the many lakes around here."

"How are you set for other rescue equipment? Like rappelling equipment and a rescue basket for the chopper." Oh shoot, he just had to ask.

"We've got some good rappelling gear. Casper Christiansen from the Wild Harbor Trading Post, a local outfitter, was able to get his hands on some stuff for us. Bought them at wholesale prices. As for the basket and chopper gear... Not good. We bought a used Stokes basket from a company in Duluth when they upgraded, but it's old and clunky. I could really use your expertise on that one."

"Yeah, I can write out a few options." Wait! What was he *doing*? He had zero intention of getting involved with this Crisis Response Team.

Frankly, after his time in Iraq and the disaster he'd seen

there, the only crisis he should consider responding to was the possibility of running out of burgers at the VFW.

"I gotta ask again. I wish you would reconsider taking the flight nurse position." Boone laced his fingers behind his head. "We've been relying on whoever is available on a volunteer basis from the hospital. We need someone more permanent. And someone more skilled. Preferably someone who is actually trained to do this stuff."

Nope, nope. Not going to happen. Even if he could keep his conviction under wraps, he was not looking to get involved.

Involvement led to background checks, which led to news articles...

Nope. And Boone needed to think that through too. "I just got out of prison. Do you think Deep Haven would trust a guy like me?"

"The people up here can be very forgiving. All they care about is that you are helping make our area safer. We need someone who is good under pressure, who has experience with this kind of thing. You'd be perfect for the job." Boone unlaced his hands and crossed his arms over his chest, leaned back.

Jack blew out a breath. "Boone, I like you, man. I consider you a friend. I'm asking you to back off on this."

Out in the main room, the front door opened, closed. He heard a pair of high-pitched voices and then two women appeared in Boone's doorway. One was blonde, shorter than her friend, and had a determined look in her eye. The other, tall and slender, had her red-blonde hair caught up in a ponytail. Cute.

The shorter of the pair was the first to speak. "Boone!" She blew past Jack like she didn't even see him, dragging her friend behind her. They planted themselves in front of the desk. "This is my friend Colleen. I don't think you've ever met. I was telling her about the flight nurse job, and I think you should convince her to apply."

Wait, this woman wanted to be the *flight nurse?* Well, hallelujah. That would get Boone off his back. He felt like doing a fist pump.

Jack shifted in his chair, relieved to be out of the intensity of Boone's focus. He noticed the friend was hanging back a little. Interesting. He tuned out the blonde as he observed Colleen from his position in the corner. She was pretty—a redhead. No, not quite red. What did women call it? Strawberry blonde. She wore a pair of faded jeans and a Blue Ox sweatshirt.

"Jack and I were just talking about that job." Boone gestured at him, and both girls turned his way.

"Hi." He gave a sheepish wave, feeling a little silly, the voyeur in the corner.

Boone rose to his feet, prompting Jack to do the same. "Jack, this is Ella Bradley, and I guess this is her friend Colleen..." He paused.

"Decker." Her green eyes gave Jack a quick once over. Did he imagine the spark of interest? Probably. He'd been too long in the pen.

Boone did a quick double take. "Wait. *Decker?* Any relation to Jason? He's got a sister who is a nurse, I think. Is that you?"

"Yeah, he's my brother." She nodded. "Wait. Boone? The *actor?*"

Boone wore a wry grin. "Not anymore."

"My parents said you did great filling in for Jason on such short notice when he got that part in California. They loved the play. Maybe you shouldn't give it up so quickly."

Boone rubbed at a scar healing near his eyebrow. "It turns out the theater is more excitement than I bargained for."

Colleen gave a swift smile. Her eyes filled with something mischievous. "Yeah, my parents told me about that too. You and Vivie made quite a splash over the past few weeks."

"I'd be happy to let my acting career die a quiet death." Boone held his hands up in surrender. "Ladies, why don't you have a seat and we can talk about this situation more."

Jack heard his cue and pulled two more chairs off the stack. He put them front and center of Boone's desk. "I think I'll take off, Boone. Thanks for the tour." Whatever this visit was about, it didn't concern him.

"Actually, why don't you stay?" Boone sat back down and waved the girls into their seats. "I could use your perspective."

He wanted to leave in the worst way, but oh shoot, he really owed Boone. Resigned, he sat back in the corner, hoping they would forget he was even there.

Colleen tossed her ponytail, and he caught a hint of an apple fragrance. "I'm afraid Ella is overselling the situation. I'm only here on a fact-finding mission. I don't know what is involved with becoming a flight nurse."

Boone nodded. "That's fantastic, Colleen—"

She held up her hand. "It's just information. I don't know if I'm ready to move back right now. I have a home and a good job in the Cities."

"She's good in high-stress environments," her friend interjected. "She has four years of ER experience at HCMC, two of which are full-time night shift. She's familiar with Deep Haven, and you can't beat having someone who grew up here. And, she's a superfast learner." Ella smiled at Colleen, who looked at her with wide eyes.

Boone moved forward in his chair. "Well, there's definitely specialized training involved, although you may have taken some already at HCMC, like the Certified Emergency Nurse certification. The bigger issue for our purposes is that our Crisis Response Team is on a shoestring budget. Many of us are filling multiple roles. We're looking for a nurse who can also do some search and rescue work, rappelling, wilderness missions, and things like that. It may even require working solo on some flights."

"I don't have experience with any of that. Except, I did go climbing at REI once."

"Are you scared of heights?"

"Nope, no problems with that."

Colleen's tall, slim limbs gave her the appearance of someone familiar with the gym. Jack would bet she played a sport. Basketball, maybe? The confident note in her voice as she talked with Boone gave him hope that she could carry herself in a trauma situation.

"We can always train you on the SAR stuff. In fact, Jack here has the certification from his time in Pararescue in the Air Force. He could probably coach you through a lot of it."

Jack straightened up. "Uh, yeah. I am certified." Way to sound intelligent...

He met Colleen's eyes. Whoa. Intense green held him captive for a moment—as if she knew what he was thinking and was assessing him right back.

Colleen turned back to Boone, releasing Jack from her spell. "Um, okay. I guess I have something to think about. But that's quite a lot to learn in a short time."

"Colleen, I'm sure you can do it," Ella said. "Remember when we took that ballroom dancing class for a PE credit? You were great at that."

Colleen snorted. "What does ballroom dancing have to do with any of this? It's not like there's much call for an emergency rescue on the dance floor."

Ella waved off the question. "Just that you're coordinated. Good at learning complicated things. And you grew up here, out in the wilderness. Physical stuff, outdoorsy stuff." She rolled her hand in an et cetera motion. "It's all up your alley."

"Let me give you the paperwork and you can think about it. Don't take too long though, as we'd really like to have someone start right away." Boone riffled through a drawer, pulled out some papers, and handed them to Colleen.

"But I wouldn't be trained yet. I wouldn't want to break any rules."

"Don't worry, this would be provisional until you passed the exams. When you feel ready to take the test, you'll have to call and set up the certification exam. I've included the list of requirements and the phone number to call."

The girls got up. "Nice to meet you, Jack," Ella said. Colleen was reading the papers as she left, giving him a quick glance and a half smile.

The headquarters grew quiet when the door shut behind them.

Boone folded his hands over his chest and grinned at Jack. "It looks like you might have competition for that job."

"I told you before, I don't want the job. I'm happy flipping burgers." Actually, maybe this *was* his way out. It was clear that Deep Haven needed someone stat and it was equally clear that person wasn't going to be him. But, just in case the thought lingered in Boone's head, he added, "Look, if she wants the job, I'd be happy to train her. It sounds like she would be a quick study. I think she could be ready by the end of October or sooner."

Boone leaned up and held out his hand. "Deal. You train her, then you can lie low all you want. Of course, if Colleen decides she doesn't want the job, I'll be hassling you again. You can't stay in the safe zone forever."

That's what Boone thought, but staying in the safe zone was exactly what Jack intended to do.

CHAPTER 3

*W*hat was she thinking? She couldn't *stay* in Deep Haven.

No matter how much the flight nurse job intrigued her.

Colleen needed to stop reading the job description Boone had given her along with a brochure about the Crisis Response Team.

She had a job—a life—in Minneapolis.

So maybe hanging out at the Friday night fish fry at the VFW, with all the delicious savory scents of grilled onions and deep fried herring hanging in the air, was a colossally bad idea.

The restaurant was packed, the gathering in full swing.

When Ella had called and suggested they catch the Blue Monkeys at the VFW, Colleen had pulled on her jacket practically before even hanging up the phone.

They sat at a high top table.

"Thanks for coming out with me." Ella took a long drink of her Coke and set it down. "Adrian wanted to work on a few things before we leave tomorrow for a business trip, but I couldn't skip town without seeing you again."

"I'm glad you called. I love my parents, but being at home has become…I don't know. Suffocating. It's only been a few days, but…" Colleen twisted the glass in her hand. The bottom left a damp trail across the table top. "I've spent all week helping my mother get ready for Grandma's big party—ordering flowers and cake, making a dinner menu, and the house is hospital clean. But tonight mom pulled out the guest list and started working on seating arrangements. Let's just say, I'm glad you called."

"You know my offer is still good, right? You can stay with me for a while if you want."

"Thank you for that. I might still take you up on it. It's probably not that my parents' house is so suffocating, just…"

Ella leaned into Colleen's pause. "Ready to get back to the excitement of Minneapolis?"

Colleen shrugged. "I can't help but feel like coming home is a sort of defeat. Or running away."

"Please. Deep Haven is the preferred vacation hub of thousands of Minnesotans, not to mention a few movie stars and professional athletes. You *know* there's practically a whole starting line of Blue Ox who hang here all the time."

"I know. It's just that I spent my entire life wanting to leave." Except, being at home had held a sort of magic healing power. The slower pace, her mother's cinnamon rolls.

So, maybe she wasn't that anxious to get back to vending machine pastries.

It could be that she just had to get out of the house, out of her room papered with boy band posters.

"It seems like you and Adrian are doing well."

"Yep." Her friend smiled, a secret look washing across her face. Colleen felt a sudden pang of envy.

She still thought Ella's story sounded like some kind of fairy tale. The rich prince, a night at the ball, then true love. Colleen's only claim to a fairy tale was winning homecoming queen her senior year. Some fairy tale that had turned out to be. Paul

Johnson, the homecoming king, tried to kiss her behind the bleachers, saying it was tradition.

Instead of a prince, she'd gotten the frog.

And then came the breakup with Tucker, her high school boyfriend. A fissure of regret sent a chill down her back. She remembered the moment at a volleyball game her first year of college. Tucker had shown up, looking hot, and she could hardly concentrate on the ball.

Why she'd then decided to dump Tucker and date someone else, she couldn't quite fathom. Especially when she'd seen the hurt in Tucker's eyes. His words to her—*You had it good and you didn't even know it*—were probably true. She'd been so eager to shuck off the remnants of Deep Haven, she didn't consider that Tucker had changed.

Sure, he'd been a bad boy in high school, but last she'd heard he was off fighting fires in Montana or something, a bona fide hero.

When she discovered her college boyfriend cheating on her, it only proved the truth—she made colossally bad choices about people. Trusted the wrong ones. Always fell for the bad boys.

"Has he put a ring on it yet?" Colleen asked.

Ella's laugh tinkled among the hubbub of the restaurant. "Not yet. I think he's waiting until the business proves to be sustainable first." Ella and Adrian ran an organic soap and cleaning supply company called *All Things New*. They had a storefront in Deep Haven, and a website, Essentially Ella, dedicated to sales. "Not that he would be marrying me for the business." Ella winked. "I think he has trouble concentrating on more than one thing at a time."

"How are Essentially Ella and All Things New really going?"

"It's been a slow start, but that's good. I don't have the time or space for a large-scale operation yet." She gave another laugh. "Our 'corporate headquarters'"—she added air quotes—"is the kitchen table in my apartment over the shop. We're hoping to figure out how to scale up production, but for now we're filling orders as fast as they come in."

They paused as the waitress brought their burgers and onion rings. Colleen inhaled the steam rising from the plate in front of her. "I know it's a fish fry, but I love the VFW burgers." She bit into her hamburger. Caramelized onions. Cheddar cheese. Candied bacon. Barbecue sauce. The sharp tang of a pickle. "Oh my gosh. This is amazing. I don't remember the burgers being this good."

Across from her, Ella bit into her food. "You're right. The food here has always been good, but this is phenomenal. Maybe the promise of burgers every Friday will convince you to move home."

"Ella, I know you mean well, but I don't think moving home is the answer."

"The flight nurse job would be perfect for you. I worry about you down there at HCMC. It's not safe."

Ella didn't even know the half of it.

Colleen picked at an onion ring. The door to the kitchen swung open as a man with dark-blond hair pushed through it. He wore an apron around his waist and made his way around the crowded tables, chatting with a few of the other diners before stopping at theirs.

"Is the food okay?"

He looked vaguely familiar. A five o'clock shadow brushed his cheeks. His blue VFW T-shirt strained against his muscular chest. Not that she noticed. She *definitely* didn't notice. But even the sleeves of his shirt seemed to strain around his biceps. What was a guy like this doing in a *kitchen*? He gave a quick smile that didn't quite reach his iron-blue eyes.

Wait, she knew him. "Jack, right? From the other day in Boone's office?"

Comprehension dawned in his eyes too. "Right! And you're Colleen. The one who wants the flight nurse job."

Well, that wasn't quite true...

"I told Boone that I could train you if you want. I know what certification you need."

"No. I was just telling Ella here"—she gestured to her friend who had oh so conveniently chosen that moment to stuff a whole onion ring into her mouth—"that I wasn't sure if I was going to stick around. They expect me back in the Cities sometime next week."

Jack seemed unexpectedly crestfallen. Why did he care if she stayed or not?

"If you change your mind, I'll be here." He started back to the swinging door of the kitchen while the Blue Monkeys crooned the chorus of "Take My Breath Away" on stage.

She didn't know why, but, "Wait!" Colleen called out. What was she *doing*?

Jack halted, turned back to her.

Um. "I just wanted to ask you to tell the cook that this is a great burger." She held up her half-eaten sandwich.

A slow smile transformed Jack's face. "It's the onions, isn't it?"

Was it her imagination, or did the room suddenly get weirdly hot?

"I...I was going to say the candied bacon, but you're right. The onions really pull it together."

Jack stepped back toward the table. "It's definitely worth the time it takes to caramelize them before adding them to the burger. Going slow can be a good thing." His magnetic eyes locked onto hers.

Gulp. "I didn't realize *you* were the chef." Sheesh, that definitely sounded like...*flirting*. What?

"Not a chef, just a short-order cook. But I take my job seriously. Speaking of which, I should get back. But thanks for noticing." Jack winked, then wove his way through the tables to the kitchen.

What…just…happened?

She looked up to Ella's wide grin. "What? Do I have something on my face?"

Ella laughed. "No, silly. *Jack*."

She took a bite of the burger. "What about him?"

Ella made her eyes wide, deadpanned, "'I didn't realize *you* were the chef.'"

Colleen's face burned. "What? I like a good burger." She took a drink. "Just because I'm not sticking around doesn't mean I can't appreciate a cute guy."

"Colleen, you've got to be kidding me. If it wasn't disloyal to Adrian, I would say Jack's more than cute. He's *gorgeous*."

Colleen bit into an onion ring. "Yeah. I'd go there. But it doesn't matter."

"Oh, stop. I think you should rethink training for that flight nurse position. You could come home and live with me. You wouldn't have to stay at your parents' place. Besides, who wouldn't want to spend more time with Muscles?"

Hmm.

If only coming back home didn't smell a little too much like defeat. And Colleen never liked waving a white flag.

◊

Why did a sleepy little town like Deep Haven need a full-time flight nurse, anyway? As far as Jack could tell, there were zero violent crimes and very few real emergencies. The worst thing that could happen here was a case of frostbite.

He'd spent the past few days lying low, holed up in his apartment, eating peanut butter sandwiches, and reading a Louis L'Amour book he'd found on a shelf in the Java Cup. He spent his nights at the VFW perfecting his burger recipes and tweaking their other menu items.

Jack surveyed the kitchen as he pushed through the swinging

door. It was small, but efficient, which was great, actually. Everything within reach. A chopping station, a flat-top grill, deep fryer, and along one wall a walk-in fridge and matching freezer. Much as he'd suspected that first day, this space just...fit.

He'd been in charge for four days and he could admit he never wanted to leave.

Running into Colleen and Ella during his mandatory sweep of the dining room had been...interesting. He found himself thinking of Colleen's pretty green eyes and gave himself a shake.

I just wanted to ask you to tell the cook that this is a great burger.

He didn't know why her words, her smile, clung to him. He was just a thirsty man is all. He'd been out of the game so long, a pretty girl with a kind smile did devastating things to his heart.

He wasn't available. At least not for someone like her. Someone who would want something permanent and lasting. But not with a guy like him.

Prison had stolen that from him.

He pulled himself back to the kitchen. Focused on the tasks in front of him.

A local teen, Mike Something-or-other, manned the deep fryer, and Katie Larson was Jack's sous chef. Not that you could call anyone a sous chef in this casual atmosphere, but she liked to think of herself that way, and Jack let her. It was easier than explaining the mechanics of a kitchen. Again.

Behind him, in the dining room, he heard applause as the Blue Monkeys finished their set. He glanced at the clock on the wall—8:15. A little less than two hours to go. Kitchen service shut down at 10:00 p.m. on Fridays.

By the fryer, Mike was drinking a glass of water. Katie was hauling a bag of frozen fries from the cooler.

The kid shouldn't drink by the hot oil. He would have to set him straight. Jack started to call over to him when Katie shut the cooler with her hip and headed toward the fry station.

In a split second, and in the longest moment, Jack saw Katie walk by, accidently jostle Mike, and then the glass slipped out of Mike's hand.

Straight into the deep fryer.

Hissing oil spattered up out of the vat. Fingers of boiling heat washed over the right half of Mike's face, chest, and neck.

Mike screamed. Went down.

Katie dropped the fries and screamed too.

"Call 911!" Jack took off for Mike, being careful not to slip in the oil on the floor. Jack grabbed Mike's shirt and pulled him away from the spitting oil.

Then he grabbed a towel, covered his hand, and shut off the fryer.

Angry red welts were growing along Mike's neck, but more concerning was the way Mike held a hand over his eye.

Jack knelt next to him.

Mike thrashed away at Jack's touch.

"Let me look at it, man. I need to see." He gently, but firmly pulled Mike's hands from his face. The skin around the boy's closed eye was puffy and already blistering.

He hauled him up and dragged him over to the sinks, hit the faucet for the cold water.

"I need a cool towel!"

Not his voice. The shout came from behind him. He turned, and out of nowhere, Colleen stood beside him. "Katie is calling 911. Let's get this shirt off him." She reached over, started at the hem, and ripped.

The entire shirt shredded at her force, and when she got to the neckline, she ripped that too.

Huh.

Meanwhile, he grabbed a towel and wet it. Gave it to her. "I'm concerned about his face and eye."

"Me too." She put the towel on his face then maneuvered

him toward the running water. "We need to cool down the wound."

He helped her put Mike's arm into the water. She bathed his neck and chest with the towel.

"He needs a burn center," she said as Mike started howling. Jack helped lower him to the floor.

"I'll get my truck."

"Not here." She knelt before Mike. "Deep Haven can handle a few minor traumas, maybe a childbirth or stabilization after a heart attack. Beyond that, we need to go to Duluth." She turned back to Mike, whose skin had already started to blister and peel off.

"Does it have a Level 2 trauma center?" Jack said. They locked eyes for a second.

She nodded.

Even though Katie had called 911, dispatch wouldn't be sending more than an ambulance at most. But Mike needed a medevac ASAP, and Jack would go straight to the source. "I'm calling Boone."

On the floor, Mike moaned and thrashed out an arm. Colleen bent to him, shushing in his ear.

Jack rose and pulled out his cell. Dialed. Boone picked up. "We have a serious burn victim at the VFW and need the chopper to Duluth." He gave a quick rundown on what was happening. Boone promised to get the helicopter pilot ready to go.

By the time Jack hung up, the emergency responders had arrived with an ambulance and stretcher. They assessed Mike and agreed with Jack—this kid needed an airlift to Duluth before he lost his eye.

Jack and Colleen got in the ambulance with the emergency responders and Mike.

Jack crammed himself into a corner while the paramedic, a Latina woman who introduced herself as Ronnie, worked on

Mike. She slathered silver sulfadiazine on his arm, chest, and neck and put a loose bandage over his eye.

Colleen sat at Mike's left side, where the teen had a death grip on her hand.

The radio squawked and then the driver called back. "The sheriff got a hold of Mike's mom. She's meeting us at CRT headquarters."

So the kid would have someone with him. Having a loved one in a time of crisis could make all the difference.

The ambulance slowed, stopped. On the CRT pad, Jack spotted a man walking around the helicopter doing a preflight check.

The ambulance driver—his name patch read Atwood—came around and opened the back of the ambulance. Atwood and Ronnie wheeled Mike out and onto the ground. Colleen hopped out behind them and Jack followed the procession as they hustled over to the bird.

The two emergency responders pulled open the doors on the side of the helo and transferred Mike onto the litter basket inside. Colleen climbed on board with them, talking Mike through what was happening. The kid had gone eerily silent.

As the emergency responders busied themselves getting Mike strapped in, Jack met the pilot.

"Bill Hooper." The man had a strong, steady grip.

"Jack Stewart."

"Are you our flight nurse?"

Um, no. Absolutely not. "What do you mean?"

"Boone said he couldn't get a hold of the other guy, Rhino or whatever, and promised he'd find someone else. I just assumed…"

There was no nurse to go with Mike? Jack's mind raced. A flight nurse or other medical personnel was required on a flight. And a two-hour ambulance ride up the shore meant Mike might lose that eye.

Ronnie called out to them. "He's ready to go!" She climbed out of the chopper.

Bill took the chopper's front seat. "I can't leave until there's someone in the back with the patient."

Shoot! Maybe one of the emergency responders would be able to go along. The deepening twilight hemmed in around them.

A van screeched into the tiny parking lot. A woman burst out of the driver's door. "Where is my son? Where is Mike?"

Ronnie met her, grabbing the woman by both arms. "Ma'am, Mike is safely in the helicopter. Calm down." Mike's mom attempted to pull away, but Ronnie put her arm around her shoulder. "Breathe now. Take a breath. Do you want to go with Mike?" The woman nodded. "Okay, we can't let you go if you are hysterical."

The woman nodded, and Ronnie led her over to the helicopter.

Perfect. Ronnie could go—

Inside the ambulance, the radio squawked to life.

Atwood answered it then yelled, "Ronnie, we've got another call. We need to move."

The dark-haired woman hesitated, looking from the chopper to the ambulance.

Atwood called out again. "It's a kid in respiratory distress. We gotta hustle."

Shoot! But what choice did he have? Jack stepped up to where Ronnie held the mother. "I'll take this. You get going." He put his arm around the mother's shoulder. Ronnie gave him a grateful smile before sprinting for the ambulance.

The emergency vehicle spit gravel from under its tires as it shot out of the lot, sirens blaring.

A brief moment of silence filled the space.

From the helicopter, Mike moaned. Jack led the mother over

to the waiting bird. Colleen, at the door, reached out for her and Jack relinquished his charge.

In the front, Bill flipped a few switches. The rotor engines began to whine. "Let's get going. Any word from Rhino? Or is one of you coming?"

Jack looked in at Mike. The boy's swelling was growing worse. There was no time to waste waiting for this Rhino character.

The mother began to groan again. "He looks so helpless. His face..." She began to hyperventilate. "What if he loses his eye?"

They had to move. And Colleen couldn't go on her own—she might be a trauma nurse, but she wasn't trained for flights.

He climbed into the helicopter and shut the door. "Well, it looks like it's you and me."

"Wait, what? Are you talking to me?" Colleen turned to him, her face white. "I've never done this before—I'm not qualified."

"You'll do great. If you can run a night shift in the HCMC ER, this will be fine. I can't do it alone and this boy needs our help." He flicked his gaze to the mother, hoping that Colleen understood that they needed to project confidence for her sake. Operating as a team would be the only way to keep the boy safe and his mother under control.

Colleen looked between the mom and the boy. Took a breath. "Okay."

Jack turned to the mother. "You can ride along, but I'm going to need you to stay strapped in. All the time, regardless of what happens. We will take good care of Mike." He helped her with the seat belt in the jump seat at the front of the cabin.

"Colleen and I will be your flight crew." He said to the pilot. Bill gave him a quick salute before turning to his instruments.

The blades whirred to life.

The bird lifted off, the familiar jolt as they swung around, forward, and then they were airborne.

Jack's palms slicked. The last time he was in a chopper...

No. He wouldn't think about that. This was a very different scenario. He needed to concentrate on Mike.

Right now, the boy was calm. He held his mom's hand on one side and Colleen's on the other. As they rose into the darkness, Jack inspected the kid's IV and rechecked that the stretcher straps were tight.

Jack's heart rate began to settle and he managed to ignore the ghosts lurking in the corner of his memories. This ride was going to be a breeze.

It had to be.

Then, just like that, the helicopter dropped. Colleen and Mike's mom shrieked and grabbed for something to hold on to. Jack crouched on the floor next to the stretcher, one hand on a stabilizing bar. The other clutched the litter, his arm around his patient.

"Woohoo! This girl's a bucking bronco tonight." Bill's voice ground out as though it scraped across the rocky shoreline of Lake Superior.

In the cockpit, Jack could see Bill's white knuckles gripping the cyclic. "I think I've got it now. Wind shear is bad tonight. Guess I should've looked at the weather before we took off."

Jack's vision tunneled. No...*no*... He released the stabilizer bar and ran his hand down his sweaty face.

A sound broke through the red mist in his mind. Colleen. Calling his name.

"Jack. *Jack*, I think Mike's blood pressure is dropping." She checked the cuff from the auto-blood pressure monitor to his arm.

Focus, man. Focus on the problem in front of you.

He moved forward, his vision clearing, and touched his fingers to Mike carotid artery. Thready and thin. "He's going into shock. Grab another blanket. There should be one in the locker." He adjusted the IV. "I'm going to push some morphine and more saline."

"Are you sure? I don't think that's necessary. My training says too much fluid can compromise his airway. Most patients don't die of inadequate fluid in the first hour."

The boy's mom began wailing again. "Mikey is going to die? My son can't die! He's a senior in high school. He's supposed to go to the U of M next year. He has a *scholarship*."

Ignore the mother's hysteria. Jack met Colleen's eyes. "I don't care what the book says, you gotta trust me, Colleen. Ignore what you know and listen to your gut."

Colleen found the blanket, laid it over Mike. "Fine. I hope you know what you're doing. Keep an eagle eye on his breathing." She turned to the mom, who was weeping in her seat.

The helicopter dropped again, almost forcing Jack to lose control of the IV. "Easy up there!"

"Five more minutes. Don't worry, I'll get you there in one piece." Bill banked the chopper. Jack felt the floor tilt much farther than it should for a rescue vehicle. Bill should know that he was making their job harder. Jack braced himself against a cabinet.

Near the front of the chopper, Colleen strained to stay upright as she continued to console Mike's mom.

In the distance, Jack saw the lights of the Duluth helipad winking out their welcome. A team of medical professionals stood to the side, hunched against the wind from the lake.

The helicopter touched down and Jack helped with the transfer of the patient.

When Mike, his mom, and the hospital staff had disappeared through the elevator to the depths of the hospital below, Jack moved to stand next to Colleen.

She had her arms wrapped around her waist, her strawberry-blonde hair blowing in the wind, wide-eyed.

"Well," she said. "That was an experience I'll never forget."

"You did good," Jack said. "I know you're on the fence about taking the job, but you have great instincts."

Colleen did a quick glance around. She lowered her voice. "I'm not so sure about flying again though. That pilot freaked me out."

And she wasn't wrong. Bill's cavalier attitude had endangered the whole mission. Speaking of whom, the pilot was walking toward them.

"What about you?" Colleen asked. "It seemed like you were spooked back there. I thought I lost you for a minute."

He turned to Colleen. "It was no big deal." Liar.

"Okay then. If you say so. Ready to head home?"

"What do you think about renting a car to get there?"

The relief on Colleen's face cemented his decision.

Because there was no way he was getting back into that helicopter again.

Ever.

CHAPTER 4

*A*nd now she definitely didn't know what to do.

Colleen leaned against a countertop in her mom's kitchen and watched her stir a mammoth bowl of pancake batter, last night still replaying in her head.

And, boy, she'd liked it. Mostly. With the exception of the couple times the chopper had hit turbulence, the feeling of flying above Deep Haven, paired with the pump of adrenaline from caring for a critical patient—yeah, she'd take that over a full ER any day.

Which meant, what, exactly?

"Are you planning to feed all of Deep Haven?" she teased her mother.

Mom pushed a stray hair off her face with the back of her hand. "Nope, just your brothers. Jason and Henry came in late last night while you were gone. Jason convinced his director to give him the weekend off for your grandma's anniversary party. Those two will eat a hundred pancakes if we let them."

"Put me to work. What can I do?" She straightened up and moved to the table in the center of the room. Warm and inviting, the kitchen was the perfect gathering place.

"You can peel and chop those apples." Her mom pointed her spatula at the bowl of bright red Macintosh apples resting on the table. "Add a little sugar when you're done and then I'll sauté them in a pat of butter. Your dad loves apples on his pancakes."

A hiss as the pancake batter hit the hot skillet, and a warm, slightly vanilla scent filled the air. Colleen picked up a Macintosh and began slicing it, the rhythmic sound of her knife accentuating the silence.

"Tell me about your emergency call last night." Her mom flipped a pancake.

"There are some things I can't tell you. Patient confidentiality and all that."

"I know. You don't have to tell me about Mike, just about your experience."

Her experience. Exhilaration, the sense of really saving a life. And then there'd been the ride home with Jack. She'd fallen asleep as he'd manned the wheel, something steadfast about his expression that made her feel oddly safe.

Maybe it was his movements in the chopper, the way he'd challenged her to trust him.

And then promptly kept Mike alive. So yes, maybe.

Fact was, Jack was an interesting, handsome, hamburger-flipping, life-saving enigma.

"You know that I can't even confirm that it was Mike, right? I have to follow the rules, even in a small town."

Her mom put up a hand. "Colleen, it's fine. You don't have to tell me about that at all. I already know it was Mike because Ellie Matthews put it on the prayer chain this morning. She had his mother's permission to share the concern with our church family. Poor boy. At least it sounds like they will be able to save his eye. I'm not so sure about his football scholarship." She gave the pancake batter a quick stir. Opening the oven, she slid the first batch of hotcakes inside to keep warm.

"Right. Anyway, without confirming or denying who the

patient was, I'd have to say I actually kind of liked it. I can see why people do it for a living. Jack was great. He showed me what to do. You have to think on your feet a lot. Those helicopters are amazing. Like a tiny ER with wings. Well, propellers, but you know what I mean."

"Are you saying that your friend Ella isn't crazy for thinking you should apply for that job? I agree with her—you really would be perfect for it. And it would be nice to have you around more."

Colleen carried the bowl of apples to the stove. She sprinkled some cinnamon and sugar over the top of the apples and stirred them together. "Thanks, Mom. But I'm just not sure I want to go back to my high school life."

"I worry about you sometimes down there. I know you live in a safe neighborhood, but anything can happen to a girl on her own. All it takes is one person who decides to step outside the law, and your life is changed forever."

Changed forever.

A veil slipped over Colleen's vision, and her breath hiccupped.

Stop. But she reached out, connected with the back of a chair, and stumbled. The chair went over with a crash.

No!

She raised her hands to her face, startled to discover they came away wet. *Calm down!*

"Colleen, what's the matter?" Her mom crossed the kitchen to her. Her concerned face came into focus. "It's okay, honey. Take a minute to breathe." She put her arms around Colleen's shoulders and pulled her to herself. Colleen shuddered but she leaned against her mother, her heart rate slowing.

Her mother finally released her and grabbed a towel from the table. She used it to wipe away Colleen's tears. Then she took both Colleen's hands in her own. "Want to talk about it?"

Colleen closed her eyes. Opened them. Focused on the

cheerful flower-strewn curtains hanging in the window. Where to start? "You were right about the danger."

Before she could say anything more, her dad came into the room. He was still in sweatpants and a cotton T-shirt, his hair mussed from sleep. He gave his wife a kiss, then looked to Colleen. "Whoa, what's the matter, sweetheart?"

At his concern, Colleen's eyes welled up again. She looked at her stricken parents. "I didn't just come home early to help get ready for the party like I told you."

Her mother sank into a chair.

"We had a serious incident at the ER during my Saturday overnight."

Her father poured a cup of coffee and handed it to her.

"Thanks." She took a sip. "A patient came in, a prisoner. We've had them before, so I thought 'no big deal.' He was accompanied by a cop. Standard procedure."

Her dad moved to stand behind her mom.

Colleen stared at her coffee. "I was giving the patient a drink of water when a commotion started in the hall. The criminal took advantage of everyone being distracted to cut himself out of his bonds."

Her mother gasped.

"He jumped out of the bed, and I didn't know what to do. He grabbed me and held the scalpel he'd used to my neck."

Her hand strayed to the Band-Aid on her neck.

Her mother got up, took two steps, and pulled Colleen into an embrace. "Oh, honey. I had no idea."

Her dad put his hand on her shoulder. "What happened next?"

"I'm not super clear on that. The cop who was in the room with us was able to take the guy out. They moved him to another room and sent me home for the night. I thought I was okay, but the next night, during my shift, I saw a guy with a tattoo and totally freaked."

That might be the understatement of the year. Her panic had felt more real in those moments than it had the night before when she was actually in danger.

"My friend Julie found me hiding in a closet. Then my supervisor made me take the next few days off. She said I needed a longer break."

Her mom held her at arm's length. "So, you've been having panic attacks? That's what those few episodes have been, right?"

The worry in her mother's eyes almost undid her again.

She nodded. "I thought I was fine. I'm in high-stress situations all the time. But something about this one really got to me."

Her mom pushed a strand of hair off her forehead, tucked it behind her ear. "I'm sure it brought back bad memories of Luis Garcia. That man affected our lives in ways we are still living with."

Silence reigned in the kitchen for a heartbeat. Then her mom spoke again. "Maybe you should think about staying and taking Boone up on his offer."

Colleen wiped her eyes. Sighed. Maybe she did need a break from the "big city" and a return to home. But she'd worked so hard to leave Deep Haven. How could she just run back, like a coward? "But am I just retreating from life to hide out here in Deep Haven? Running away doesn't sound like a good idea."

"Honey, I don't think it would be running away. Sometimes God gives us safe spaces to retreat to so we can come back healed. Maybe He is providing a safe space for you right now."

"I just don't know. I used to think I was so confident, but now I'm questioning everything."

She saw her mom and dad give each other a long look.

"What?"

Her father took a breath. "We wanted to wait until after the party to tell you. Actually, your grandma asked us to wait, but I think this could be an answer to prayer." Her dad looked away for a moment, his eyes wet.

"What, Dad?" A note of panic crept into her voice.

He met her gaze. "Honey, your grandma's cancer came back. That's why we're having the anniversary party tonight instead of waiting until a more traditional ten years."

It took a moment. She looked at her mom, back to her father. Took a breath. "What is her prognosis?"

"The doctor said it's stage 3 and will require chemo and then possibly radiation. She's starting treatment next week." Her mother's quiet words rang so loudly in Colleen's head she almost didn't hear the next part. "The doctor also said her prognosis is good. Grandma Helen has been seeing the doctor frequently for her lupus, so they were able to catch this recurrence early."

Her dad sighed. "Frank is going to need help caring for Grandma. I think we told you he recently fell? He sprained his arm and fractured his hip. He's not going to be able to do much around the house. In fact, he may need some care too. We didn't want you to worry, but we were thinking of asking you to come home and help. We decided not to because it was such a big ask. But, if you're thinking of staying…maybe you might be willing to help?"

In the sink, the faucet dripped an accompaniment to her thoughts. The cinnamon apples bubbling on the stove wrapped her in the scent of home. Safety.

Moving home suddenly seemed like the perfect answer.

"I'll call Nicole on Monday and take a leave of absence. She said I could have a month, maybe more without a problem."

The worry on her dad's face eased. "This means so much. Thank you."

"What about your apartment, honey?" Her mom laid a hand on her arm.

"There's a nurse on the OB floor who's looking for a place.

Maybe I can sublet to her for a while. I have a few months before my lease is up. I can push that decision off for a while." Her mind started clicking through the details. "Actually, maybe I should drive down on Monday. That way I can pick up some more clothes and get things settled. I'll call my coworker this afternoon to see if she wants to rent my place, then stop by the hospital on Monday to talk to Nicole in person."

"Well, that's a load off my mind." Her dad rose from his chair just as Henry and Jason came crashing into the room.

Jason tousled her hair. "When's breakfast? I'm starving."

Colleen laughed. Her too. But apparently, she'd come to the right place.

∼

Jack jerked awake in a predawn darkness, drenched in sweat, the covers wrapped tightly around him. Shoot—he thought he'd beaten this demon.

It had been almost a year since he'd had this nightmare. He'd thought his time in prison had seared this horror out of him. Or replaced it with others just as terrible.

It seemed he was wrong.

He couldn't even remember the dream, just snatches of it.

A helicopter in a spiral.

Gunfire and dust.

Someone screaming.

He shut his eyes, but an image still remained, in brutal outline. Ryan, bleeding out.

He stared at the ceiling, willing his heart rate back to normal.

The helicopter flight the night before with Mike crept into his mind. If he never flew with that incompetent Bill Hooper again, it would be too soon. Boone would be getting a full report the next time they saw each other.

Thinking about the near disaster of the flight to the hospital in Duluth was jacking his heart rate up again. *C'mon, Stewart, get it together.* That trip was a one-time thing. A fluke.

He unwound the covers, sat on the edge of the bed, scrubbed a hand across his face, then flipped on the bedside lamp. The shadows scuttled back into the corners of this small room above the coffee shop. Maybe a novel would settle his mind.

He propped himself up against his headboard and opened his latest Louis L'Amour. He reread the same paragraph over and over. Stared at the wall. Tried again. But even the fast-paced Western story by the master writer failed to capture his attention.

Giving up, he rose, went to the tiny bathroom, fumbled for the spigot in the bright white shower, and turned the water as hot as possible. He shucked off his clothes and tested the water. A shade cooler than lava. Stepping under the spray, he braced his arms against the tile and allowed the scalding water to wash the sweat of the nightmare away.

He finally got out, toweled off, pulled on some jeans and a sweatshirt, and checked the time. Perfect. The coffee shop downstairs would be serving any minute. There were some benefits to this rental.

The smoky, earthy scent of coffee rolled over him as he stepped into the Java Cup. At the counter, the barista-slash-owner, Kathy, arranged some donuts in the bakery case. She peeled off her gloves and moved to the cash register.

A big man with long, dark hair and a lumberjack beard stood in line. His blue flannel shirt stretched over broad shoulders. "I'll have a large dark roast, black, please." He moved off to the side as Jack stepped up to order.

"I'll take an Americano. Black, extra shot." A short stint at the Aviano Air Base in northern Italy had taught Jack to appreciate a dark, full-bodied coffee.

The big man turned to him. "I like a man who doesn't drink

a foofoo coffee. Hey, pardon me for asking, but are you Jack Stewart?"

"Actually, yes I am. How did you know?"

"I'm Peter Dahlquist, Deep Haven's fire chief. Sorry, small town. Boone mentioned your name at a recent meeting and that you were going to be staying in the apartment here." He gestured at Jack's feet. "Since you're not wearing shoes... I kind of put two and two together."

He wasn't wearing shoes? He looked down to discover that he was, in fact, shoeless. The dream—no, nightmare—had messed him up more than he'd thought.

"Um, excuse me a minute." Jack's face felt like fire as he jogged up to his apartment. When he got back down, Peter was accepting his drink from Kathy.

Peter gave him a friendly smile and lifted his coffee in a salute. "Want to share a table for a few minutes? I don't have to be down at the firehouse for a half hour."

Jack wasn't really in the mood for a heart to heart, but he didn't have an excuse either. He gave a quick nod. Maybe this was some kind of ritual. Invite the new guy for coffee and make sure he's not an ax murderer. He briefly wondered if Boone had filled Peter in on his history. He certainly wouldn't get a clean pass.

Besides, he thought it was probably best not to get on the wrong side of the local fire chief. Restaurant fires were nothing to mess around with, and he didn't want some strange local tradition to get in the way of him receiving aid if it ever came to that.

Jack nabbed his coffee and sat across from Peter. Their table rested in the corner, where both men could see the door.

Peter gave him a brief smile. "In the interest of honesty, I should probably tell you that I got the incident report from last night. Sounds like you had quite an evening."

"Yeah, that was pretty bad." He sipped his coffee.

"The way I heard it, you're a hero. You might have saved that kid's eye."

A hero? Yeah, right. "Right place, right time."

"Still, the whole town is grateful."

The whole town? That was a bit overstated. "It was great that Colleen Decker was eating there and came in to help. She's the one the town should be grateful for. I couldn't have done it without her. She kept Mike calm, and then his mom. If it wasn't for her jumping in at the first sign of trouble, the whole thing could have gone very differently."

Both men quieted for a beat.

Peter eyed him sideways. "I heard she might be considering taking the flight nurse position."

"I don't think so. She seemed pretty adamant about not sticking around." At least that's how it seemed to him. He remembered the toss of her pretty hair as she had insisted on it several times back in Boone's office earlier that week.

"I don't blame her." Peter slugged back the dregs of his drink in one long gulp. "Must be hard for her to be back home with its memories."

Jack couldn't let a statement like that go by. "What do you mean?"

"Just that she had it pretty rough her last few years of high school. None of us were surprised when she hightailed it to college as soon as she graduated."

Well, well, the pretty girl had a past.

Jack waited a minute. Two. Took another swallow of java. Stared steadily at the big man across from him. Finally, Peter cracked.

"Look, I probably shouldn't be telling you this, but when Colleen was sixteen years old or so we all found out that her mom had been in WITSEC. Basically, her mom had been hiding in Deep Haven for almost twenty years."

Huh. So he wasn't the first one to hide out here.

"That wasn't the worst of it, though. Colleen found out about her mom when the ex-con who wanted to kill Annalise took Colleen hostage at knifepoint. I wouldn't be surprised if she never trusted anyone again."

"Wow. I had no idea."

"Normally I wouldn't be telling a virtual stranger something like this, but if she does decide to stick around and train for the flight nurse job, I figured you should know about it. We watch out for our own up here." The big man set his cup down on the table. Met him with a long look.

What?

"Um...I don't... What's going on here?"

"Nothing. Just a friendly tutorial about Deep Haven." Peter smiled, stood to his feet. As he passed by Jack, he laid a heavy hand on his shoulder. Sheesh, did he need to squeeze quite so hard? Or give Jack another one of those long, inscrutable looks?

Fine. Jack got it. He needed to tread carefully.

Well, don't worry, Deep Haven. He had no intention of getting involved. Besides, every time he tried to act like a hero, he just got hurt in the process. In his experience, good guys finished last.

A lesson he'd never forget.

CHAPTER 5

*H*er life was changing so fast a girl could be forgiven for having a little whiplash.

In the week since her parents had told her about her grandma's diagnosis, Colleen had helped with the anniversary party, gone back to Minneapolis to take an official leave of absence, sublet her apartment, and moved back home.

Into her old bedroom.

With the boy band posters.

She'd gone to her grandma's doctor's appointment and to a chemo treatment. Then cleaned her grandma's house since Grandma Helen and her husband, Frank, were both out of commission.

So, yeah, a big week.

Which totally explained why she was sitting outside the Crisis Response Team Headquarters in the cold and not going in. When she'd called Boone to ask if she could take the training on a provisional basis, he'd readily agreed and asked her to come in on Saturday, today. Boone said he'd hold the position while she worked toward her certification in the hopes she would decide to stick around.

The building loomed in front of her. The early morning sun glinted off the two-story structure, casting a shadow over the front door.

Now all she had to do was push open the door and start this next part of her new-slash-old life.

She was still sitting in her car a minute later when another car pulled into the lot. Ronnie, the paramedic from the emergency at the VFW, got out and walked over. Her long, dark hair was pulled back in a French braid. A few wisps had escaped and now brushed her light brown skin. Ronnie's eyes registered pleasure when Colleen opened her door.

"Hey, Colleen, right? Good to see you." Ronnie put her hand on the car door. "Are you starting with Jack today? I heard through the grapevine that you two were going to be training together."

And, see, that was the thing about small towns. Nothing stayed private for long. "Yep. Big training day." If she could manage to walk into the building.

"Great! I have training later today too. I came in early to get some work in beforehand, so we'll see a bit of each other." Ronnie headed to the entrance. "Are you coming?"

Colleen swallowed hard. Yes. Yes, she was coming.

She took a good look around inside. She hadn't paid much attention when she'd been here with Ella before. The two-and-a-half-story bay was anchored by a huge climbing wall at one end. Workout equipment and other gear were arranged in groupings around the rest of the space. She could see a stairway leading to the second floor where Boone's office was.

Jack jogged over from where he'd been lifting weights. His dark blond hair was mussed. A dusting of beard darkened his chin. He must have been here a while lifting weights because his shirt betrayed a hint of sweat down the front. "Glad you could make it today."

Suddenly, she was very glad as well. Maybe that had something to do with the blue eyes washing over her with their intensity. *Get it together.* "No problem. Where are we going to start?"

Jack led her to the climbing wall. Near the top, a strange bar apparatus jutted out into the air. "Ever seen one of these before?"

Good thing Boone had told her to wear workout gear. "Well, I've seen a climbing wall, if that's what you mean. What's the bar?"

"That's to simulate a helicopter. We'll use it to teach you how to attach the basket for rescue." He gestured to a pile of equipment. "This is the rigging and hanging basket. Let's get to it."

Over the next hour, Colleen got a crash course in climbing gear, rappelling equipment, and patient transfer.

They worked together at the base of the climbing wall to set up the Stokes basket for their practice run. Jack showed her how to attach the rigging that secured it to the "helicopter" winch attached near the ceiling above the climbing wall. She clipped a line to an opening on the basket. It hung slack against the side.

"Tighten that strap." Jack leaned over and adjusted a rope tie. He brushed against Colleen and she jumped back. Her heart rate ratcheted up. "Uh, sorry." His confused voice cleared away the ringing in her ears.

"No. It's no problem." Sheesh. What was that about?

"Okay. I think we've got it. Time to practice on the wall." Jack stepped into a rappel harness, cinching the blue nylon straps around his thighs and adjusting the belt around his waist. He reached for the other rig hanging from the ceiling. Colleen moved over to him.

"So, just step into this." He held the green rig open and gave it a half shake. She lifted one foot into the harness and then stumbled a bit. Jack reached a hand out to steady her, but she pulled away, yanking the harness out of his hand in the process. Jack shot her a look. "Everything okay?"

Her face flamed as she nodded. What was wrong with her?

He held a line for her to clip onto.

"Technically, we could use the stairs to get up to the helicopter, but it will be good for you to get some climbing practice in. And for me to see what we need to strengthen in the next few weeks."

Colleen nodded. She hoped her one time up the wall at REI wasn't a fluke. She gave silent thanks for her spin classes. If she didn't make it, it wouldn't be because her legs weren't strong enough.

She buckled a helmet onto her head and pulled on a pair of fingerless gloves.

Ronnie approached the wall. "Need a spotter?"

Jack nodded. "Yes, that would be great." He turned to Colleen. "We'll be using an auto belay, which means the winch near the ceiling will be taking up the slack as we climb. It will also catch you if you fall and slowly lower you to the ground. We use a spotter for newbies, but once you've done a few climbs, you won't need one. When we get out into the field, one of your teammates will belay you."

Ronnie got into position as Colleen assessed the wall. She knew one of the secrets to a good climb was to seek out her path and then follow it.

There. A few of the lower grips looked right for her size frame. Hugging close to the wall, she began her ascent. Jack started up the wall a few feet over and slightly below.

She came to a stop midway up.

"How are you doing?" It really wasn't fair that Jack didn't sound even remotely winded.

"Just need a short pit stop." Her fingers were starting to feel the burn and she mentally reminded herself to use her leg muscles more.

"Over to your left a little should be a great hold," Ronnie coached from below.

Colleen looked up and spotted the grip. Pushing up on her legs, she just touched the top. She pushed a little more and wrapped her fingers in place.

"Atta girl." Jack's praise warmed her through.

They both reached the top of the climb and Jack talked her through making her way across the top to the simulated helicopter. Two stories below, Ronnie chimed in with an instruction or two.

They reached the helicopter platform and Colleen willed her legs to stay upright. Across from them, and so very far down, she could see into Boone's open office door. He was sitting at his desk shuffling papers. Suddenly, Boone stood up and the loss of perspective made her light-headed. She teetered once and Jack grabbed her elbow.

"Steady now."

And of course, electricity zinged up her arm.

She shot him a weak smile. "I got it, thanks."

"Okay. We're going to attach our lines to the winch and rappel down as though we are jumping out of a helicopter in flight."

Jack showed Colleen the lines, both of them carefully moving next to each other on the small platform two stories above the bay floor. "Today we'll just do a simple rappel to give you the feel of it. I'll teach you how to do it in an emergency environment over the next few weeks." He handed her a pair of gloves, then reached out for the line and clipped it into the figure-eight rappeler connected to her harness.

"Keep one hand on the rope, about shoulder high. The other goes behind you, here." He wrapped it around to her hip. "You brake by pulling it in toward your body, and loosen by moving it away."

"Hanging in midair?"

"Yes." He clipped himself in. "For now, Ronnie has her eye on you, so don't worry." He looked down. "You all set, Ronnie?"

"Belay on!"

"Super. I'm going to step out, and then I want you to follow me."

She knew her eyes widened, because he smiled again, so much warmth in it she couldn't help but hear his voice from that night in the chopper. *Trust me.*

Maybe.

He stepped off the ledge, hanging from the pole. "Come out. It'll be fine."

Right. Fine. She leaned back on her brake hand and found the figure eight rappeler held her.

Then she pushed off.

Dangled from the top, just like Jack.

"See? Not so hard. Now, just let it out, a little at a time." He showed her how, dropping a few feet, then stopping his descent.

It couldn't be that easy. Except, as she let out, she found herself moving slowly down. "Oh!"

"If you go too fast, just bring it in."

She started sliding down, past him, faster—

"Pull in, Colleen!"

She yanked in, and somehow, the momentum not only stopped her, but pitched her forward. Suddenly, she was upside down, staring at the floor.

She let out a scream.

"You're fine." His steady voice was right by her ear. "Keep your hand on the brake—although Ronnie has you—and simply grab the rope with your right hand."

She looked up at him.

Oh, for Pete's sake. He was upside down, too, his brake hand holding him as he leaned back, his leg wrapped around his rappel rope. The other hand he stretched out to her. "Take my hand, Colleen."

She looked at him, his eyes holding hers, so blue.

So unafraid.

She reached out and took his hand. He moved it to her rope. "Okay, pull yourself up." He grabbed her arm and helped.

And then, just like that, she was upright. She hadn't fallen to her death, twenty feet below, hadn't slipped into a panic attack.

"See? You got this," he said, unhooking his leg and pulling himself upright too. So incredibly easy for a guy with his ropy muscles.

"Slowly now." He stayed even with her all the way to the bottom.

"Great job," Ronnie said as she waited next to the Stokes basket. "I'll be your patient."

They worked together to strap Ronnie into the basket, and then Jack showed Colleen how to winch the stretcher up to the helicopter while attaching herself to the lift.

She went up, and then moved the basket into the "helicopter."

She and Ronnie took the stairs down.

"A few more run-throughs of those steps and you'll be ready to do it on your own. You're a quick learner." Jack's compliment sent a wave of pleasure washing over Colleen.

He started winding up the ropes and gear, packing them away into a bag.

She rounded up the harnesses. "Thanks. I can see how this will take practice. But the steps themselves are simple enough."

"Not everyone feels that way. Some of the guys in my candidate squad never did get the hang of it." He stowed the equipment in a nearby locker.

"I think that might say more about the guys on your team."

Jack smiled at her quiet sarcasm, his eyes crinkling at the corners. "True. There were some real winners in my unit." He grabbed his water bottle. "Want one? There's a case in the kitchen."

She followed him into the kitchen. A box of donuts sat on the counter. He opened the fridge and pulled out a bottle.

She reached for a donut and sat on one of the high top chairs. "What made you want to go into Pararescue?"

He leaned a hip against the counter. Grabbed his own donut. She waited as he took a huge bite. He looked at the donut as though it held the answer to her question.

Finally, he spoke. "My dad and his dad were both in the Air Force. They were fighter pilots. I wasn't interested in doing that, but not being in the military wasn't really an option. I settled on saving lives. Plus, there's nothing like that moment, when you're hanging in the air and everything goes quiet."

Colleen met Jack's gaze. She noticed brilliant blue flecks mixed in with the darker iron near his irises. "That sounds almost magical."

Abruptly, his eyes shuttered. "Well, it was for a while, anyway."

Huh, what was that about?

"We'll have you flight certified in no time." He pushed away and headed out of the room.

Was it something she said?

∼

Jack wasn't sure how he'd found himself manning a grill in front of the Crisis Response Team headquarters on his only night off this week.

It must have been the lure of the near-perfect fall evening. Or the siren song of the waves crashing along the lakeshore. Yeah. That was it.

It definitely wasn't the sense of camaraderie that had swept into him as he'd helped train Colleen, and even Ronnie, on proper transport techniques this morning.

Or the way Colleen had looked at him when he'd helped her

out of her rappelling catastrophe. Big green eyes latching onto his, so much trust in them, it had swept the breath out of his chest.

Nope. Nope. He wasn't interested in a relationship, thank you. Been there, done that. He never could get the hang of baring his soul to a woman just to have her walk away. He wasn't interested in repeating that any time soon. Or ever.

Jack had spent the last week trying to lie low, and succeeding. There had been no more incidents at the VFW, just long boring nights working the 2:00–10:00 p.m. shift, flipping burgers and fiddling with recipes. He'd resisted all of Katie's attempts to get him to open up about himself.

He wasn't in town to make friends.

So, why had he agreed to come to this party?

It certainly wasn't a swinging ponytail or a pair of green eyes. Nope. Colleen Decker played no part in him deciding to join the group.

"Are you coming to the barbecue tonight?" She'd asked him during their training session that morning. Yeah, it was tempting to take her up on the offer to stick around, eat some burgers, and relax after a long day of training. But an event like that usually meant bonding, and bonding meant team building.

And no, he definitely wasn't going to be part of any team building. Especially for a team he wanted no part of. "I don't…"

"Of course he's coming." Boone had appeared from some dark corner and slapped him on the shoulder. "Who else is going to cook the burgers?"

"Boone—"

"C'mon, man. It's a beautiful night for a couple hours to relax with friends. You can't say no."

Hmm. One of these days, the debt to Boone would be paid and he could say no with a clear conscience.

Oh, who was he kidding? He owed Boone everything right now.

"Fine. I'll be there."

"Excellent. I hope you're up for making two dozen of your Juicy-Lucys."

Right. Now Jack lifted the edge on one of his cheese-stuffed burgers. Almost there.

The town couldn't have picked a better spot for their team's headquarters. The cement pad the grill sat on looked straight out over the lake. The gentle shoreline sloped away, ending at the rocks piled on the water's edge. Nearby, the team had found space to put in a sand volleyball court. A rowdy game was already taking place while they waited for the food.

Peter Dahlquist, the burly man he'd met at the coffee shop, came over to the grill. "I heard Mike's gonna be okay." He wore a pair of jeans, boots, and a blue Deep Haven Fire Department T-shirt.

"I heard that too. Looks like he won't miss much of the season either." Jack had gotten a call from Mike's mom thanking him for helping her son.

"Well, that's good news. I don't think they could afford to send him to college if it wasn't for the scholarship he was awarded."

"It was a close call. I'm glad it worked out."

On the volleyball court, Jack watched Peter rejoin the chaotic match, both teams shouting good-natured insults and encouragement.

"That's game!" Kyle Hueston called as the ball skittered off the court after a well-aimed spike.

Jack waved his spatula to draw the players' attention. "Burgers are ready!"

The group ambled over, laughing and teasing. Boone was hand in hand with Vivien, his girlfriend. Jack had met her a few nights ago at the VFW when the couple had come in for dinner. He'd never seen his friend look so light-hearted. Happy.

"That last serve was totally inside the line," Boone said.

"Give it up, Blue Eyes. You're never gonna convince anyone." Vivien bumped him with her shoulder. "We won fair and square."

As Boone started protesting, Jack caught the look in his eye. Oh, Boone was a goner. Jack felt a quick pang at the look that passed between the CRT coordinator and his feisty girlfriend. Lucky dog.

Colleen stepped up, the last in line for a burger. She held her plate out for him to load her bun. "I have high hopes for this hamburger, Chef. After the last one you served me, I expect good things."

He added a patty to his own bun and followed her to the picnic tables set near where the helicopter bay would eventually be built onto the building.

Taking a place across from Colleen and next to Boone at the table, Jack quickly assessed the eaters. Everyone seemed to be enjoying their burgers.

"Have you met everyone?" Boone asked, gesturing to the others. "You know Viv, Colleen, and Ronnie, of course. The others are Peter Dahlquist, fire chief, and Dan Matthews, a pastor here in town. And at the other table are Kyle Hueston—the sheriff—and Jensen Atwood. He owns a resort in town." He gestured to more members, giving names like Cole and Megan, but after a while the names began to blur together. No matter. It wasn't like he was going to be on the team anyway.

Jack saluted each one in turn with the red plastic cup in his hand. "I've seen some of them around and I met Peter at the Java Cup." The information Peter had shared about Colleen flashed into his mind. He'd kind of forgotten about it. He had to give her credit for how well she'd handled things today.

"I saw you on the wall, Colleen. You're a natural," Peter said. "I always feel like I'm a breath away from falling off that thing."

"Aw, thanks. I guess I still have some athlete in me after all. Plus, it helps to have a good teacher." Colleen winked at Jack.

And something funny happened to his brain. Or maybe it was his ears because he was having a lot of trouble hearing what Peter asked next.

"Is there a lot for you two to work on?"

Colleen outlined the plan they'd established. They would train together with the hands-on stuff for a few days a week while Colleen studied for the written exams on her own. She'd promised to get in touch if anything in the manual didn't make sense.

"You should get Jack to teach you some orienteering," Boone commented.

"Orienteering?" Colleen shot him a look.

Boone took a huge bite of his burger so Jack filled in the answer. "They taught us that in the service. It's basically using a compass or other fixed points to find your way quickly from one place to another. Boone's right. We should include that in your training."

He still wasn't sure why Colleen had agreed to the training. He'd have put money on her hightailing it back to civilization. She'd been adamant enough in Boone's office that day, not to mention at the VFW.

"Hey, Colleen, how's your grandma?" Pastor Dan asked from the end of the table.

And then the light in her eyes just...went out. "It's not looking good this time. The cancer is back and more aggressive." She hunched her shoulders. "My parents are worried. Frank is worried. They've asked me to stick around and help with her care. I think she's going to need a lot of help before this is over."

"I'm sorry to hear that." Dan nodded gravely. "I'll keep her in my prayers."

Well, that explained her sticking around. Maybe she figured she'd get the certification to fall back on. She'd probably take a flight nurse job out of Minneapolis when her grandma recovered.

An even worse thought occurred to him. She'd been carrying this burden all day and hadn't said *anything*. He felt like a heel for not noticing she was going through some stuff. But wasn't that exactly what he wanted? To keep his head down, not get involved in other people's problems. Why should he care if Colleen's grandma was sick? He was here to train her to do the flight nurse job and that was it.

Still, he did care, and as the crew cleared away the mess from supper, Jack approached Colleen. "Good job out there today. I'm sorry about your grandma. I didn't know."

Colleen stacked used paper plates and walked with Jack to the garbage can. "How would you have known? Sure, we live in a small town, but the gossip doesn't always spread that quickly."

"Do you mind if I ask what kind of cancer?"

"Breast cancer. Stage 3. It's metastasized to a few of her lymph nodes." Colleen reached up and tightened her ponytail.

"That stinks. Let me know if there is anything I can do."

Wait—what? But the words were out.

Colleen paused and seemed to be considering something. "Thanks. I...you were great today. I appreciate your help climbing."

"Anytime." And now he just sounded desperate.

She walked out to her car. "Thanks again!"

"You bet." Jack held up his hand.

He returned to the grill, cleaned it, and packed it away. By the time he was finished, most of the team had gone.

"Thanks again for dinner." Turning around, he spotted Boone, who held out a plate covered with tin foil. "Leftover Lucies."

"Thanks, Boone."

"Thank *you* for agreeing to train Colleen. It looked like you had a good first day."

"Her friend was right. Colleen is a quick learner. She's fearless and spunky."

"You two make a good team. You know, I could maybe make two part-time jobs available for the flight nurse position." Boone raised one eyebrow.

"I told you I don't want to do it. Besides, I don't think Colleen will want me hanging around."

Boone raised his hands in surrender. "Can't blame a guy for trying. If I hadn't just eaten three burgers, I'd say you're wasted being a cook over at the VFW. As it is though, you've proven that grilling is a God-given talent. I'd hate to take you away from using that gift."

"I don't think God is in the habit of handing out burger-flipping talents. Especially not to guys like me."

Boone frowned, made a funny sound. "That's *exactly* what God is in the habit of doing. He takes ordinary things in our lives and changes them into something holy, something that can be used for Him. Also, enough with the 'guys like me' attitude. God is in the redemption business. No matter what you've done, He offers fresh starts."

Could Boone be right? Could God use his talents despite his history?

"You know, Jack, sometimes God uses a person *because* of what they've done, not *in spite* of it. Do you think you're the first person to go to prison because of someone else's mistake? Maybe God wants to take that experience and ask you to minister to someone who is trapped."

Jack looked at him. "I'm just here to flip burgers."

But Boone's gaze hung onto Jack as he headed to his truck—and long after he'd driven back home.

CHAPTER 6

*M*aybe being back home would work out after all.

Because sitting in church listening to Pastor Dan—yes, this felt right.

Colleen had woken early this morning buoyed by the good training the morning before. Learning the procedures had been a breeze, and she wasn't too ashamed of her performance on the rock climbing wall. Not too shabby for a newbie. Jack had seemed pleased with her progress, and he'd called her brave.

Twice.

She had lain in bed for a few minutes, reliving the evening hanging around with the team for the barbecue and the fun of their volleyball game. After Ella had moved up to Deep Haven, Colleen had never found a different friend group in Minneapolis to hang with. Working the night shift wasn't really conducive to making new friends. She had to admit, it got lonely in that little two-bedroom apartment in Robbinsdale.

It didn't hurt that her flight nurse instructor was straight up hot. She may have been distracted by her own problems on the rock wall, but not too distracted to appreciate watching him stretch to reach a high grip. His biceps had strained against his

T-shirt, revealing some real deal muscles. He had the body of an athlete, honed by self-discipline. His dark blond hair and scruff of a beard added to the man's mystique.

And then he'd sort of saved her.

Yep, coming back home just might be the best decision she'd ever made.

Colleen gave herself a mental shake. She'd missed church the first Sunday she'd been home, but had been determined to make it this week. So this morning she'd forced herself out of bed and her mind off of Jack. She'd pulled on a skirt and sweater and had headed to church with her family.

Now they sat in the same worn pew they'd sat in all through her high school years. Around her the church glowed with light gleaming through the stained-glass windows. On the altar in the front, the women's guild had put out the usual fall arrangement. She'd bet they'd changed it to that gold, red, and burgundy floral arrangement on the first Sunday in September like clockwork. Throughout the service, they sang a few old familiar hymns and Pastor Dan spoke truth from the pulpit.

Just like always.

Not that she wasn't grateful for the sameness. There was comfort there, like an old worn blanket tailor-made to fit. She didn't have time to reflect though, as right after the final hymn, she felt a tapping on her shoulder.

Colleen turned to her left. She'd slid into the pew next to Edith Draper at the beginning of the service, but hadn't had time for much more than a quick smile in greeting.

"So, you're back from the big city," the older woman said by way of greeting. "I didn't get much chance to say hello at your grandma's party last week."

"Hello to you too." Colleen smiled at Edith. The older woman's white hair framed her face. Laugh lines crinkled at the corners of each eye. Edith had to be pushing 85, but she was still spry and alert. "Yes, I'm home for a little while. I'm glad you were able to be at the party. It was such an honor for Grandma and Frank to have so many of their friends there."

And it had been quite the party. Her mother had outdone herself with the decorations, flowers arranged by Claire Atwood, and food provided by Grace Christiansen Sharpe. The room had filled with laughter throughout the night as people packed in to deliver well-wishes. Near the end of the night, Frank had stood, using his crutches for support, and given a toast to her Grandma Helen. His tender words of love had brought tears to Colleen's eyes.

"Are you still worrying your mother sick by running around with that bad boy, Tucker Newman?" Edith eyed her sharply.

The question threw her for a moment. It had been *years* since she and Tucker had broken up. Although that didn't stop his voice from creeping into her mind at odd times. "Um, no. We actually broke up a few years ago."

"I'm glad you aren't with that crowd anymore. Oh dear, I'm sorry. I didn't mean to bring up old memories. It's so hard to keep up with everyone's lives sometimes."

"It's fine. I don't mind." The old memories weren't bad, exactly. In fact, Tucker was probably right—she hadn't known what she had in him until he was gone.

Edith gave her one last long look. "I see. Well, I'm glad you're back up here and not getting into trouble at the U of M. I'll see you around." She toddled off.

That was...strange. Edith had seemed to think she was still in college. Maybe her parents hadn't really talked about her graduation.

Three years ago.

In the pew in front of her, she glimpsed Darek and Ivy Christiansen. Standing next to them was Joy, their daughter. She'd grown a foot since Colleen had seen her last. "Hey, stranger!" Ivy smiled warmly and wrapped Colleen in a hug. Joy tucked herself half behind Ivy. "This is the second weekend in a row you've been home. We saw you at the party."

It seemed everyone had seen her at that party. She didn't know why they hadn't greeted her then, but it had been a busy night and she'd spent a lot of it in the kitchen, making sure the food was perfect. It made sense she hadn't seen many of them in return.

A throat cleared behind her. She spun around to see Ingrid Christiansen and Meredith Johnson standing there. The older ladies beamed at her. Ingrid held out her arms, and Colleen leaned over the back of the pew for an awkward hug.

"Colleen, it's so nice to see you!" Ingrid's warm welcome was an embrace in itself. "Tell me about volleyball. You're still playing, I hope."

Wait a minute.

A brief flash of…something blazed through Colleen. It was hard to be annoyed at Mrs. Christiansen, but did Ingrid *really* think she was still in high school or something? She should know better. Colleen was the same age as Amelia, the Christiansen's youngest daughter. Did the whole town only think of her as the volleyball girl who'd dated Tucker? Every time she came home, it was the same thing. No one recognized that she'd grown up. "Um, no. I stopped playing volleyball in college. I had a shoulder injury my first year and had to give it up."

Ingrid put her hand to her face. "Oh, that's right. Silly me. Of course you're not still playing volleyball. I knew that you had to give it up a few years ago. I guess I was hoping after college you'd be able to pick it up again."

"You moved to Minneapolis, right?" Meredith Johnson put in.

Before Colleen could answer, her mom came to her rescue. She slid into the pew next to Colleen and put her arm around her. "She has moved back home for a bit. She's training to be a flight nurse on the Crisis Response Team." Her mom gave her shoulder a little squeeze then dropped her arm.

"So, you're going to be around?" Meredith Johnson reached out and took her hand. "My son Sammy will be glad to hear it. He always liked watching you play volleyball. I'm sure he'd love to know you're in town." She patted Colleen's hand. "I'll tell him to give you a call." Meredith let her hand go and started to shuffle out of the pew.

Her mother wore a funny smile. "Sammy is cute. And he's a good boy."

"Mom." She drew the word into several syllables. "Sammy is a lumberjack."

"What's wrong with a lumberjack?"

"Nothing exactly. But the last person I want to be with is a lumberjack-slash-snowplow driver living in a small town in a shack in the woods. Blaze orange is not a good color for me."

Her mother shot her an amused look, raising her eyebrows. "A lumberjack in a shack? Really? Did I raise a snob?"

"Okay, he probably doesn't live in a *shack*. And there's nothing wrong with being a lumberjack. But, Mom, this is the reason I moved down by Minneapolis. I want more for my life than what is always expected. I never wanted to stay in this small town."

"I guess I can understand that. Don't be too quick to overlook small-town life though." She put her hands on Colleen's upper arms. "Just because you live in a small place doesn't mean you have to live a small life. And it doesn't mean you can't find exactly what you've been looking for. Look at your dad and me. Neither one of us thought we'd end up here, but we couldn't be happier."

"Yeah, I suppose."

"Just think about it, honey. I want you to be happy with your choices in life. I'm glad that those choices led you home for now, and if you choose not to stay, I'll be content with that also.

But I wouldn't want you to overlook something just because you assume something about it. You might be wrong."

Yeah, well, her mother didn't know how it felt to grow up in a small town with a long memory. She wasn't the rebellious girl who'd left Deep Haven. If only everyone else could see that.

She pushed out of the pew and through the groups of people clustered here and there between her and the door.

The open door to the parking lot beckoned. She'd almost made it through when she felt a hand on her shoulder.

"Colleen?" She turned to see Ellie Mathews standing there, clipboard in hand. "I'm glad I caught you. I'm signing up volunteers for the Fall Festival. I heard you might be staying in town. Can I put you down for running the rubber duck pond? It's a fairly straightforward job. We just need someone to make sure the water stays in the kiddie pool and not dumped all over the church carpet." Ellie held up a pen, eyes wide.

Colleen stared at the woman.

Unbelievable.

The one person who actually acknowledged she was a grown up didn't actually see her as an individual and instead only wanted to rope her into one of the crazy, small-town festivals.

"No, thanks," she managed. Turning, she pushed through the door and fled into the cool fall air.

Maybe this had been a terrible idea.

～

Just one more set of reps and he would quit for the day.

Around Jack, the weight room at headquarters was quiet. He'd only turned on the half bank of lights above him, and late autumn sunlight filtering into the windows cut through the darkness and shadows of the rest of the bay. He'd come in early. Snuck in, really. He knew that many of the team attended church on Sunday mornings and he would have the place to himself.

He preferred it that way.

Besides, if he wanted to do right by Colleen and the promise he'd made to train her, he needed to stay in shape. So he'd put himself through his normal routine before ending up here, on the bench press.

He planted his feet firmly, pushed against the bar across his chest. His back tightened against the bench he lay on. Two more reps and he'd meet his goal.

The training exercises the day before had worn him out more than he'd expected. And it wasn't all physical fatigue either. Taking Colleen through the steps of tying up the rescue basket and securing the safety lines had reawakened a part of his brain he'd thought he'd buried in a star-spangled casket.

He had tried to drown the memories in a long, hot shower, but they insisted on resurfacing. Standing in his bathroom, he was suddenly right back in training with Ryan Nelson. Jack smiled, remembering the way Ryan would razz Jack when he couldn't get the double figure eight fisherman's knot to come out right. *"C'mon, Win. How many times do we gotta go through this?"*

"Sorry, Ryan. It's not Win anymore." He spoke into the quiet air to banish the memory.

Yep. Those thoughts bubbling up had made it hard to breathe.

Thankfully, he'd shoved them right down again. He'd even slept like a baby last night. He'd dreamt of green eyes and a strawberry-blonde ponytail. Colleen had impressed him on the climbing wall. And he hadn't been kidding when he'd said she was a fast learner. She'd caught on to the knot tying with little practice. It wouldn't take her long to finish up her training and be ready for her exams.

The laughter from the barbecue wended its way through his mind.

If he wasn't careful, he'd learn to like being on a team again.

Last push on this set.

Halfway into the raise, as his arms locked upright, Jack knew he was in trouble. In trying to push himself, he'd put too much weight on the bar.

He needed to move it onto the stand, but if he missed, the bar would crush his chest.

His arms shook with the effort. A roaring echoed in his ears. He squeezed his eyes shut. He wasn't going to make it.

Without warning, the bar lightened. Jack's eyes popped open.

"Whoa there, buddy. Let's get that secured."

Leaning above him, bearing some of the weight, was Cole Barrett. Jack had been introduced to the ex-Army Ranger the night before at the barbecue. He'd been friendly enough then. The look on his face now was decidedly not friendly.

Together, the two men lifted the barbell into the J-hooks on the rack.

Jack sat up on the bench, sweating, breathing hard.

Cole scowled at him. "What. Were. You. Thinking?" Each word growled out of him. "That was an incredibly stupid thing to do. You were lucky I saw the lights on in here and came in to check the place. Do you have a death wish?"

"You're right. I'm sorry." Jack flushed with heat. "I'm used to working out without a spotter." Well, at least he'd gotten used to it in prison. He was too white-collar for the hard-core criminals and too hard core for the white-collar guys, so he never had a gang. He'd ended up just trying to keep out of everybody's way. When he'd had gym time, he'd had to make do on his own.

"That's not going to fly around here. No solo lifting, man." Cole's face was closer to its normal color. "It's against the rules to lift weights without a partner. Besides, you don't need to do it on your own anymore. That's what the team is for."

Jack got up, grabbed his towel, and scraped it down his face. "Listen, I'm not on the team. I'm just temporarily helping out." His protest sounded a little whiny even in his own ears.

Cole let out a breath. His face relaxed from its last trace of anger. "Look, you've got to understand the MO of everyone in this town. Once you're here, you're family. We watch out for our own."

Huh. An unfamiliar sensation wound through him and squeezed a part he'd thought long dead. A piece of him that desired a place to fit in. Where, maybe, he could belong.

He met Cole's gaze. "I'll remember that."

The feeling stuck with Jack through a quick shower in the locker room after Cole had left. He was still thinking about it as he made his way to the Java Cup and ordered an Americano to go. He planned to work out a few more recipes at the tiny bistro table that sat in his galley kitchen upstairs.

Climbing the stairs to his apartment with a coffee in hand, Jack had to do a juggling act to answer his ringing cell phone. His dad's face was on the caller ID.

"Hey, Wi—Jack, how are you?" His congressman father, Christopher Stewart, always sounded like he was giving a campaign speech. Jack pictured him on the other end of the line. Likely wearing a suit, fresh from church, with his dark hair slicked into a news anchor worthy style. His piercing, light blue eyes, intent on business papers spread before him.

His dad was a consummate multitasker, but somehow he still gave the impression that each individual was consuming all of his attention. Jack supposed that was how he'd won reelection so many times in a row.

"Doing okay, Dad." He tucked the phone into his shoulder as he unlocked his door. He'd talked to his dad twice since moving to Deep Haven. Dad had reluctantly agreed to call him Jack, though he argued that Jack shouldn't be ashamed of being called Win. It was a family name—he'd been named after his grandpa on his dad's side. "I worked out that new recipe for fried chicken. I'll have to make it for you some time. You can tell me if you think it tastes like the stuff we had down in Louisiana at Mama Creole's place."

After his mom died, Jack and his dad had visited Mama Creole's several years in a row. The last time they'd been to Louisiana, they'd discovered that Mama had lost her restaurant to Hurricane Katrina. He'd been tinkering with a breading recipe, trying to get it to taste like the iconic fried chicken he remembered.

"That's great. Maybe I'll come up to your VFW to try it out." His dad cleared his throat. "I'm glad to hear things are going well. Have you seen much of your friend Boone?"

"Actually, I'm over at his workplace a lot. I'm training a woman named Colleen to be a flight nurse."

"It sounds like your certification is coming in handy. Maybe you should take that job yourself."

Jack set down the coffee on the table. "I never want to fly in a helicopter again, Dad. You know that."

"Right. Right. I just thought maybe it would be different as a civilian."

"Nope. That hasn't changed a thing." His dad had been supportive of his decision not to re-up after his last tour. He'd claimed that he understood. And maybe he did. After all, Jack came from a long line of military men. His dad and his grandpa had both been Air Force pilots. His grandpa had seen action in Vietnam and his father had flown during the Gulf War in '90. They both knew the toll it took.

Jack suspected his father had never approved of his decision to train as a medic in Pararescue instead of as a fighter pilot. But Jack could never stomach the idea of taking lives. He believed in saving lives at any cost.

His dad had also hoped Jack would follow him into politics. Now, one bad choice had ruined that too.

Jack walked over to the window. Below, the water was a deep blue, the trees along the shoreline a burst of color. Not a bad place to hide.

"How are Melissa and Ethan?" His stepmom and half brother were a semi-safe subject.

"Good. They're good. Ethan is starting as halfback at Kellogg High this season." A hint of pride rang through the tinny phone connection.

Jack glanced at the photo of the three of them where he'd propped it up on his dresser.

"Dad, when I'm finished up with this training, I'd love to come home for a visit. It's been a long time since I've seen Ethan. He's probably shot up three inches since I was last there."

He'd welcome a chance to get to know his brother. After all, he'd been shipped off to boarding school shortly after Ethan had turned a year old. That had been Jack's fault though—another time where no good deed went unpunished. He'd only been trying to give his brother some breakfast. As a ten-year-old he hadn't known that babies shouldn't eat honey. Or whole grapes. Now, as an adult, he understood his stepmom's reaction, but at the time it had felt like his father was choosing his new family over him.

He still wasn't sure about that last part. His dad did a lot of choosing his new wife and younger son and very little of choosing Jack.

His father cleared his throat. "I don't know, Jack. I've got a lot of engagements coming up, and your brother is busy at school. Maybe we can work something out after the holidays."

Translation: He didn't want his ex-con son to come home and ruin any photo ops. Especially in an election year. Jack pinched the bridge of his nose.

There was a muffled voice and some rustling on his dad's

end of the phone. "Okay. Listen, Jack, I've got to run, but let's have a longer catch-up soon. I'm glad you're doing well in Deep Haven. It sounds like a good place to start over. Maybe that's what you need right now."

"Thanks, Dad. Fine. I'll talk to you later." Jack ended the call and sat on the edge of his bed, holding the device in his hands.

His dad wanted him to stay put. He didn't say as much, but then he never had to. His disappointment was always clear to Jack.

And maybe he was right. Maybe it was time to start putting down roots. It was obvious he couldn't ever go home. Perhaps Deep Haven was home now.

Jack stood and crossed to where a pile of laundry lay on the table. He neatly folded the shirts and put them in the dresser's second drawer, a space that fit them exactly.

Deep Haven was going to be home for a while. He just had to figure out how not to screw it all up.

CHAPTER 7

*C*ould this day get any worse?

Colleen stood in her grandmother's kitchen as smoke poured from the oven. She'd stuck a casserole from a neighbor in before taking her grandma to her doctor's appointment. But the chemo treatment had run long and by the time they got home, the tuna noodle had turned into tuna crisp—extra burnt.

Colleen raced around the room opening up all the windows, the fire alarm shrieking, keeping up its noise. She grabbed a sheet pan from the drawer under the oven and waved it beneath the box. Maybe the air flow would shut the dumb thing off.

When at last the kitchen became mercifully quiet, she went around and shut the windows again. At the table, Grandma Helen shivered.

"I'm so sorry! This is no day to have the windows open." Colleen snagged a knitted afghan from the nearby couch and draped it on her grandmother's shoulders.

She glanced at the calendar on the wall. How was it Wednesday already? Monday and Tuesday had disappeared in a blur of Colleen helping both Grandma Helen and Frank to doctors' appointments. And then the three of them had spent time writing thank-you notes to the guests at the anniversary party. They took frequent breaks for Grandma Helen and Frank to rest.

This morning, John Christiansen had picked up Frank, claiming he needed some guy time. He had promised to have him back later in the afternoon. Colleen hoped they were having a better time—and a more palatable lunch.

Grandma Helen sat in a straight-backed chair at the table. "No problem, dear. The chemo has that effect on me. I'm cold all the time." Her grandmother broke into a chuckle, her shoulders shaking.

"What? What's so funny?" Colleen couldn't find any humor in their situation.

"I've always hated tuna noodle casserole. Looks like you found a way for me to avoid eating it." Grandma's smile warmed Colleen to her bones. Her chuckle turned to a laugh. "And you looked so funny trying to shoo that smoke right out of here."

"Why do you have a tuna casserole if you hate it so much?"

"People keep bringing me things. I don't have the heart to tell them no."

Colleen sat next to Grandma Helen at the table. "What should we eat instead?" She covered her grandma's cold hand with her own, hoping to transfer some of her warmth.

"I've always been partial to a peanut butter and jelly sandwich."

That was one thing Colleen could certainly manage.

By the time they had eaten half of their sandwiches, Grandma Helen was looking very wan. Colleen wrapped up her uneaten half in plastic wrap and carried it to the master bedroom. "Let me help you into bed for a nap. I'll leave this here in case you get hungry when you wake up."

As she walked her grandma down the hall, she paused to

look at the photo gallery hung on the walls. Grandma Helen touched the photo of a graduate in his cap and gown.

"Nathan's graduation was the proudest day of my life. Until you kids came along. Your brothers are great, but there is something special about watching a granddaughter grow up. It pleases me to see you making such good choices. I'm so proud of you, honey."

"Thanks, Grandma. That means more than you know." She helped her into bed and pulled the coverlet up over her thin shoulders. She'd have to make sure that there was plenty of interesting food in the house to tempt her appetite. "Gotta go, Grandma. My next training session starts in twenty minutes. Frank should be home in an hour or two. I'll check back in with you tonight." She bent and kissed her grandma on the cheek.

"Stay safe now. Thanks for helping me today."

"I will. And you know I'm glad I can be with you."

Outside, Colleen zipped up her jacket, the frigid air startling her a little. They might have an early snow. She looked up at the gun-metal gray clouds whisking through the sky. Yep. Snow for sure. Hopefully it wouldn't be too much. An early storm usually passed quickly but could be dangerous for drivers not yet used to winter driving.

She got into her car and turned on the radio. The Beach Boys sang about good vibrations as she drove through town. She was still humming to herself as she parked in the lot at headquarters.

This time she had no trouble pushing through the door. She was already looking forward to putting some of her newfound skills to the test.

Inside the gym area, Peter and Kyle were sparring, some sort of complicated routine. She watched them a moment until she saw the pattern emerge. In another corner, Ronnie and Cole pored over a clipboard. Where was…?

There. She spotted Jack halfway up the climbing wall.

Colleen stood there and took a moment to admire his, um, climbing form. He wore a pair of compression shorts, climbing shoes, and a sleeveless shirt that showed off his muscled arms. The guy made rock climbing look *easy*. One handhold followed another in rapid succession, very Spider-Man.

In just the few minutes that she stood there, he finished the wall. Suddenly she realized he had been taking it easy on her the other day.

Heat blazed through her. She stalked over to where Jack descended and landed on the mat.

"Hey." She got right up next to him and poked a finger in his chest. "You can't treat me like that."

He held up both hands in surrender. "Whoa. Treat you like what? What did I do?"

"You were going easy on me. Telling me I was brave and doing a good job. Well, I saw you on that wall just now, and it's *very* apparent to me that I was *not* doing a good job. I was doing a very *mediocre* job."

His mouth quirked into a smile. And, darn it, he had a really great smile. "Colleen, how many times had you gone rock climbing before that? Or even been on a climbing wall?"

The single time at REI flashed through her mind. "Um, once."

"Right. That's what I thought you said. Most people can't even make it up a wall this high on their *second ever wall climb*. I meant what I said. You did a great job."

Oh.

"I just don't want you to treat me like I'm made out of glass or something. I want to know how to do it right and do it with excellence."

"Trust me. I won't go easy on you. And I would never think you are made out of glass." He slipped out of his harness. "You have too much iron grit. You're more like a finely crafted steel blade."

SUSAN MAY WARREN & ANDREA CHRISTENSON

And there he went again, telling her the truth she longed to hear about herself. She didn't feel like iron or steel. She felt like a slightly burnt tuna noodle.

Jack broke into her thoughts, oblivious to the feelings he'd sparked. "Kyle volunteered to be our victim, so if you're ready to start training, we'll interrupt his sparring."

She nodded mutely.

At Jack's call, Kyle jogged over to them. "Where do you want me?"

Colleen directed him to lay near the rescue equipment. Together, she and Jack ran through the steps of securing the "patient" in the Stokes basket. Colleen adjusted the straps, pulling them tight, then doing it all over again at Jack's urging.

By the time Jack made her run through the steps a third time, her brain was swimming and her fingers were rubbed nearly raw.

"Now we need to climb up and winch the basket to the practice helo." Jack was already stepping into his climbing harness.

Colleen reached for her harness, fumbling to put it on. The leg straps twisted as she drew them up over her jeans. She huffed and started over. This time, the harness lay flat.

She tied herself into the rope and approached the wall.

"Why don't you move down to this side?" Jack gestured to the more difficult end of the climbing wall. "You could use some more reps with the wider spacing."

"Don't worry about me," Kyle called from his prone position on the floor. "I had a late night last night. I'm just gonna take a nap down here."

Colleen laughed, some of the pressure disappearing. She studied her route before taking her first step onto the wall. Jack stayed below to spot her.

Hugging close to the wall, she slowly made her way up and across the tougher route.

Halfway up, she knew she was in trouble. All the retying

she had done had left her hands tired and sore. The busyness of the week caught up with her and she couldn't suppress her fatigue.

She tried using her legs to take the pressure off her hands and fingers, but she could feel her thighs begin to burn.

"Hey, Jack?" she called down to him. "I don't think I'm going to make it up."

"You're doing fine. Keep going. Look to your left. There's an easy hand grip there."

She saw the grip he indicated and reached for it. The handgrip was farther than it looked. She stretched her arm as far as it would go, shifting her leg to match, putting all her weight on the left side.

But then, her leg just gave out and she was falling.

The belay slowed her down, but she hadn't climbed far, so Jack let her glide all the way to the ground.

Then he caught her, his arms going around her before she went *splat* on the floor. Or worse, landing on Kyle, still playing the part of the patient a foot or two away. She closed her eyes. How humiliating.

Jack smelled good. Yes, a little sweaty, but mostly manly, a hint of soap still on his skin.

Oh. She squirmed out of his embrace. "Thanks. I can't believe how stupid that was."

"It's no big deal. I had you. I'm just glad you weren't injured."

"Yeah, nothing hurt but my pride."

Jack's mouth twisted into a half smile. "At least that heals quickly. Probably without a scar."

Okay, yeah, she could think about that. But right now, the humiliation stung.

"Let's take a break for today. We've accomplished a lot." Jack walked away to wind up the climbing gear as Colleen released Kyle from his safety straps.

In the rescue basket, Kyle sat up. "I'm impressed, Colleen."

"Impressed by what? My complete screwup? It's a good thing you weren't really injured or you would not have survived."

"C'mon, don't be so hard on yourself. It takes time and patience to perfect anything. You know that."

"Fine. I guess you're right. I'm just used to things being easy for me."

"Not many good things are easy." Kyle began clearing away the rescue basket equipment supplies and Jack returned to give him a hand. "I should think you would know that after all the trauma you went through in high school. You've really come a long way since then."

Colleen caught Jack looking at her. Of course Kyle knew about the crazy WITSEC story, but she didn't need it broadcast to Jack.

"Would you like to talk about it?" Jack asked quietly. "Maybe...over a Coke?"

She sighed. But if they were going to be partners, it wouldn't hurt to let him in a little. After all, the man had caught her. Made her feel safe.

"All right."

When their gear was properly stowed, the two entered the kitchen.

Colleen sat at one of the small tables.

Back to her, Jack studied the vending machines before feeding in a dollar bill. "Want a Snickers bar too?"

"No, just the Coke." Her stomach needed to settle down before she added chocolate.

"Cheap date."

He joined her at the bistro table.

Twin hisses sounded from their pop bottles. Colleen took a long swallow. The sweet fizz rolled over her tongue and down her throat. She closed her eyes and sighed. Opened them to find him staring at her.

"Sorry, I guess I really needed that drink." She gave him a quick grin.

"Looked like it." He took a long drink of his own. "Listen, about earlier—"

"I'm sorry." They both spoke at the same time. She gestured for him to go first.

"What happened on the wall today was totally normal for a new climber. You recovered well."

"Pssht. I screwed up. Again. First the rappel, now the climb. I'm not sure I'm ever going to get this. You don't have to try to make me feel better." She stared at the bubbles making their way up the soda bottle. Each one struggled to the top before popping in a miniature explosion. Boone had asked her today when she was going to schedule her certification exam, but she'd put him off. Again.

"It really was no big deal. Even your fall was done with skill. You remembered to push away from the wall, you kept your knees bent to absorb the hit, and you exhaled on impact."

Yeah, the impact into his arms. And her exhale was merely her shock.

He did have a nice set of muscles.

"I'll do better next time."

"Actually, I think next time we are going to climb a real wall. Kyle told me about a place near here, Palace Head?"

"Palisade Head," she corrected him. "He's right. It's not too far. But I don't think I'm ready."

He tipped his Coke toward her. Winked. "You're just going to have to trust your teacher."

She didn't have a reply to that.

"Uh, so you asked about what Kyle said about high school. It's kind of a long story." She took another swig of the pop. "And it begins before I was born." She gave him a brief sketch of how, as a young woman, her mom had fallen for the wrong guy. After he'd killed someone, she testified against him and was given a new life, a new name, in Deep Haven.

Jack looked appropriately shocked.

"Then she married my dad, settled down, had us kids, and lived her new life."

"Brave lady." His admiring tone didn't escape her.

"Yeah, I can see that now, but when I was sixteen I didn't feel that way." She didn't need to tell him *all* her high school secrets. It was kind of nice to have someone who didn't see her just as high school Colleen, always in trouble with "that Tucker boy."

"During my junior year, the guy who my mom testified against was let out of prison. He figured out where she was and caught up to us here." She paused, remembering how naive she'd been, thinking her problems were the biggest thing in her life. No wonder people had a hard time respecting her. High school Colleen had been awful.

"The guy—Luis Garcia—lured me into his car and threatened me with a knife. He wanted me to tell him where my mom was. When I refused, he hit me then made me go to my volleyball game and act like nothing had happened. He said if I didn't, he'd kill my whole family. Anyway, my family had a lot of mending to do after all of that."

Starting with her admitting she had been stupid to get into a stranger's car. She waited for Jack to say as much.

"You're lucky to have such a close family. It's no wonder you have so much grit and determination."

Oh.

"I was incredibly lucky. I made a huge, stupid mistake, and lots of people could have gotten hurt because of it."

"It doesn't look that way to me. It looks like you did what you had to in order to keep yourself and your family safe. I think you're brave."

His words sank deep. Found a sore spot in her heart and wrapped like a balm on the tender area.

Except he didn't understand. She pictured her run-in with Joseph Terranova, the glimpse of a tattoo peeping out from under his shirt sleeve.

"I'm not brave. I still freak out at the worst times, actually." And she didn't know why telling him felt so important right then. "I recently had a really bad experience with a patient." She peeled the label from her coke bottle. "I was held hostage with a scalpel by a guy who had just been in a shoot-out with the cops. The criminal was subdued but not before he gave me a souvenir." She pulled her hair back, giving Jack a look at the mark on her neck.

His face completely changed. "Who did that to you?"

"Just a guy in Minneapolis."

He sat back, his mouth pinched. Shook his head.

Yeah, he thought it too, probably. "I was so stupid."

Jack looked up at her. "Stupid? Hardly—"

"Yes. I totally trusted him and I shouldn't have. I felt *sorry* for him, broke protocol, and got close enough for him to grab me. Stupid is exactly what I was."

He was shaking his head. "No. You were doing your job— being a nurse. And sometimes that backfires. But it doesn't mean you were stupid."

He drew in a breath, then glanced away for a moment.

That hooded look again.

"Jack?" She couldn't breathe as his dark blue eyes moved back and studied her. He shifted in his chair, and for the space of a heartbeat she thought he was going to reach out and take her hand.

Instead, he reached for his drink. "Okay, so ready to run it again?"

Right.

She nodded. He got up and headed out to the climbing wall.

But she couldn't help but think that somehow she'd stumbled into something more than his arms. A wound maybe.

And Colleen was a nurse. She couldn't deny that deep inside her...she wanted to fix it.

~

Jack couldn't have planned a nicer day.

Palisade Head was located at the end of a spit of road off Highway 61, which ended at a sheer two-hundred-foot cliff that was apparently the highlight of all the local climbers.

He parked his truck and he and Colleen retrieved their gear and hiked out to the edge.

"We're climbing that?" She looked over the edge.

The rock face below them rose up dry and craggy. But there were plenty of easy handholds for a beginner. "No problem, Colleen. You can do this."

Overhead, clouds studded through a blue sky. The trees lining the top of the cliff showcased their rainbow colors.

They'd spent two more days climbing the wall at headquarters, and she'd gotten better at managing her weight and then rappelling. It wouldn't be long before she'd pass her certification and his job would be over.

Job. Felt more like a friendship, really.

Maybe even something more, although he was too smart for that. Still, hearing her tell her story of being attacked had ignited something almost dangerous inside him. The image of someone with a knife to her throat had nearly caused his own to close up. And the fact that it had happened to her more than once knotted his gut.

So, maybe he cared. A little. Why not? She was pretty. And brave. And seemed to enjoy hanging out with him too.

And, she didn't ask any personal questions.

Next to him, Colleen was already gearing up, her eyes bright, her normal ponytail swinging. She looked fresh today. A hint of apple shampoo caught his senses when her shoulder brushed his. She wore leggings and a tight, easy-moving top under her green puffer jacket.

He finished tying off his anchor lines for the belay. "Let me check to make sure your harness isn't twisted." He did a quick visual check of the Black Diamond harness she'd already stepped into. He would lower her down, and then she'd climb back up.

In a clearing nearby, a family—mom, dad, and two elementary-aged school kids—threw a Frisbee around, taking advantage of a rare, beautiful Saturday in October. The dad called out encouragement to the younger boy when the plastic disc sailed over his head.

Watching them a moment, Jack swallowed against the tightness in his throat. *Focus back on your climbing partner, Stewart. Getting sentimental helps no one.*

"This won't be much different than what you did on the wall back at headquarters." Jack looped her rope in a double figure eight knot around a carabiner and clipped it to her belay loop. "Obviously as we are starting at the top of the cliff instead of the bottom, you'll begin by rappelling down, then climbing back up. But the main difference out here is that instead of the belay device holding you steady as you rappel down, it will be a combo of me and a sturdy tree."

"The what device?"

"The pulley system attached to the ceiling."

"Oh, right."

The sun glinting off Colleen's ponytail cast a glow around her and distracted him for a moment. "I'll be controlling the slack on the rope from up here, letting it out as you descend. Then, pulling it in when you climb back up."

"So we do this as a team." The smile she shot him matched the glow of her hair.

He quickly looked away. Cleared his throat. "Let's do a quick run-through of the terminology again."

Colleen ran a hand around the harness strapped to her waist. "I think I have it. This is my climbing harness. The rope is the rope." She shot him a smile and the day grew even brighter. "Going down is rappelling and coming up is climbing."

"Good. You remember the signals?"

She pulled on a pair of fingerless gloves. "'On belay' when I am ready, 'rappelling' as I get started, then 'off belay' when I get to the bottom."

"Right."

He walked over to his anchor line, then clipped into it with his carabiner, sat down, and wove the rope around his back.

Colleen walked to the edge of the cliff and turned to face him. The rope pulled taut. She grabbed it with both hands. "On belay." Her voice was steady.

"Belay on. Okay, lean back. That's it. You're basically going to just walk backward down the face."

"Rappelling."

"Rappel on."

Colleen stared into his eyes as she leaned back, out over the open air. Keeping her eyes fixed on him, she took a cautious step down, then another. Soon she was half-hidden by the rock.

Keeping the line taut, Jack scooted to the edge to watch her progress. He let out the tension in the rope in small amounts, matching her descent.

"Doing okay?" he called to the top of her head.

She looked up, grinning wildly. "This is great! As long as I don't think too hard."

He smiled in return and then leaned backward as he let her complete her descent in quiet.

He felt the rope loosen as she touched the ground at the base of the rock wall.

"Off belay." Her voice echoed up the rock.

"Belay off. Good job." He peered down the cliff at her. She stood in a shaft of sunlight, perched on a rock between the cliff and the sparkling water of Lake Superior. "Take a minute to get your bearings, and then you can come back up."

Far below, Colleen did a few deep knee bends, then rolled her shoulders. "I'm ready."

"Okay, just like back at HQ, look for good handholds. But more importantly, find places for your feet. You don't want to use your arms to pull yourself up—you want to push up with your feet like you're climbing a ladder."

"Easy for you to say, all the way up there." Her gentle sarcasm coaxed a smile to his face.

"Belay on?"

"On belay."

The rope tightened, and Jack adjusted his grip. "Belay on."

"Climbing." Her tone was strong, and she wasn't winded, which was a good sign.

"Climb on." The intermittent tugs on the rope indicated Colleen was finding her groove.

They worked in silence for a few beats, Colleen making steady progress up the rock.

"How you doing?"

"Good!"

He brought in the line as she ascended.

The wind rushed through the trees, the smell of autumn in the breeze. He drew in a breath, something free and clear.

He liked it here. With the team, with her.

He hadn't had a panic attack in weeks, and maybe he'd put that in the past.

In fact, maybe he'd put it *all* in the past. Jack Stewart, new man.

"I don't think I can go any farther!" Her shout sounded closer, maybe halfway up. "I'm stuck."

"You're doing fine. Do you have a good base?"

"Yes, my feet are fine. I just don't have a new place to go."

"Okay, you're going to want to take a breath. Close your eyes for a moment and then look again. Sometimes you just need to shift your focus."

"Okay." The way she drew out the word told him she didn't quite believe what he said.

In the clearing, the family had stopped throwing around the Frisbee. From the corner of his eye Jack saw them sitting down next to a cooler. A cold drink and a sandwich were starting to sound pretty good.

"Hey, you were right. I do see a new spot for my foot." Colleen began moving again. "I think I'm getting this."

He drew in the slack.

Twin yelps rang out.

Below him, Colleen slipped. He quickly drew his brake arm across himself to stop her from free-falling.

On top of the hill, there was also a commotion. One of the kids was screaming. Probably playing.

"I can't get a grip." Colleen sounded near tears.

"I've got you. You can do this." Even while coaching Colleen, he risked a glance to the side. The mom and dad were frantically searching through their backpacks.

On the ground, one of the boys writhed. It looked like the younger one.

Something was very wrong.

"I got it." Colleen's exultant cry was almost lost in the activity from the family.

"Colleen, I need you to get up here. Right now."

Maybe it was his tone.

"What's going on?"

"I don't know, but someone needs help. I can't help them until you are topside."

"I'm coming. I think I can see a path to the top."

In the clearing, the kid had gone silent. Jack risked another glance. The mom had thrown her pack aside and was tugging off the small boy's jeans. The dad had pulled out his phone.

He saw Colleen's hands crest the cliff, and then her head, and then her whole self as she pushed her way onto solid ground.

He wanted to pull her in but waited until she crawled over to him.

"Off belay," he said and unclipped from the anchor.

She was on her feet in a moment. "What's going on?"

"I'm not sure—I think he had an allergic reaction." She gave him a look, her eyes a little wild. "Hey, don't worry. We'll see what we can do. Field medicine is the same as working in a hospital. Stick to the basics and go from there."

She nodded once. Good. He wouldn't have to worry about her too. He already knew she would rise to the emergency.

They came up the family in time to see the mother jam an autoinjector against the boy's thigh and click the trigger.

Colleen immediately knelt beside her. "We're nurses. How can we help?"

"He was stung by bees. We don't know how many." The mother pushed away tears as she focused on her son. "He's allergic, and I usually have two EpiPens, but I think the extra is with his grandma."

The boy was wheezing, his eyes swelling.

On the phone, the father was describing their emergency to someone on the other end of the 911 call.

"They're going to send a helicopter," the father said, moving the cell phone slightly away from his mouth. "I have to stay on the line."

"Oh, thank God." The mother held the little boy's hand to her chest. "Hold on, Elijah, help is coming."

Jack moved to the father. "I'm Jack, that's Colleen. How can we help?"

The lines in the father's forehead eased. He clutched his son and the cell phone, raking his gaze over Jack. "Maybe you should take this call."

SUSAN MAY WARREN & ANDREA CHRISTENSON

Jack took the cell phone. "Hi, this is Jack Stewart."

"Hey, Jack, Sabine Hueston. I met you once at the VFW. What's the situation there?"

"Young, Caucasian male, having an anaphylactic reaction to a bee sting. He is pale, but responsive." Cradling the phone between his ear and shoulder, Jack felt for the carotid artery in the small neck. The weak pulse fluttered below his fingertips. He glanced at his watch. "Heart rate 120. He has tachycardia and we've already administered the only EpiPen we have."

The boy's breath wheezed in and out. It was becoming much too labored for Jack's liking. He moved away from the small family so they couldn't hear him. "This boy is still struggling. Have you got that helo in the air, Sabine? We need some help here, stat."

"I'm sending the chopper to you now. Can you give me an idea of where you are at?"

"We're in a small clearing not far from the parking area at Palisade Head. It should be big enough to land in." He checked the GPS unit he'd clipped to his belt and gave her the coordinates.

Jack tossed the phone back to the father. "Help is on the way. Stay on the line until they get here."

"Do you know where he was stung?" Colleen was asking, pulling up the boy's shirt. He looked about eight years old, brown hair, skinny.

"He must have gotten several," his mother said. "He usually responds to one epi shot."

Jack knelt and pulled the boy's shirt off, sitting him up to examine him. Several angry welts peppered the young skin. "We have to get these stingers out."

"Do you have a credit card?" Colleen's question to the father fell flat in the air. When he just stared at her, she repeated the question. He nodded.

She held out her hand.

The man retrieved a slim plastic card out of his wallet and handed it to her. She slid the edge of the card over the red welts.

"If you try to pinch or tweeze these out, you risk releasing more venom." Colleen spoke quietly, unperturbed. "A credit card does the trick without the harm."

The mother let out a quiet moan. "I can't believe I forgot! The ER nurse told us about that procedure."

The boy was still wheezing when they laid him back down. Jack met Colleen's grim expression with his own.

In the distance the *whump, whump* of helicopter blades cut through the air. Jack would be glad to hand this over to the rescue team.

Soon, they were shielding their eyes as the blades of the helicopter whipped up the dust around them.

Moments after touchdown, Bill Hooper swung out of the cockpit. No one exited the back.

"Where's the flight nurse? Or Rhino?" Jack, angry now, stood to his feet.

"He didn't show up. They said you were up here and could help out. Sabine said it was urgent and to just get here. She said to fly the boy back to Deep Haven. They have a team waiting for him there."

"That's not cool, man."

Bill raised his hands in surrender. "Wasn't my call. Besides, last time Rhino flew in my bird, he threw up all over the place. Took us hours to clean it up."

Colleen stood too. "Hey, let's figure this out another time. Jack, get the litter. We gotta go."

She was right. Focus.

Jack worked with Bill to move the litter basket out of the chopper. On the ground, the boy's breathing had become steadier. Deeper.

"Looks like the epinephrine might be working," Jack said.

His mother gave the boy a quick kiss and then stood back,

her arms around herself as they loaded him into the litter. "Last time Elijah was there, the doc said his allergy could keep getting worse. I can't believe I didn't remember that second EpiPen."

Jack didn't have time to reassure her as they secured the boy and Bill slid into the cockpit. Jack and Colleen moved the patient into the belly of the bird. The rest of the family held each other just outside the door, peering through the open space. The older brother was wide-eyed as he looked around the chopper.

Colleen closed the door.

And just like that, it happened. The walls suddenly closed in, turned hot. Jack would've bet cash money that this bird had been bigger the last time he was in it. His vision began to blur around the edges, and he swayed.

He dug his thumb and forefinger into his eyes.

Colleen put a hand on his arm. "Are you all right?"

He grunted something.

"Jack, look at me."

"Nope." He braced himself on the cabinet lining one wall. His breath came quickly now, and he worked to calm it.

"There's no way you are going on this flight."

His eyes flew open. He'd once had a bullet hit him square in the stomach, dead center of his Kevlar vest. Somehow hearing her say those quiet words punched ten times worse.

"I'm fine."

"You are *not* fine. Don't forget, I saw you on the other flight." Colleen kept her words low, and he was grateful that the family couldn't hear what she said. "This is a routine anaphylactic shock case. I'll be fine on my own. We saw them all the time in the ER."

He held her gaze. His heart rate slowed. "You're right. You're ready. You can go on your own." Maybe he could finally keep that promise to himself about never flying in a helicopter again. Colleen could do it—he had faith in her.

Outside the bird, he saw the parents. They were shaking. The brother had gotten over his fascination with the helicopter and his face was turning red. He was blinking furiously, and Jack knew he was holding back tears.

Here was an escape.

"I'll drive the family to the hospital. I'll explain to them that you're on your own, and they aren't able to ride along." Colleen shouldn't have to worry about calming a desperate parent while also attending to the kid in distress.

She nodded once and opened the door, and he was out.

"Let's get this bird in the air," Bill called from his seat in the cockpit. At his words, Jack shut the door. Colleen was already getting the IV set up to run into the boy's arm. The boy's eyes were open and alert. His breathing had settled into a more normal pattern. His face, though puffy, held good color.

She could handle this. She'd be fine.

Bill looked over at him, gave him a thumbs-up, and the chopper roared to life.

The father gratefully handed over the keys with a shaking hand as they turned to make the trek to the parking area.

Jack swung and picked up his harnesses, his webbing ring of carabiners, and quickly grabbed his ropes.

By the time he reached his truck and secured his gear, the family was in their minivan, waiting.

He slid into the driver's seat and glanced at the father. "She knows what she's doing. I trained her myself."

He didn't know why, but the man's grateful, dark nod felt a little like redemption.

CHAPTER 8

*C*olleen checked the IV inserted into the boy's arm.

"How old are you, Elijah?" She had to yell at full volume over the chopper's noise.

She leaned her ear next to his mouth to hear his reply. "I'm nine." Elijah's quiet, labored response told her he was nervous.

"Have you ever flown in a helicopter before?" She smiled at him. If she was calm, he would be too.

"No. This is my first time flying anywhere."

"I'm sorry it's under such bad conditions. You're going to have to try it again when you can sit up and enjoy it." She turned to attach the bag of epi to the hook on the wall, which substituted for an IV pole. "What grade are you in, Elijah?"

He didn't answer.

"Elijah?" She turned back to him.

The nine-year-old was breathing heavily now, the signs of stridor beginning.

Colleen frantically searched the patient for signs of an injury they'd missed. Back on the ground, she and Jack had stabilized his breathing, and *he should be fine.*

Not struggling to breathe.

She didn't find any other injuries. Her mind raced over the protocol. She'd done this before. Being five thousand feet in the air didn't change how she'd treat anaphylactic shock. She pushed the epi through the IV, going as quickly as possible without endangering Elijah.

He coughed, gasped, then fell silent.

"You picked a fine time to abandon me, Jack Stewart!" she yelled. Even as the anger rushed through her, she knew it wasn't fair. She'd insisted he not be on this flight. The ashen look on his face had told her there was something going on. She'd have to figure out what it was later.

"What was that?" Bill asked, turning his head to see her. His hand on the collective moved with his head. The helicopter dipped and Colleen banged her head on the wall.

"Hey! Eyes on the sky."

"Whoops. Sorry 'bout that." The pilot adjusted his grip and brought the helicopter under control.

The boy was wheezing now, the stridor getting more pronounced.

Now would be a great time for a miracle. She turned her thought into a desperate prayer.

Even in the close confines of the helicopter, with the roar of the engine, it was hard to hear herself think, let alone pray.

Elijah's breathing grew more labored. She saw his little belly pushing in and out, trying to help his lungs get enough air.

And then he flatlined.

What—?

"No!"

She began compressions. "How much farther?" Her shout to Bill went unnoticed. "How long before we are on the ground?"

"Another ten minutes or so. You all right back there, missy?"

Ten minutes was about nine minutes too long.

She got a rhythm back, but he was still fighting.

Only one thing to do.

Even if it meant breaking the rules, she would have to intubate the boy.

She searched the area around them for an intubation kit, pulling out drawer after drawer in the vertical supply chest near the front of the small area.

There. She grabbed the kit, opened it out onto the small tray positioned at Elijah's head.

She could do this. So what she'd never done it herself—she'd seen hundreds, maybe thousands of patients intubated.

Problem was, she needed special training and certification to intubate people.

Certification and training that she didn't have.

On the table, Elijah's back arched.

Giving Elijah a dose of Ketamine through his IV, she prayed for a miracle.

Just as she tipped Elijah's head back and was opening his mouth to insert the tube, the helicopter bucked again, knocking her off her feet. She fell, hitting her chin on the tray as she went down. The instruments scattered onto the floor. She picked herself up and ran a hand over her chin.

No blood.

Elijah had passed out. His blue lips shocked her back into action.

Stripping off her gloves, she pulled the drawer open for a clean intubation kit. Hands shaking, she tore open that kit and repeated the procedure.

Colleen planted her feet in case Wild Bill caught another pocket of air and tilted Elijah's head back again. Blocking out all sound and anything in her vision other than Elijah's mouth and throat, she walked herself through the steps she'd seen others do.

She inserted the laryngoscope, lighting the path the esophageal tube would take down, then threaded that through. Partway down, she met minor resistance. She closed her eyes briefly, prayed she was doing the right thing, visualizing the cords, then pushed the tube through the area into position.

Working swiftly, she removed the laryngoscope and attached an Ambu bag. This one was equipped with a sensor that turned color when the lungs had properly inflated. She gave the bag a few squeezes at regular intervals, approximating breath repetitions.

The sensor turned gold.

Colleen blinked against the hot pinpricks in her eyes and continued to rhythmically squeeze and release the Ambu bag.

Elijah's lips began to pink up.

His eyes flew open.

"Shh, shh." She put her hand on his shoulder. With the other hand, she held a finger to her lips. If he struggled or tried to move, he risked injuring his throat. She bent to his ear, so she could speak to him without shouting. "I had to put a tube in your throat to help you breathe. Blink twice if you understand." She watched his face.

The boy's eyelids fluttered twice.

"Good. Brave boy. This tube won't get out of the way to let you talk, so I'm just going to keep my eyes on you to make sure you're okay. How does that sound?"

His eyelids flickered again.

Keeping a steady rhythm on the Ambu bag, Colleen leaned close again.

"Okay. The pilot said we don't have too much farther to go, so I'll just help you breathe, and when we get to the hospital, the doctors will help you too. You're doing a great job."

Right on cue, Bill called back to them. "We're approaching the hospital now."

Through the window, the austere brick and concrete building appeared. Colleen's shoulders dropped a fraction and her back started to unknot.

"Elijah." She waited until the boy met her gaze. "We're going to land now. When we do, the doctors will be there to help you." A crease formed between his eyes. "My friend Jack is helping your mom and dad and brother get to the hospital. They will be here very soon."

Tears pooled in his eyes.

"Don't be scared. I will be with you as much as they let me until your parents come." She reached out one hand and took his tiny, cold one. He held it tightly.

The helicopter came to rest on the ground with a thump.

Men and women in scrubs swarmed the chopper. Colleen told them the things she'd done on the flight, listing the doses and timing of the meds she'd given the small patient.

They pulled Elijah out of the bird and placed him on a gurney. Colleen clung to his little hand and hurried along beside them. The hospital staff pushed him into an ER room, making swift work of unlatching him and transferring him to a hospital bed.

A doctor bent over him and slid a stethoscope over his chest. He called out the numbers to his colleague. Another nurse began hooking up a heart monitor.

"We need to make room," said the nurse, and Colleen stepped back, hating that she had to let go of his hand.

She sank into the straight-backed chair at the edge of the room as the doctor and nurses continued their complicated dance, inserting IVs, calling out medication doses, and working to keep Elijah stable. As the minutes passed, she held herself back from jumping into the fray. A few times, she was able to reach through a gap in the medical personnel and pat Elijah's hand. She hoped it was enough reassurance.

A commotion in the hall caught her attention, and then the boy's mother rushed in.

"I'm here, honey," she said and grabbed his hand.

Colleen slipped out. She made it three steps down the hall before sinking to the ground.

Her whole body shook. She took in gulping breaths of air.

She'd done it. Saved a life all by herself.

She hadn't freaked out. Hadn't gone running. Hadn't hid.

Looking down, a tender, crazy giggle twined through her even as tears formed in her eyes.

She was still wearing her climbing harness.

~

Turned out, not getting involved was not a sustainable game plan.

Jack stood outside the Deep Haven hospital attempting to retrieve his hand from where the father stood shaking it. At the moment, it appeared he wasn't going to let go.

On the drive up from Palisade Head, Jack's hands steadied on the wheel of the family's Dodge Caravan. Focusing helped him calm down. His breathing had normalized while talking the parents through what they could expect at the hospital. The wife had assured them that they knew the drill because this was the third time that Elijah had needed to be rushed to the ER. Even so, she'd kept a white-knuckled grip on the armrest and had closed her eyes often, maybe offering a whispered prayer.

Driving into Deep Haven had felt strangely like coming home. The buildings held a peculiar welcome. Lake Superior lay placid in the sunshine, winking in and out of view. Despite the trauma he still found himself in the middle of, Jack's chest eased after entering the city limits.

Maybe he had finally found a place he could call his own.

When they had pulled up outside the Deep Haven hospital emergency room, Jack had breathed a sigh of relief to see the helicopter perched on the white X of the helo pad.

Now the wife had already gone into the hospital, and the older brother clung to his dad's side.

"Don't thank me. It's Colleen you should be thanking."

"Believe me, I'll thank her too. But if you hadn't been there…"

"Right place, right time," Jack said.

The sliding ER doors opened, and Colleen came out. She looked…uh oh. Not good. Her face was tearstained and pale. And was that a bruise on her forehead? What had happened in that helicopter?

"There you are!" The dad transferred his grip to Colleen's hand. "Thank you for what you did for my boy."

Her quiet reply was almost lost on the cool breeze. "You're welcome."

The father pulled Colleen into a hug. Over his shoulder, she met Jack's eyes. Her pupils almost blotted out the green of her eyes. She blinked furiously. Aw, no. Something was definitely wrong.

Time to stage a rescue.

Jack tapped the father on the shoulder. "You should go see your son. I bet the doctor will want to go over things with you and your wife."

The father seemed to snap back into place. "Right. Of course. C'mon Simon."

"Last room on the right," Colleen said to his back.

When she turned back to him, Jack took her hand. It trembled. "What's wrong?"

"He lived."

He raised an eyebrow. "And…how is that bad?"

"It's not." She blew out a breath. "It's not."

"What happened?"

"He flatlined in the chopper."

"What—?"

"Yeah. Elijah had a relapse about two minutes into the flight. He stopped breathing."

No wonder she looked unraveled. "But you got his heart started again."

She nodded. "The kid's a fighter."

He saw a bench near the door and led them to it. Over on the helo pad, the helicopter roared to life. Colleen scrubbed her hands over her face.

"Tell me what happened."

"Wild Bill showed his true colors again. I don't know if he's qualified to be a rescue pilot." She gave a little shrug. "But I just don't think Boone would have hired him if Bill didn't have the credentials."

"Yeah, I've been wondering about that too. That guy can be dangerous. I'll bring it up with Boone."

"That wasn't really the worst of it, though." She told him about Elijah's airway closing again, how he'd turned blue, and how she'd hit her chin while trying to intubate him. "Honestly, I was terrified."

"You must have done similar things in the ER before."

"Yeah, but then I wasn't stuck with just a reckless pilot in the middle of a flying tube. I had doctors, other nurses and people around. And, you know, people who have actually placed an endotracheal tube before." She exhaled, hard. "I'm not certified."

"You will be."

She shot him a look. "You really think I can do this?"

"You just did." Unable to stop himself, Jack took her hands in his. Held them, then rubbed slightly to warm the twin ice cubes. "Listen to me. I can see how this must have been scary for you." He let go with one hand, reached out and tipped her chin up until she looked him in the eye. "What you did up there was courageous. You saved that boy's life. And you did it all on your own. I'm confident you could do it again." He put his hand back on top of hers.

She blinked at him. Took a shuddering breath. Nodded. "It did feel pretty amazing. Maybe I'm just overthinking this. You must have done this kind of thing all the time."

The desert outside Mosul in Iraq flashed through his mind.

"Yep. I made what felt like a thousand trips in a bird much less cushy than the one the CRT owns."

Her hands began to warm up between his. Good. The adrenaline drop must be fading.

"Did that have something to do with what happened in the chopper?"

Oh. That. He let go of her hands.

"Sorry. I don't want to pry. It's just..."

Something about Colleen made him want to open up. Just a little bit. "I was in a helicopter crash."

She blinked at him.

He looked away, seeing it. "Working Pararescue meant hundreds of missions behind enemy lines. My buddy and I were sent to the most dangerous regions to extract personnel and equipment. The day of the crash, we were called out to air rescue a civilian contractor who had been backed into a tight spot behind enemy lines in Iraq."

She slid her hand into his. He closed his fingers between hers.

"There were three of us in the chopper—the pilot, my buddy Ryan, who was also a medic, and myself."

That day had been hot, the sun a torch on his back as he'd scuttled from the helicopter to the patient, head on a swivel looking for unfriendlies. The air had been thick with dust stirred up by the helo's spinning blades, and a hint of diesel oil had added a thick tang.

"We landed in a dense neighborhood in the Old City of Mosul, west of the Tigris. The walls of the houses crowding the road were silent, like they were guarding their secrets. The civilian was lucky to be holed up near an open town square, otherwise we might not have been able to set the bird down."

He'd heard the chatter of gunfire a few blocks away and estimated they had little time to rescue the injured man before the fighting circled back around to them.

"We got to the wounded man and Ryan provided cover while I grabbed the patient." He skipped over the discovery that the civilian's arm was shredded. "We got him on board and secured and the pilot got the bird in the air in under five minutes."

Her hand in his tightened.

"The missile came out of nowhere. One of the insurgents must have been hiding in a building we were flying over."

Colleen gave a soft gasp.

"The shot took out our rear rotor. The pilot half landed, half crashed about a half klick from our field hospital. After the dust cleared, we evac-ed with our patient and took refuge in a building on the outskirts of town.

"Were you hurt?"

"Not much. Bruises. But whoever shot us down had followed us. We saw a group of men moving toward us from an abandoned building." He could still taste the dust of that street. Smell the heat in the air.

He swallowed. Hard. "I had to get the civvie to the hospital or he would die. I slung him over my shoulder and Ryan laid down cover as I ran for the safety behind our lines. I didn't stop running until I reached our makeshift hospital." A wave of grief crashed over him. He forced himself out of the wave, buried it deep. He looked out over the helo pad and the parking lot beyond.

"What happened?"

So much. But he couldn't go there. Not yet. Maybe never.

Instead, "The guy lived. Our doctors were even able to save his arm that was injured. Last I heard he was stateside with his wife and five kids." Taking a risk, he met Colleen's eyes. They were shining. The pale, overwhelmed look completely gone.

"You're a real live hero."

"I wouldn't say that. I was just doing my job."

Colleen's gaze dropped to his mouth. Color rose in her cheeks as she leaned forward.

And then she kissed him.

The shock of it stilled him. What—?

Except, her kiss was sweet and soft and—

He cupped his hand around her neck and kissed her back.

She tasted like apples.

He liked apples.

He put his arm around her and moved in closer.

She made a little noise at the back of her throat and sank against him.

As if she trusted him.

Wanted him.

Wait—! He pulled away, his eyes hard on hers, breathing quickly.

Her eyes widened. "Oh...uh, I'm sorry." She pressed her hand to her mouth. "I don't know what came over me."

Aw, what? She was apologizing? Jack was the one who should apologize. "No, don't. It's fine." Shoot. Better than fine.

Except, her kiss had awakened feelings long buried. Forbidden.

What had he done?

A hint of nervousness layered her voice. "I don't usually go around kissing men, even if they are handsome and brave."

He turned away, lacing his hands around the back of his neck. "Colleen, you hardly know me."

Silence. The October air that had chilled her earlier now swept between them.

Finally, "Well, I know you're brave. Your story confirms that."

"You can't base everything you know about me on one story." He got up. "Let's get going."

The last thing he wanted was to somehow let her tug out the truth.

He was nobody's hero.

CHAPTER 9

*B*eing her grandma's care attendant took more energy than Colleen had anticipated. Or maybe it was the trauma and drama of the two days before that had done her in.

At least today was going better.

Colleen and her grandma entered the house to the rich scent of baked lasagna. After the tuna casserole fiasco, she had been reluctant to use the Time Bake feature on the oven again, but her mom had promised to run over from her house across the street if the doctor's appointment ran late.

Today's chemo treatment marked the mid-point of this round of therapy. Soon Grandma Helen would have a short break before they started the therapy again. After her second round, they would decide if she had to do radiation as well.

By that time, Frank's cast would be off and he would be more mobile. These health problems were wearing everyone down. He'd ridden along to the chemo treatment today, but then Colleen had dropped him off at the VFW to meet some of the guys for lunch. He had promised to text her if he needed a ride home afterward. She mentally patted herself on the back for resisting the urge to peer through the windows looking for Jack like a lovesick teenager.

Colleen settled her grandma in an easy chair in the living room and went to check on the lasagna.

No smoke, no burning. She stood at the window, staring out at her parents' house across the street, the maple tree turning a brilliant red, and stifled a yawn. It had taken a long time to fall asleep last night. Her mind kept replaying Saturday's events in a continuous loop. First, her near fall on the cliff face. Then, Elijah's screams and his mom's panic. The helicopter and her own near panic.

Then, her crazy dive into Jack's arms.

She'd chalked it up to an adrenaline drop, and with it the vanishing of her common sense.

Because she wouldn't forget for a long time the way Jack had nearly leaped out of her arms.

Well, after he'd kissed her back with something she would have called enthusiasm. So, what was *that* about?

She wandered back into the living room. Her grandma's eyes were closed.

"Grandma." She whispered, not wanting to wake her if she was sleeping. But, also, if Grandma was just resting her eyes, it would be good for her to eat before a nap. "Are you feeling all right?"

"Yes, my dear. I just needed a little shut-eye."

"The lasagna will be ready in about fifteen minutes."

"Sit with me. I'll rest my eyes and you can keep me company. I want to hear about how things are going with the flight nurse training you've been working so hard on."

Colleen sat in the armchair next to her grandma. The living room was casually comfortable, a large room at the front of the house. Colorful knit afghans draped over the couch and scattered knickknacks gave rise to interesting conversation without being clutter. At the far end was the fireplace. Its red brick warmed the room, and the rough wooden mantlepiece boasted dozens of family photos. A place for hot cocoa and fireside chats. Throughout her teen years, Colleen had often found herself seeking refuge wrapped in one of the blankets and pouring out her teenage troubles to her grandma.

How laughable some of those troubles seemed now.

"Mostly good, but Saturday was a humdinger." As she filled her grandma in on the traumatic events of the day, she found that she was feeling better about the whole thing. She really had made a difference in that boy's life.

"It sounds like you didn't let panic get the better of you. You used your training and that stubborn, adventurous spirit you were born with. I knew it would come in handy someday."

Better than a knitted afghan, the pride in her grandma's voice warmed Colleen down to her toes.

"Tell me more about this boy who is training you."

"Jack? I don't really know much about him." She thought back over their conversations. "I know he was in the Air Force and served as a medic or something, but I think that ended a while ago. He's really good at what he does. He's calm under pressure and always encouraging. You should have seen him handle that family on Saturday. I do know that he's great at cooking, or at least with stuff you can make on a grill."

"Mm-hmm. And, is he cute?"

"Grandma!"

"I'm just saying. Maybe a little romance wouldn't be such a bad thing."

"I have to admit, I am attracted to him." That was putting it mildly. The more time Colleen spent with Jack, the more he invaded her head. His quiet *"I think you're brave"* threaded through at the oddest times.

"Yeah, okay. He's very easy on the eyes. And he's a hero. He told me about rescuing this one guy during his time in Iraq, which sounded straight out of a Hollywood movie. And even though he doesn't want the flight job, he's always quick to help people in crisis."

"He reminds me of my Frank. I like him already. Bring him by someday."

"I don't know. When we get you better, I'm thinking of going back to Minneapolis. I haven't entirely given up my job there."

Her grandma sat up in the recliner and turned toward her. "Oh, pish. There will always be jobs. Good men, now they're harder to find. Besides, Deep Haven is changing, growing. It's not the same town it was when you were little."

Colleen thought about her grandma and Frank. What they had would be enviable in any town. "You could be right. Maybe I should give it a chance."

She heard footsteps on the porch and remembered that her dad had asked if he could join them for lunch. He came through the door just as Colleen said, "I guess staying in town and making a life here wouldn't be such a bad thing, not if I could have what you and Frank have."

"Don't forget about your mom and me," her dad said, shucking out of his light jacket and tossing it on the sofa. "We have a great life, even in this small place."

Colleen knew her dad had once dreamed of moving down to Winona State for college and studying for the bar exam until his mom's first bout with cancer had prevented that move from happening. But staying in Deep Haven had meant he was around to meet, fall in love with, and marry Colleen's mom. They never would have met if he had gone to Winona State.

"Why would you ever want to leave? Everything you need is right here. Your old dad, for instance." He gave her a wink, then leaned over Grandma Helen's chair. He kissed her softly on the forehead. "Something smells great."

"Ingrid Christiansen brought over a lasagna." Colleen rose. "I'll go get it on the table."

As she walked into the kitchen, she heard her dad ask, "How

are you feeling, Mom?" Her grandma's answer was too quiet to hear.

A few moments later, her dad came into the kitchen. "I think it's going to be just you and me for lunch. Grandma is falling asleep in her chair. I covered her up with an afghan."

"I'm worried about her, Dad." Colleen pitched her voice low, unwilling to disturb Grandma. "She's so tired all the time. I'll be glad when this round of chemo is over."

"That's how it was before too. But she was always cheerful, even after losing a bunch of weight and her hair falling out."

"Look what I found." Colleen went to the counter and grabbed the box sitting next to the toaster. "It's a red wig." She pulled the garish item from its wrappings. "Grandma said she'd always wanted to be a redhead like Lucille Ball and that this time when she loses her hair she wanted to be prepared."

Nathan started laughing. "That's about ten shades brighter than Lucy's. I can't wait to see her in it."

Colleen joined in. "I know, right? She wants me to put it somewhere so Frank doesn't find it. She plans to surprise him."

"Oh, he'll be surprised all right."

She wrapped the wig back up then went to the cupboard and took out two plates. Her dad grabbed some silverware. After she had dished up a slice of lasagna each, her dad said grace and they began to eat.

"I meant what I said earlier, you know." Her dad's nonchalance didn't fool her for a second. She knew his serious voice when she heard it. "I found everything I ever wanted in this small town."

Her stomach churned. Colleen cut her pasta into smaller and smaller bites. "I know, Dad. It's just that I get restless sometimes. It seems like this town won't ever let me grow up. I want more than to just be the volleyball champ."

"Sometimes we feel restless because we haven't discovered what it is that God wants for us. We keep searching for things to fulfill the longing He has put in our heart, but we miss that the longing is for something He has called us to do."

Colleen studied her fork, made a trail in the tomato sauce on her plate. "So, what is He calling me to?"

"That's between you and Him. But I suspect He put that love of a challenge and adventure in your heart for a reason."

Her drive for adventure had always seemed like a negative thing, but now her dad made it sound...holy. Like her impulses to jump in, seek adventure, *and* do the right thing could be a sacred calling. Could God really use her restless spirit? And could He do it here, in Deep Haven? She did feel loved and accepted here. Being smothered once in a while by her old life suddenly seemed like a small price to pay.

Her thoughts turned to a certain good-looking burger chef. Add one large check to the stay-in-town column. If she stayed, she might be able to untangle his strange post-kiss behavior.

Maybe take another crack at it.

Like Tucker had said, she didn't know what she had until she lost it. She didn't want to lose it this time before she figured out what it could be.

"You know, Dad, you're right. Everything I could ask for might be right here in Deep Haven." She gave her dad a wink. "Except maybe a decent movie theater."

He laughed.

Deep Haven was home. It always had been. Maybe it was time to figure out if she could stay.

~

Jack was in big trouble—and he knew it.

Shoot. Why had he let himself kiss Colleen?

Jack stood in his apartment at the table, folding his weekly load of laundry. In the two days since rescuing that kid and the kiss, he had avoided headquarters and the Crisis Response Team.

Because he wanted it—the life that suddenly felt real and whole and...

Despite his best efforts, he liked the team. Liked his life here. Liked Colleen.

Very much.

But being with her—and the team—would eventually mean telling the truth. And not about the military.

About his stint in Stillwater. His crime.

Yep, no.

Except, he was having a harder and harder time dodging the idea that maybe he was supposed to be here. The words he'd said to Elijah's dad kept winding through his brain—right place, right time.

And it seemed he wasn't the only one to share that thought.

Earlier today, while walking back from the laundromat with his duffel full of clean clothes, a sheriff's cruiser had pulled up next to him. Kyle Hueston had stepped out.

"Hey man, I heard about your adventure at Palisade Head." Kyle's uniform jacket had been zipped up tight against the cold breeze blowing in from Lake Superior.

"Yeah, that climbing trip didn't turn out quite how I'd expected." A double meaning, as the end of that adventure was unexpected too. Not that Jack minded being kissed by a pretty girl. In fact, he'd love to repeat that part.

He just didn't want to get them both in over their heads.

"You were right about the location, though. It's a great place for climbing. Boone drove me back to get our gear and my truck, and I spotted another place I'd like to try." Jack had shifted his laundry to the other hand. "I'm looking forward to giving it a second chance." He'd also given Boone an earful about Bill Hooper's casual attitude toward in-air safety. Boone had said Bill came highly recommended but promised to look into the situation.

"I'm glad you were there when you were. Sounds like a case of right place, right time. God's ordained timing, used for His purpose."

God had a purpose for him? That was certainly hard to believe most days. His skepticism must have showed because Kyle had given him a smile as he'd turned to get back into his car. "Believe what you want. My opinion is that God had you right in position where He wanted you. We could use a guy like you on our team permanently. I know Boone has been after you. I'm adding my voice to his. Consider staying on."

Consider staying on. Only one problem with that—he didn't want to be pulled back in to being on a team.

Or so he tried to tell his traitorous heart.

Jack folded another shirt, tucking in the sleeves and then rolling it up like he'd been trained to do. His thoughts kept straying back to that moment when Colleen had kissed him. *"You're a real live hero."*

Oh boy. Maybe he could just not tell her. Even as he thought that, he rejected it.

Relationships needed to be built on trust.

So, there was that.

On the table, his phone rang.

Unknown Number popped up on the screen. He debated a minute, but so few people had this number, maybe it was an emergency. He swiped it open and put the phone on speaker. Unless it was a "drop everything" emergency, he wanted to get this laundry finished.

"Hello?"

"Is this Staff Sergeant Winston Stewart?"

He didn't recognize the voice. Paused a moment before, "Yes."

"Staff Sergeant Stewart, you probably don't remember me.

This is Thomas Silver. You rescued me in Iraq after my arm was mangled?"

Sounds of gunfire, the grunt of his patient as he carried him over his shoulder echoed through Jack's mind. "Mr. Silver, I do remember you."

"I saw the rescue of that boy with the bee sting on the news and felt I had to track you down. I hope you don't feel it's an invasion of your privacy, but I did a little googling and found your dad's campaign office. When I called and explained who I was, the gal there gave me your number."

It *was* sort of an invasion of privacy, but what was done was done, he supposed. "I see. How can I help you?"

"Actually, I'm calling to see if I can help you. My family and I just celebrated the first birthday of our sixth child last week. She wouldn't be here if it weren't for you saving me. My whole family owes you a debt."

The pair of pants Jack wrestled with resisted their tight fold. He shook them out and tried again. "I was just doing my job. No need to thank me."

"Listen, I have some friends in high places, and I know what it cost you to rescue me. When I saw the boy on the news the other day, I was glad to know that you are back to saving lives. If there's anything I can ever do for you, let me know."

"Thanks for the offer. Have you been stateside for a while?" There. The pants held tight this time. He laid them in a tidy stack with the others.

"Yep. I never went back. I retired from the military contract business. The high-stakes game of gathering intel got to be too much for me. I'm loving every minute I spend with my wife and kids. I run a specialty balloon bouquet business now, if you can believe it."

"That's hard to picture, but I'm sure it's rewarding."

"It really is." On the other end of the line, Jack heard kids squealing and a muffled holler. "Sorry, I've got to run. I'm serious about the offer. If there's anything I can ever do for you, just give a shout. Promise?"

"Sure. Thanks." He hung up.

Crossing to his dresser, he laid his laundry in neat piles, sorting the pants and shirts into their own drawers.

Outside, the lake was in turmoil, the waves crashing hard on the shore, the scent of storm in the air, the clouds dark.

Right place, right time. God's ordained timing, used for His purpose.

Yeah, well, he had a good thing going here.

He wasn't going to screw it up with the truth.

CHAPTER 10

The smell of deep-fried onion rings was a music all their own. The tune the Blue Monkeys played only added to the aroma. The Saturday evening crowd at the VFW pulsed with life.

Colleen sat at the right end of a string of tables pushed together to make one long seating arrangement for the Crisis Response Team. They'd just finished up a long day of training, including CPR certification with the volunteer recruits. Ronnie had asked Colleen to assist her in teaching the newbies and she had eagerly agreed.

She'd been disappointed that Jack hadn't been at the training. Like he wasn't a part of the team or something. Or maybe, avoiding her?

And frankly, that just bugged her. So what if she'd kissed him? He'd kissed her *back*. And that deserved at least a conversation. So, she'd come to the VFW to do just that—wait until he got off shift and…well, if all went well, maybe tell him that she liked him.

Why not? She'd already said yes to staying, right? She was on a roll.

After the training, she'd grabbed a quick shower, pulled on some jeans and an orange blouse. She'd decided to let her hair hang down over her shoulders for once, the slight curl after her shower giving it bounce.

The past five days had deepened her conviction that Deep Haven was going to be her home. Permanently. She kept returning to the words her father had spoken over her like a blessing. *"He put that love of a challenge and adventure in your heart for a reason."*

If Deep Haven was where God was calling her, then she was all in.

The restaurant and bar hummed with activity. People in town loved when the Blue Monkeys played. A few couples swayed together in front of the band on the patch of the restaurant that served as a tiny dance floor.

Colleen bit into her onion ring. Crisp, savory breading and then the tang of the onion filled her senses. Was it crazy to think that even the VFW onion rings tasted better now that Jack was cooking them? Probably. She'd barely kept herself from groaning aloud at the first bite of her burger. She'd ordered the unnamed special but when Signe Netterlund delivered it to the table, she'd said Jack called it the Colleen.

Interesting. Sweet. Oh, she didn't know what to think.

Except the burger was delicious. Slathered in a sweet teriyaki sauce with a big hit of spice at the end. Topped with a pineapple and snuggled into a brioche bun. Sweet and spicy.

Okay, she could embrace that.

She wished he'd come out into the eating area so she could say hi—she hadn't seen him since their, um, kiss, a week ago.

Was he *really* hiding from her?

Around the table, the team talked about today's training and the batch of volunteers.

Ronnie and Peter sat to the right of Colleen. The big man

had his arm around the back of Ronnie's chair. He leaned in close to hear what she was saying, a smile playing on his face.

The chair to Colleen's left sat empty until someone pulled it out and sat down. She turned to see Sammy Johnson dragging the chair closer to her. Burly and tall, Sammy could be Paul Bunyan's younger, more normal-sized brother. Or Peter Dahlquist's brother for that matter. She briefly wondered if Sammy and Peter were cousins. Probably. Peter was related to everybody.

Back in high school, she and Sammy had shared a few classes, including a science lab where they were partners. She remembered him as being eager, but not very good at science. He'd almost set her hair on fire with a Bunsen burner. And, just as his mother had reminded her, Sammy had attended all of her volleyball games.

She'd thought he was just into sports. Apparently she was wrong.

The big man had been at the training day, but until now, Colleen had successfully avoided engaging him in conversation.

Maybe it was time to play nice. After all, he was a friend.

"Hey, Colleen." He reached over and took one of her onion rings. "I heard you were home. Thanks for helping out today."

She moved the plate slightly, put her arm on the table between it and Sammy. Playing nice didn't mean she had to share her rings. "I was glad to do it. I didn't need to update my own certification, so it just made sense to help everyone else earn theirs."

"I tried to talk to you all day, but you were pretty busy."

Colleen tried for a laugh. It fell flat. "Yeah. It was crazy today." And it had been. Trying to get twenty people through all the material was harder than climbing Palisade Head.

"Since this chair was empty, I thought I'd corner you to say hi. Is this water taken?" He gestured to the full glass that sat midway between her plate and the empty space in front of him.

It was her water, but she'd been working on a Coke, so she shrugged.

"Take it if you want."

He downed half the glass in one huge gulp. "Thanks. I haven't seen you much since you left for college. What brings you back to Deep Haven?"

"Aw, you know. The burgers."

The door to the kitchen swung open, and she shifted in her chair, trying to spot a glimpse of Jack. Rats. He must be working on the other side of the grill.

"So, how about you? What have you been up to since high school?"

"I started working full time up at Turnquist Lumber."

"Really? That's great."

"Yup. I've made it onto day shift. I'll actually be driving a truck starting tomorrow. I've filled in from time to time, but now they've made it permanent."

Colleen pictured the lumber trucks that passed through town, remembered their loads of huge logs strapped tight with chains. She gave a little shiver. "Be careful. It's deer season."

Sammy drank the rest of the water. "I'm always careful."

"Are you still living with your folks?"

"Naw, I got my own place now. I bought a little trailer and a few acres in the woods outside of town. I'm planning to build myself a cabin. My land touches the Superior National Forest. Perfect for hunting." He leaned back in the chair, stretched his legs out a little.

"It sounds like you're building a nice life for yourself." She gave him a smile. On stage, the Blue Monkeys started playing "Brown Eyed Girl." She tapped her foot in time to the music. Lost in the lyrics, she almost didn't hear Sammy speak again.

"I just need a little lady to share it with."

Had he really just said that? "What?"

"Do you want to dance?" Sammy held his hand out. "I've always loved this song."

Sammy wasn't the person she wanted to dance with tonight, but she also didn't want to be rude. One dance couldn't hurt.

"Let's do it." She slapped her hand into his and allowed him to pull her up and out onto the tiny floor. He stepped close and she put her hands on his shoulders. Yes, he was a big man. But standing next to him only reminded her of being this close to Jack.

Jack might not be big, but he was built.

They swayed to the beat for a measure or two. Sammy curled his arms around her waist and leaned in close.

"Colleen, I like you. Would you ever consider going out with me?"

Uh oh. This was not the plan. The plan was to wait for Jack to get off work and tell him that she liked him. Not be cornered by some old high school friend who owned a trailer in the woods.

Okay, okay. That wasn't fair. Sammy was a good guy, and the fact that he owned his own place was cool. It just wasn't what she wanted for her life.

She wanted...

What did she want?

Jack.

And her thoughts stopped there. Jack and his smile and cool head and encouragement and she was getting waaay ahead of herself.

She pushed away from Sammy, trying to figure out how to turn him down when she spotted Jack.

He had come out of the kitchen wearing a waist apron, a black shirt that outlined those amazing shoulders, and a hint of a beard. He clearly had stopped by their table, because he put his hand on Peter's shoulder, then swept his gaze across the room.

Over here. She gave him a little wave, but he must not have seen her because he headed back to the kitchen without stopping.

She shifted her focus back to Sammy, who still waited for an answer to his question. "I'm sorry, Sammy. I don't want you to get the wrong idea. It would never work out between us."

"Oh." Sammy cocked his head. "You sure? We almost had a thing in high school."

"Sammy. We danced together. Once." She took his arms off her and stepped back a half step. The music changed to "Sweet Home Alabama."

"C'mon," he said. "One more dance. I could never resist this song." He started doing a funny little shimmy.

Okay, he was a little cute. Colleen laughed. "Fine. One more dance." She moved back into his arms. "Hey, remember when you almost set my hair on fire in Mr. Hanson's science class?"

"I got distracted by my buddy. He was making kissing faces at me from across the classroom and pretending to give someone a hug. I guess I had a crush on you back then too."

"Well, I'm glad we're not in high school anymore. Things sure have changed around here."

"You've changed too."

"How can you say that? You've only spent time with me for a day."

"I don't know, you just seem different. More settled. Less...I don't know...restless maybe. Back in high school you were always trying to be the best, to be noticed all the time. Today you were content to let others try things. It was fun to watch you training people. Sorry. That was maybe too personal."

Huh. "No, I liked it. I'd like to think I've changed since then. I hope it's for the better."

"Oh, it is. It is."

She leaned back and saw the grin on his face, something of desire in his eye—and now this dance needed to be over.

Thankfully, Ronnie called out and waved them back to the

table. "We're splitting up the bill, and then most of us are taking off."

Colleen reached for her purse. She counted out the cash to cover her portion. She was hoping to stay until the end of Jack's shift.

"I'm going to hang out here for a while," she told Ronnie. Turning to Sammy, she crossed her arms over her chest. "Thanks for the dance."

"That's two now. By the time I get my third, you'll say yes to me."

"Maybe another night."

He gave a little salute. "I'll hold you to it."

She laughed, and he grinned at her, but she had a feeling he wasn't kidding.

Sammy left with the rest of the group and Colleen sat back down at the table to wait.

The clock ticked closer to 9:00 p.m. and the Blue Monkeys called out that they had two songs left in the set.

Signe came over and refreshed her Coca Cola. "Anything else for you?"

"No. I'm good. Just waiting for Jack to get off his shift."

"Jack?"

"Yeah, is he still around?"

"Colleen, Jack left ten minutes ago."

He'd...what? Just left?

"Is he coming back?"

Signe made a face.

So yes, he was hiding. Well, hello, that was just *enough*.

He'd called her brave. He hadn't seen anything yet.

∼

Just. Calm. Down.

Jack stared at the semi-destruction of the contents of his

dresser drawers, now flung on his bed, his duffel bag open.

So, he'd been a little upset when he'd seen Colleen dancing in the arms of the local lumberjack. Of course she'd be drawn to the hometown boy, someone who had known her forever.

It didn't mean he had to go off half-cocked, destroy the good thing he had going here.

Breathe.

Really, it was probably for the best. Think what would have happened if he'd told her the truth about himself.

Shoot. Even so, he'd spent most of the past week wondering if he shouldn't have run away from her so quickly. Maybe they *did* have a chance. Jack had spent his shifts at the VFW silently rehearsing what he might say to her, how he would explain his prison time and how it was in the past. It wasn't who he was anymore. He'd alternated between believing that she would forgive him and that she would hate his guts.

See, this was why it was better not to get involved.

The worst part was he'd thought Colleen maybe cared about him, at least a little.

And then he'd seen her dancing with Sammy. He bet that orange blouse topping her boot-cut jeans brought out the green in her eyes. He'd never seen her with her hair down before. She looked gorgeous on the dance floor. Then he'd seen the moment she'd put her head back and laughed, her eyes sparkling at Sammy.

How terrible was it that he wanted her to look at *him* that way?

Breathe.

Right place, right time. Wrong girl. It didn't have to destroy him.

He shook out the clothes from his duffel, started to refold them.

He was getting way too bent out of shape for a guy who had practically dodged her for the past week—and especially someone with his kind of secrets. Frankly, she was probably better off with the lumberjack.

So, someone tell that to his stupid heart.

A knock came at his door. Who could that be? Probably Katie, asking him if he was okay. He had sort of stormed out without a word.

Still. His shift was over. It was his business.

"What?" His angry word died on his lips as he yanked the door open and saw Colleen standing there. Her hands were pressed into the pockets of her puffy, white jacket. The overhead light turned her strawberry-blonde hair golden around her face.

"Hey." She gave him a smile, then caught her lower lip. "So... you weren't at practice today, and then tonight...anyway, I was hoping to see you. You okay?"

Was she serious right now? "Super. Glorious. Happy as a heart attack."

Her eyes widened.

"Sorry." He shook his head. "I just..." And now he felt like a fool. She could dance with whomever she wanted. Sheesh. What was wrong with him?

"Jack. What's going on? Ever since...well, we *kissed*, you've been avoiding me. Can we talk?"

He wanted to wince. To shake his head, close the door.

Walk away.

But the image of her laughing in that guy's arms just... "Who was that guy?"

She blinked. "Who—Sammy?"

He nodded. "An old—or maybe current—boyfriend?"

She gave a short laugh. "No. Just a friend. We were reminiscing about high school. I was reminded of why I'd never want to go back to those days." She cocked her head. "Why?"

And that was the golden question, wasn't it?

She glanced out at the lake. The storm a couple days ago had cleared the sky, and stars glimmered in the arch of night. "Are you up for a walk? It's such a beautiful night."

"It is." Okay. "Sure." He grabbed his coat, zipped it up, and followed her out the apartment door, closing it behind them.

Colleen led them down the stairs, through the parking lot, and across the street until they reached the harbor park.

They hit the beach, their feet scattering the tiny rocks that comprised the shoreline.

"I've always like walking here. There's something peaceful about the waves, the rhythm, the steadiness on the shore."

Maybe that was it. Here, he felt safe, hemmed in, the world expected, easy.

He glanced at her, the moon in her eyes, the soft flow of her hair. Or not.

"I'm sorry. I've been kind of a jerk."

She frowned at him.

"I have been avoiding you."

"Oh." She tripped on a rock, and he grabbed her hand to steady her.

She glanced at him as she pushed a stray lock of hair out of her face. "Thanks."

He let her go. They walked in silence, his heartbeat nearly deafening.

Tell her.

"Colleen…"

"There's nothing between Sammy and me. Just so you know."

Oh. Um. "Good." Good? What was that? "I mean, it's none of my business."

Stop talking.

She looked at him, frowning.

Sheesh.

Colleen headed over to a wide, flat rock, high enough above the water to avoid the spray.

He sat beside her, one leg stretched out, arm dangling on his other knee. The waves a short distance away lapped at the shoreline.

"Crazy storm a couple days ago." What was he doing? Talking about the *weather*?

"The storms here can be doozies. It's the lake effect. I remember one time I was at the park with my brothers. We were having a great time on the swings when huge, black clouds rolled in over the water." She shifted her hands on the rock, leaned back to her elbows. "It went from daylight to twilight in moments. As soon as the first fat raindrops began to fall and the lightning streaked across the sky, my brothers ran for home. They called for me to follow them, but I was too scared. I hid underneath the merry-go-round."

"Not a metal one, I hope."

She smiled. "No. Ours used to be made out of wood. I think they've taken it down now, which is good because that thing was a death trap."

"What happened?"

"I stayed under there for a really long time. Like probably ten whole minutes." She flashed a wry grin at him. "The water started pooling in the groove where kids would run to make the thing turn. Pretty soon the puddle was too big for me to cross. Like a reverse moat, keeping me in instead of out." She leaned forward again, pulled her knees up and crossed her arms around them.

"I remember the rain banging on the merry-go-round above me, and then I heard my name being called. I couldn't move, I was so scared of that water and the lightning that continued to flash across the sky.

"Suddenly two arms reached under the equipment and pulled me out. It was my dad. He'd come out to rescue me. I don't know why, but right then, I felt invincible. Safe, maybe, but then he put me down, grabbed my hand, and we ran through the puddles, soaking wet, laughing. I think it was just the fact I was holding his hand."

Yeah, he got that. "I had a dad like that. For a little while, at least. It was just him and me—my mom died when I was three."

"Oh, Jack, I'm so sorry."

"Cancer. She had it when she was pregnant with me and by the time I was born, it was too far along. My dad was in the Air Force, but after my mom died we moved to Kellogg where he worked as a civilian for a while before running for Congress."

He leaned back too. Okay, so this part wasn't so terrible. He might be able to work up to the rest. "Every year, we would take a vacation to Louisiana. Our favorite place to eat was Mama Creole's."

"Fun."

"Yeah, well it closed when I was nine."

"Oh, that's too bad. Did you find someplace new?"

"No, by the time the next summer rolled around, my dad had remarried, and then a year later my half brother was born. We never went on trips after that."

Silence.

"Sorry." She slipped her hand into his. Squeezed. "Sorry you lost your dad. Sort of."

"It's okay. I still have happy memories of eating Mama Creole's blackened grilled chicken. I've never tasted anything like it before, despite trying to recreate it ever since."

He lost his train of thought then because Colleen was twining her fingers between his. "That must be why you're so good at cooking."

"Yep, always trying to chase the taste of my youth." He turned so they faced each other on the rock, being careful not to unlace their tangled hands. "But I haven't been very successful. Story of my life, I think."

She blinked at him. "You can't really mean it."

"Sure, why not? I haven't had a lot of good things happen in my life." He tried for a nonchalant shrug. Failed. And shoot, to make things worse, he sounded like the center of his own pity party.

"Jack. You have a lot of things going for you. You're a great teacher, a kick-butt cook, and a good friend. You moved up here when Boone asked you to, and despite your obvious desire not to, you keep saving people's lives. And you have...I mean, I hope you can see that you have...well, you have me." She licked her lips, looked at him from under her eyelashes. A breeze lifted a few tendrils of her hair.

Oh. "Do I?"

She met his eyes. "Do you want me?"

Oh boy. And yes. Very much, yes.

He shifted closer. Brought their entwined hands up to his chest and held hers against it. Then he cupped his hand under her head, leaned down, and covered her mouth with his.

Her lips softened as she responded to him. Her other hand came up and gripped his shoulder.

She tasted tangy, like the o-rings, and sweet, like Coke. Smelled like the apple stuff she used on her hair. Behind them, the waves were singing along the shore, the night wind soft around them.

Yes, he wanted her. And maybe she didn't mean it quite the way she'd offered, but he didn't either. He wanted her trust. Her friendship. Her laughter.

And yes, okay, her.

And it seemed she wanted him right back, the way she relaxed in his arms, playing with his hair, giggling when he pulled away, only to pull him back.

Calm down.

Breathe.

Relax.

For a long moment, he lost himself in the embrace. When he

finally pulled away, he was breathing hard. He put his forehead on hers.

"See? Good things, Jack," she said. "Lots of good things going for you."

Maybe he didn't have to go back to the past and unravel it. Maybe he started right now.

Right place, right time. Right girl.

Right life.

"Mm-hmm." He nuzzled her nose a moment before he dove in again.

CHAPTER 11

$\mathcal{H}$eat raced through Colleen's body as she tried to catch her breath.

So, this is what she got for being brave.

Hooah, as they'd say in the Air Force.

One of Jack's arms was around her back, the other braced over her on the rock. Somehow she'd curled herself around him, her hand in his hair.

Wow, he knew how to kiss. Slow and yet consuming, passionate and yet lingering just enough for her to want more.

If any question remained—no, she would never be content with a guy like Sammy. She wanted Jack. Handsome, delicious, mysterious-yet-safe Jack.

He leaned away again, met her eyes.

She swallowed. "Um, you've definitely got that going for you too. Good kisser. Add it to the list."

He gave a low chuckle, the sound sending heat racing through her again. "Noted." He leaned back, took a breath. "It's getting late—"

"Jack, I like you." Oh. Had that really come out? Oh, man. But if she was going to be brave... "Maybe it's corny to say or too forward, but I don't want there to be any secrets between us, or any games. I like you and…I want to spend more time with you."

He drew a breath. Wrapped a hand around his neck. "Yeah." He sighed then, and oh no, got up.

What—?

"Colleen, I've done some stupid stuff."

"Who hasn't?"

But it was the wrong thing to say, clearly. His mouth tightened.

"Okay. I'm sorry." She scooted off the rock, came over to him. Took his hand. "You can tell me."

He glanced at her, his eyes glistening in the night.

Oh. "Jack?"

"It's just…I don't even know where to start."

"How about starting with why you don't want to join the CRT? We had training today, and you were nowhere to be seen. What's going on?"

"Aw, that. I shouldn't be on a team—"

"Why not? You and I worked great together."

He winced, looked away. "Remember the helicopter crash I told you about before?"

"The one where you got that guy to the hospital under gunfire? I remember."

"I didn't exactly tell you the whole story."

Oh?

She waited. He swallowed hard, absently stroking the back of her hand with his thumb.

"I told you my buddy was in the chopper along with the pilot. When the bird crashed, the pilot was injured. Knocked unconscious, and something had happened to his leg. I didn't have time to figure it out."

She watched his face closely. His eyes were far away. He was looking at Lake Superior, which churned in the moonlight, but she didn't think he was seeing it.

"Ryan was fine." Jack paused and cleared his throat. "But when we saw those insurgents coming at us, we knew that someone would have to stay to protect the pilot, and someone would have to carry that civilian to safety. Ryan insisted that I go. He would stay behind and cover me, keep the pilot safe until rescue. I promised him I would come back for him."

The breeze blew a little harder. Colleen shivered.

"Maybe you can guess the rest. I let my buddy talk me into bringing in our patient. After I'd dropped the guy at the hospital, I ran back to the edge of camp, but some of my team held me back. They'd heard too much gunfire to let me go back out there to help Ryan."

A hole grew in the pit of Colleen's stomach.

"We found the pilot and Ryan the next morning. They were dead."

"Oh, Jack. That's terrible. I can see how that would haunt you."

He tightened his grip on her hand. "I should have kept my promise. Broken free of the others and ran back to save him. Or, maybe I never should have left in the first place. I should've waited until we were all rescued."

"You had no idea if that would happen or not. If you hadn't run for the base, you might all be dead right now. You were completing the mission. I'm sorry you lost your friend, but that wasn't a 'stupid thing' you did like you want me to believe. That was heroic."

He shook his head.

"Listen, being on a team means everybody plays their position, right? I used to play volleyball. If I didn't play my position, if I tried to jump in, or even held back, I would miss out on the play I was supposed to do. Sounds to me like you were just doing your job."

He drew in a breath.

"Join the team, Jack." She stepped in front of him. "I could use more training." She slid her arms up around his neck.

He met her eyes. "You're so beautiful. Did you know that?"

She fisted her hand into his shirt and pulled him down to her, kissing him fiercely. His arm went around her back and suddenly gone was the gentle passion from the rock.

He practically inhaled her, drawing her hard against himself, deepening their kiss, as if he suddenly couldn't get enough of her.

Oh boy. It was like hanging in midair, both the thrill and the eerie safety of the rope because for all his passion, and the way he pulled her back with him to the rock, sank down with her, she knew...

She could trust him.

He made a growl sound in the back of his throat. Lifted his head. "Colleen, we need to slow—"

Suddenly a bright light shone on them. "Hey, you two! Break it up!" a voice shouted from farther up on the shoreline.

Colleen's eyes widened.

And Jack practically leaped away from her.

She hadn't seen such panic since high school when her father had found her kissing Tucker.

Yeah, this felt weird. Shielding her eyes from the light's beam, she peered up at the voice. "Kyle?" The light bobbed closer. Kyle Hueston held an industrial-sized flashlight in their direction.

"You kids need to get off the beach and go home."

"Kyle, it's me, Colleen." She scrambled to her feet.

Jack was practically hiding in the darkness. This was embarrassing.

"Hi, Colleen." Kyle lowered the beam so it illuminated the area without blinding them. "I thought you were a couple of kids making out over here."

Kids? No. Making out? Kind of.

"Well, as you can see, it's just Jack and me. Two adults. Being adults." She let out a giggle that belied that statement.

"You know, Colleen, I think I remember my dad catching you once or twice with Tucker out at the lighthouse." He waggled his eyebrows at her.

And...he had to go there, didn't he?

Behind her Jack said, "Tucker?"

She waved a hand in a dismissive gesture. "Old boyfriend. Long story."

"*If* the two of you *were* teenagers, I'd remind you that these rocks get pretty slippery at night and to be careful. I'd also remind you that this is a public beach and anyone can walk by. Keep it family friendly." Kyle looked at Jack who had come into the light. "Both of you."

They were silent as his footsteps crunched away.

Jack didn't touch her. "Kyle is right."

Oh man. That Tucker comment was probably wedged into Jack's head.

"I left my car at the VFW."

"I'll walk you back."

When they'd made it onto the sidewalk, Colleen reached out for Jack's hand. Felt her chest relax when he took it.

So maybe he wasn't going to hold her past against her.

"Jack?"

"Hmm?"

"Would you be interested in coming with me to church tomorrow?"

"Church? Why?"

"I'd love for you to meet my grandma. Having dinner together or something would be a little intense, but a casual meet and greet after church wouldn't be too terrible."

"I don't know. God and I aren't exactly on speaking terms right now."

"A great place to remedy that is church."

143

He glanced at her. "You are persistent."

"Some might call it stubborn, but I definitely go after what I want." She tightened her grip.

He grinned, just enough. "So. Your grandma, huh? Are you sure she'll like me?"

"Positive. She's great. She raised my dad as a single mom while fighting cancer the first time. Several years ago, she remarried. The guy was my mom's WITSEC agent, if you can believe it. She's an excellent baker and her favorite TV show is *I Love Lucy*." She told him about the red wig. "I decided not to tell her it looks more like Bozo the clown, but then I think she already knows that. She's just going for shock value."

"Sounds a lot like someone else I know." He leaned over and kissed her head.

They reached the VFW parking lot. The lot was empty of other cars and the building was dark. Colleen leaned her back against her car door. Jack faced her. Overhead, the half-moon shone bright. A breeze blew over them, bringing with it the loamy scent of decaying fall leaves, and the wind ruffled Jack's hair.

"So...church?"

"I'll think about it."

"At least that's not a no."

In lieu of an answer, he bent to kiss her. She wrapped her arms around his neck. He planted his hands on either side of her, his touch sweet and lingering.

Nothing, however, of the thirst of before.

But maybe that was okay. Maybe she didn't always have to be the girl who fell for the bad boys.

Maybe this time, she'd found a good one.

❧

He was in serious trouble.

When Jack got out of bed this morning, Colleen was first on his mind. Their conversation last night had been bittersweet. He was really starting to fall for this spunky, grit-filled girl, and he loved hearing her say that he was a hero. He loved a lot of things about her, actually. Maybe he even loved...her.

Which left him with a problem.

He'd totally chickened out.

Last night's conversation had been going so well. He'd planned to tell her about his incarceration.

He wasn't entirely sure how he'd been derailed into talking about Ryan.

And then he'd kissed her. And it was sort of all over.

He should probably be thankful Kyle came by because kissing Colleen had suddenly been the only thing he'd wanted to do.

Ever.

And his story of nearly killing a man just didn't fit with the future he'd drawn for himself while in her arms.

Maybe he didn't have to tell her at all, right?

Maybe he simply started over. New man.

Jack Stewart.

A man who went to *church*.

He'd showered and dressed in his only pair of slacks, buttoned himself into a shirt, and even tied a necktie around the collar.

And drove up to Deep Haven Community Church.

Where Colleen was nowhere to be seen, thank you.

Now he was sitting in a pew, sandwiched between Peter on one side and a squirming kid on the other. Yeah, he felt like squirming too. The last hour had been...interesting. It seemed like things were almost over now. At the pulpit, Pastor Dan was reminding the congregation that God watched over everyone.

Yeah, that might be true for some people, but Jack knew that God's eye sometimes strayed.

"A lot of you know the verse in Matthew about each of us being of more worth to God than a sparrow, but another selection I love to read is in Psalm 84, where the Psalmist reminds us that each one of us, even the smallest sparrow, finds a home in God's dwelling place. And that for those who trust in Him, God does not withhold good things."

God had a place for him? Wanted good things for him?

Hardly.

Jack looked around the sanctuary and spotted the faces of many people he knew. It surprised him to realize that in such a short time, and while trying to hide away, he had gotten to know so many people. Even to like them. A few pews up, Jensen Atwood bent to shush a small child. He pulled the little girl onto his lap.

"Let me leave you with the truth God impressed on me many years ago." Pastor Dan put his hands on the pulpit. "We are never out of God's reach, never out of His sight, never out of His love. We can trust Him to pull us through."

Jack rolled his shoulders. Maybe he could believe that if something went right in his life for once.

Out of the corner of his eye, he saw someone staring at him. He moved his head slightly to improve his peripheral vision.

What in the world?

What was Adrian Vassos, heir to the Bear Creek corporate empire, doing here? Adrian's eyes widened, his mouth opening.

Fabulous.

Around him, everyone was rising for the final hymn, an unfamiliar tune. The pastor dismissed them and Jack found himself shaking hands along the pew. Cole and Peter and Ronnie and a few others they introduced him to—Seb, the town mayor, and a guy named Casper.

Then suddenly, Adrian was standing there. Still dressed like a snob, in a pair of suit pants and a pressed shirt. Didn't he notice everyone else in flannel?

The dark-haired man stared him down. "What are you doing here?" At his side stood a blonde woman who seemed familiar. "I thought you were still in Stillwater—"

Perfect. "Hey, can you keep it down? Not too many people here know about that."

"Come with me." Adrian grabbed Jack's arm.

He shrugged it off. "Hands off. I'll go with you."

"I'll be right back," Adrian said to the blonde. Right then, Jack recognized her. Ella. Colleen's friend.

His stomach clenched.

Adrian led the way through the crowd, and Jack followed, fighting the urge to bolt.

Oh yeah, church had been a fantastic idea.

Along the way, Adrian called out to Ronnie, Peter, and Boone to come with them.

Boone frowned at Jack, who shook his head.

The group made their way down to the Sunday school rooms. Finding an empty room, Adrian all but pushed Jack inside then rounded on him.

"What are you doing in my town?"

"Hey, what's this all about?" Peter asked as he came in. "Have you got a problem with Jack?"

The rest of the crew had filed in.

"So, you changed your name. Because you didn't want anyone to know—"

"No." But that was a lie, wasn't it?

"Know what?" Ronnie asked.

"Know that this guy should be in prison."

"What are you talking about?" Ronnie put in. She looked from Adrian to Jack and back again.

"Meet Winston Stewart, everybody," Adrian said. "Now we know why you changed your name."

"Adrian," Boone said quietly. "Leave him alone."

But Adrian stepped up to him. "David Barelli is my dad's cousin."

Oh boy.

"You know he still has problems talking. He's on disability. Can't even walk."

Jack held up his hands. "Listen, Adrian, I'm really sorry for what happened."

Boone broke in. "Jack, there's no need for you to explain. You don't owe them anything."

"Is someone going to clue us in on what is going on?" Ronnie thrust her hands onto her hips. "What is Jack sorry for?"

Silence, a beat between them.

"Third-degree assault. But in my book, it was attempted murder," Adrian said quietly, his eyes on Jack. "He's a convict. And now he's hiding in our town."

All four of them turned to look at Jack. His mouth dried up. He didn't need their admiration, but he couldn't live with their disgust.

"It's not like that," Boone said, but Jack held up his hand.

"It doesn't matter."

He'd done what the papers accused him of. He'd committed the act he was convicted for.

Adrian was right. He didn't belong here.

"You're right, Adrian. This is the last place I should be."

He turned to go.

And standing there, in the door, her eyes wide, was Colleen.

CHAPTER 12

*C*olleen couldn't breathe, the words screaming through her head. The last place he should be... What did he mean by that?

Maybe she'd misheard. She just needed to breathe, to step back.

To rewind the last hour and start over. Back to the moment when she was sitting with her family at church, singing.

Feeling invincible. And beautiful.

You're so beautiful. Did you know that?

Her only disappointment had been that Jack hadn't taken her up on her offer to join her at church. She'd thought for sure he'd see her sitting in the front with her parents. And it felt strange to keep glancing back to search for him.

Maybe he wasn't ready. Well, she'd wait, then.

After all, she wasn't going anywhere.

So yes, she'd shaken hands with Meredith Johnson and complimented her dress, mentioning that she'd enjoyed spending time with Sammy yesterday and was glad that they would be friends.

She'd even told Ellie that she'd be willing to help with the Fall Festival. If she was going to stay, she may as well be all in.

Pastor Dan's sermon about the sparrows hit home too. She had wandered a bit from her faith, but no more. She'd be like the sparrow and trust in God's plan. She'd made the decision to stay in Deep Haven and was feeling great about it.

And maybe a little—or a lot—of that had to do with Jack and the future she imagined for them.

"Colleen! There you are." Ella's squeal reached Colleen just before the girl herself. "How have you been?"

She reached out and pulled her friend into a hug. Releasing her, Colleen searched her face for signs of trouble. She found none. "I'm great! How was your conference?"

"It was amazing." Ella's hands talked as much as she did. She accented her words with big gestures. "I recommend a trip to Colorado in the late fall every year. It's so beautiful out there in the mountains."

"Even though you've only been gone for two weeks, it feels much longer. So much has happened."

Ella waggled her eyebrows at Colleen. "Anything happening with Medic Muscles?"

Colleen rolled her eyes. "Stop, we're in church. Someone will hear you." But she couldn't control the blush she felt spreading across her cheeks.

A delighted gasp escaped Ella before she put her hand to her mouth. "That is so exciting." She dragged Colleen into a quieter part of the sanctuary and pointed at the pew. "Sit. Tell me everything."

"There isn't much to tell. I've scheduled my licensing exams."

"Excellent news, but that's not what I mean and you know it."

Colleen looked pointedly at Ella's left hand. "I see you're still unattached."

"Oh, knock it off, silly. As a matter of fact, I have it on good authority that Adrian has a velvet box just waiting for the right moment. Stop deflecting the question."

"Okay, okay. I give." Colleen held her hands up in surrender. "Kyle caught us kissing last night."

"Ha! I knew there was something between you two. That's so exciting."

"Well, it's early days yet, but I like him. I really do."

"I'm so happy for you. You deserve a good boyfriend, especially after that scumbag who cheated on you in college."

What a disaster that had been. She'd been so foolish to dump Tucker for that silly upperclassman. She'd believed she wanted more than a hometown boy. Turned out that her oh-so-cool boyfriend had taken a liberal view on fidelity. She'd walked in on him making out with her roommate their second semester.

"I should've known better than to trust a guy who drove a Prius."

"How is Jack taking the news that you're going for the flight nurse job?"

"What do you mean—how is *he* taking it?"

"When I mentioned the job to Adrian, he told me that Boone said he'd already found someone for it. I assumed he meant Jack."

She'd stolen Jack's job? She rubbed her forehead. Jack had never breathed a word of that to her. No wonder he hadn't wanted to join the team. She felt like a jerk. She needed to clear this whole situation up. Immediately.

She stood. "Where's Adrian?"

"I'm actually not sure. He dragged Jack somewhere." Ella stood too.

"Wait, Jack is here?" He'd come after all! Colleen wove her way through lingering worshippers. At the door to the sanctuary, her mom and dad stopped them.

"Honey, I just got a call from Frank. Your grandma isn't feeling well." Her dad put up a hand. "It doesn't sound like it's anything to worry about, but he asked if you could stop by, maybe even spend the night."

Colleen's gut clenched. "I'd be happy to do that. I need to talk to a few people, then I'll head straight over there."

"Mom is refusing to call the nurse line, but Frank insisted on calling us. Your mother and I are going over too."

"I'm glad he did. It's not a problem."

"Thank you, Colleen." Her dad bent and kissed her cheek.

Jack wasn't in the fellowship hall, so she headed down the hallway toward the Sunday school rooms.

Loud voices echoed from the room on the right.

"It's not like that."

"That sounds like Boone," Colleen said.

"It doesn't matter." Jack's voice.

Colleen pushed her way into the classroom. Boone and Jack stood facing off with Adrian, Peter, and Ronnie.

"You're right, Adrian. This is the last place I should be." Jack again.

What?

She couldn't move.

Even when Jack turned and headed for the door.

He nearly ran right into her.

His eyes met hers. And shoot, hers filled. "What did you say?"

Apparently everyone was engaged in a high-stakes game of Don't Blink, because no one acknowledged her or even took their eyes off the group they stood across from.

It wasn't hard to decide whose side she was on, so Colleen stood by Jack and repeated her question. "What's this all about? What do you mean this is the last place you should be?"

Church?

Without looking her way, Boone answered. "Don't worry about it. It's just administrative stuff."

"Yeah, well, I know all about the *administrative stuff*." She looked to where Ella stood in the doorway. *Silent*.

Fine. She'd put it out there. "Why didn't you guys tell me you wanted to hire Jack for the flight nurse position? I would never have put in for it if I had known. I don't want to get in the way."

More silence, and Boone looked at Adrian. Maybe routing the source of the leak.

"I don't think Jack is fit for that job." Adrian managed to speak the sentence without unclenching his jaw. She'd only met Ella's boyfriend a few times but she'd never seen him with such an intense, angry look.

And Boone radiated a sort of sharp energy. "Cut it out, Adrian. Don't you trust my judgment?"

"I'm really not sure. But I *am* sure that Jack doesn't belong here."

And that was just *it*. "Church is for everyone, Adrian. Please." She shook her head.

"It's not..." Adrian sighed. Turned to her. "Jack has a *secret*." He turned to Jack. "Want to tell her your secret, Jack? Or should I call you Winston?" He made Jack's name sound like a curse word.

Oh. She got it. Adrian had found out about Jack's time in the Air Force and how his friend had died. Excuse her, but that didn't disqualify him from church. Or redemption or even starting over in Deep Haven. Former playboy, I-drove-my-Porsche-into-a-lake, Adrian Vassos should know a little about that. Sheesh.

"Get over it, Adrian. It's no big deal. I mean it's a sad story, but it's not like it's his fault. It's in the past. Jack has nothing to be ashamed of."

"He *told* you?" Adrian said, his eyes dark.

"Yep, he told me the story last night." She didn't feel the need to add the part about the kissing. "So, if there isn't anything else, I still have a question about Jack applying for the job."

"Seriously." Adrian rubbed a hand over the back of his neck. "I don't know you well, Colleen, but I have to admit, I would have thought it mattered to you."

She met his eyes. "Everyone deserves a fresh start."

He let out a huff. "Fine. But this isn't over." Adrian took Ella's hand and made his way out of the classroom. Peter and Ronnie trailed behind.

The silence in the air stretched.

Finally Jack spoke. "I didn't apply for the job, Colleen."

"I asked him to take it, but he refused," Boone put in.

"But Ella said she thought that they were giving you the job until I applied. She wondered if it was because I had a local connection. I didn't want to be the reason you didn't get the position."

Jack glanced at Boone, back to her. "Don't worry about that. I don't know how Ella got mixed up in it, but I never wanted the job."

He was still acting weird. Hurt, maybe. She took his hand and he finally met her eyes.

"Well, good. I'm glad there isn't any awkwardness about training me then. It would be awful to have to train the woman who stole your spot."

A warmth came into his gaze. "There is nothing awful about training you."

Colleen felt her cheeks heating in pleasure.

"I think I'm gonna go..." Boone pointed his thumb toward the door. "You two don't seem to need me anymore."

"Actually, I need to go too. Grandma isn't feeling well today and I said I would go over and spend the night. I'm going to help clean up the house, make dinner, stuff like that."

"Colleen, wait." Jack's hand tightened in hers. "Hold on a minute." Turning to Boone, he said, "Thanks for standing up for me." The two men shared a long look. Weird.

Boone nodded once, then left the room.

Jack turned to her. "I'm sorry about your grandma. I hope she's feeling better soon."

"Thanks, I appreciate that."

"My dad said that when my mom was sick, the only thing she would eat was ginger cookies from Hart's Bakery from her hometown in Wisconsin. He would have them delivered for her."

"My grandma loves ginger cookies. Your dad is amazing. That might be the most romantic thing I've ever heard. He must have really loved her."

"Yeah, everyone tells me they had something special." He reached for her other hand. "Do you have a few more minutes? I really need to talk to you."

Colleen glanced at her Fitbit, turning her wrist without letting go of his strong fingers. "I'm sorry, I can't right now. Rain check?"

He drew in a breath. "I—"

"Listen. I'm not sure why Adrian is being such a jerk, but don't let him get to you. He's obviously got something else going on. Maybe the pressure of starting that business with Ella is getting to him."

"I don't care what Adrian thinks of me." Jack made a dismissive gesture. "But, I do care what *you* think of me. We really need to talk—"

"You don't have to worry about me. Your past is in the past. And like I said, everyone deserves a fresh start." She stepped up to him. "I hate leaving, but I really need to check in with my grandma. Maybe we can meet for coffee tomorrow?"

He sighed. "Okay." Jack kissed her.

She longed to reach up and draw his head down to hers and kiss him like she meant it. Maybe they could find a quiet spot after coffee tomorrow.

"Until tomorrow," Jack whispered in her ear.

Yep. Coming home had been the best decision she'd ever made.

∿

Jack was living on borrowed time. The more he was with Colleen, the more he was falling for her.

But he was living a lie.

Clearly Colleen thought his biggest secret was the mishap in Iraq those few years ago. He knew how she felt about secrets—and criminals.

He only had to remember Adrian's words in church yesterday morning to know how she was likely to feel about him. *I would have thought it mattered to you.*

It would matter. Jack knew it in his heart. And yes, he really wanted to simply...not tell her. But that was no way to start a relationship. And he really, really wanted what they had to be a relationship.

Jack paced around his apartment waiting for her text. After the confrontation, or maybe showdown, at church yesterday, he'd holed up in this box above the coffee shop.

Licking his wounds.

He couldn't believe that Adrian was related to David Barelli. Of all the tiny towns in all the world, and they'd ended up in the same one.

He could understand Adrian's anger and scorn. He loathed himself too.

So many stupid choices, starting with breaking his promise to go back for Ryan, and ending that night at the restaurant.

The night he'd nearly killed David Barelli.

If only he'd never gone to dinner that night...

His phone pinged with a text. Colleen. *I'm finishing up at Grandma's. Heading home in a few minutes. Still on for coffee?*

Jack imagined her bright smile under a high ponytail. He was definitely still on for coffee.

He could only pray she'd forgive him at the end of it. His fingers quickly moved over the phone keyboard. *I'll meet you at your house. We can take a walk.* A thumbs-up emoji and an address popped up in response. He keyed it into his phone's GPS and saw that the Decker home was only a few blocks away. He set the directions for walking and tucked the phone into his pocket.

A smell of dark roasted beans enveloped him as he entered the Java Cup a few moments later. He placed an order and within a few minutes was leaving with a black Americano for himself and the specialty coffee of the day for Colleen—something with caramel and pumpkin spice. Kathy had also talked him into two apple scones, wrapping them up in a white paper bag.

As if he needed another reminder that it was fall, which on Lake Superior's North Shore meant it was basically winter at any moment. Overnight the weather had turned. All around town, the trees were shedding their leaves, and the cold clouds rolling in from the north threatened a fall snowstorm before the day was out.

He'd memorized the route and balanced the bag and two coffees as he headed up the hill to her house, shoulders hunched against the wind and nearly second-guessing the walk he'd proposed. But, no. He wanted privacy when he talked to Colleen and he wasn't going to find that at her place or at the coffee shop. And he certainly wasn't going to invite her up to his place. He may forget just why they were together if they were cozied up at his tiny kitchen table.

Or anywhere else.

He passed a few bungalows, a Victorian, a couple log cabins —the eclectic mix that was Deep Haven. He found her street, and for a moment stopped and enjoyed the view.

So much beauty here in the deep blue lake, the rim of jeweled colors, the puffy clouds, the deep green pine. It was the perfect place to hide. But also start over.

Build a life.

Please, let this go well.

In his pocket, his GPS announced that he'd reached his destination, a 1970s ranch house with bushes that flanked the walk turning a deep red, and a pumpkin by the door. He double-checked the house number, then walked up the driveway, the front walk, stood on the porch, and rang the doorbell with his elbow. His phone pinged in his pocket but he didn't have a way to check it with a coffee in each hand.

The door opened and an older man came out.

"Mr. Decker? I'm here to see Colleen. Has she made it back yet?"

"You must be Jack. Call me Nathan. I just got a text from her. My mom spiked a fever and she didn't want to leave her."

Right, the ping in his pocket. "She may have texted me too. Would you mind holding these?" Okay, that was awkward, but he couldn't check without free hands.

Nathan took the cups.

His phone read, *Sorry. I have to cancel. Grandma got really sick.*

And now he was the world's biggest chump, standing on his girlfriend's porch with her dad staring at him. The tiny spear of relief that he could postpone having this discussion with Colleen passed in a brief moment. Now that he'd committed to telling her, he just wanted to do it as quickly as possible. Then he would know for sure if there was a future for them.

"Jack, I'm actually glad Colleen isn't here. Maybe it's old-fashioned, but I'd like to get to know the guy my daughter is spending so much time with."

Definitely old-fashioned, but Jack could understand it. "We were going to take a walk. Perhaps the two of us could go instead?"

Nathan handed the coffees back.

"Would you like this one? I'm afraid it's a little foofoo, something with caramel and pumpkin, but I already drank out of the other one and can't offer it to you."

Nathan chuckled. "I'll give it a go. Come in and I'll grab my jacket."

Jack waited in the hall as Nathan found his jacket and called to his wife that he was taking a walk.

The two men headed outside and up the sidewalk back toward town. Nathan sipped at his drink.

"Y'know, this pumpkin thingy isn't that bad." Nathan took another appreciative gulp. "Colleen tells me you were in the Air Force."

"Yes, I trained as a PJ. Pararescue." At Nathan's understanding nod, he went on. "I enlisted straight out of high school. I served for two tours. Chose not to re-up and came home."

"I never served in the military, but I imagine the experience is like nothing else."

"It changes you, that's for sure. I mostly served in Iraq. It got so I thought I'd never get the sand out of my clothes or ever be cool again." Jack shivered. "I guess days like today remind me that it does get cold." A blast of wind punctuated his words.

"We're probably going to get a storm. Weatherman predicts we may even get a few inches of snow."

A beat passed. Then another. Both men sipped their drinks.

"I hope I'm not crossing some kind of line here, but, Jack, I want to know how you see your relationship going with my daughter."

Nathan's bluntness stopped Jack from taking another step. Nathan halted as well.

Well, he could be blunt too. "Honestly, I think I'm falling in love with your daughter." He turned to look Nathan in the eyes. "She's courageous and spunky, smart and generous."

"You don't have to tell me." An amused light crept into Nathan's eyes.

"No, I suppose not." Jack gave him a brief smile. Oh boy, this next part was not going to be easy.

But frankly, Nathan deserved to know, as much as Colleen did. "But there is something you should know. I came over here today to tell Colleen the whole story of my life, but I think you should know too."

Nathan began walking again. "Okay. I'm listening."

Jack swallowed the last of his now cold coffee. He crushed the cup in his hand.

"When I was released from the Air Force, I went straight home to Kellogg. My dad lives there and I needed a place to crash for a while. Since I'd been deployed most of my eight years in, I didn't have a permanent place to live in the states." They'd reached downtown. Jack threw his empty cup into a garbage can stationed on the corner. "I'd been home about a week and I decided I'd go out for a bite to eat." Why, oh why hadn't he taken his dad up on the offer to accompany him to that fundraising dinner instead? "I went to a local bar and grill. There was an older guy there who was obviously inebriated. He was with a date. Throughout their meal, he was making rude and suggestive comments to her. I was on my way out and as I went past their table, the old guy accused me of looking at his date. I made the mistake of saying something I shouldn't have."

Nathan looked at him, an eyebrow raised.

"I told him that I wasn't looking at her, but that he'd better treat her right or he wouldn't be looking at her either. I know. Stupid. It would come back to haunt me."

Jack and Nathan passed The Trading Post. The wind gusted along the street, blowing a stray napkin in front of it.

"Sounds like an honorable thing to do, standing up to him like that." Nathan tossed his cup into a garbage can as well.

"Yeah, well, the guy thought I was being rude and took a

swing at me. I blocked the punch and set him back down in the chair. I thought it was over and left, but after I exited the restaurant, he followed me. He confronted me in the parking lot, yelling about how I should mind my own business."

Nathan's face was neutral, but Jack got the feeling he was listening, waiting to hear the full story before passing judgment.

"I could tell he was drunk, and I really didn't want to fight him. Although, I can admit that I wanted to maybe teach him a lesson about how to treat women. But I didn't hit him. I kept backing up until I was against a car."

Out in the harbor a boat swayed, caught by the high waves. Jack could see people on board scrambling over the rocking boat, trying to tie it to the pier. One guy jumped off onto the dock holding the end of a rope.

"He took another swing at me, and I ducked. His hand hit the car. That just made him even madder. He came right up to me and was yelling in my face. I just wanted to go home. I stood up, put my hands up. Told him to back off. He came in for another shot, but by this time I was over it. I gave him a shove to get him away from me. And, I don't know, maybe some of my frustrations over leaving the military spilled over." The image of that shove was burned into his brain. A scar he would never lose.

"I don't like where this is going."

The boat drifted from the dock, resisting the pull of the rope.

"I don't really know how it happened. I think his reflexes weren't sharp, but he stumbled over the curbing and fell. Hard. Brain bleed."

"Oh no."

"Yeah. It was just that one shove, but he was in a coma for a month. When he came out, he was severely impaired. He can't walk or talk."

"I'm sorry. That's a terrible thing to have on your

conscience."

"Yeah, well, it doesn't end there."

He looked away. This was it. This was where Nathan Decker would tell him to never be in the same room as Colleen ever again.

"His family pressed charges. There were witnesses, and apparently, he had high-ranking friends—judges, lawyers, wealthy friends. Because I'd been in the military, I was charged with third-degree assault and sentenced to one year in prison. I just got out of the Stillwater prison." There it was, in the open. "I'm a felon, Nathan."

The silence stretched. *C'mon, man, say something.*

Nathan rubbed his chin. "That's a lot to take in."

On the dock, the boatman wound his rope around a sturdy post, finally pulling the boat steadily into its slip.

"How does your family feel about it?" Nathan looked him in the eye.

He raised one shoulder. "My dad is a congressman. I think he's ashamed of me. He kept in touch during my incarceration, but never came to visit. Too afraid of the press, probably."

Nathan put his hand on his shoulder and squeezed. "I'm sorry to hear it. Who else knows all this?" He dropped his hand and started walking back toward the Java Cup.

Jack followed. "Boone knows. He was there that night. And Adrian Vassos is related to the guy."

"I can understand why you would keep that a secret. I've kept a few secrets in my life too."

What was he saying?

Nathan went on. "Y'know, this reminds me of the story of David."

"A little guy who kills a giant. Not very helpful."

Nathan chuckled. "No, not that part of the story. I'm thinking of the parts where King Saul kept accusing David of being all these terrible things. David went out of his way to respect the king and just kept getting beaten down for it. But David never let what Saul said get inside his heart. He continued to trust God."

"If you're comparing me to a guy in the Bible, you don't know me very well."

"We're all guys in the Bible, in one way or another. But you're right—I don't really know you. But I do know Boone, who trusts you, and I know my daughter, and she sees good in you. I guess what I'm trying to say is that you don't need to let that event define you."

Jack let the words sink in. They felt like a strong rope, pulling him to safety. "I don't know. Feels pretty defining. In my quest for honor, I let my anger take over."

"Just think about it. God knew David's heart, and He knows yours too. What's on the inside of a man is more important than his circumstances. I'm sure Colleen will see that too."

A clap of thunder rent the sky and rain began falling in sheets. The two ran for the shelter of the Java Cup.

But as he stood, shivering, watching the sky weep, he couldn't deny that he felt oddly cleansed. As though the confession and the rain had washed some of the shame away.

His phone pinged with a text from Boone. *We need you at HQ stat. All hands on deck. We've got a situation and I don't know what we're walking into.*

"I'm sorry, Nathan, I've got to go." He shook Nathan's hand. "Thanks, man."

"No problem. Thanks for your honesty today," Nathan said.

No point getting into his truck when he was already soaking wet—he'd just run the few blocks to HQ.

With every beat of his feet against the pavement, Nathan's words pulsed in his mind. *You don't need to let that event define you.* And never in a thousand years did he expect that conversation to go that well.

Maybe he should just stop worrying already.

CHAPTER 13

*C*olleen couldn't remember ever being this fatigued.

The night spent at her grandma's was fractured at best. The chemo rippling through her grandma's body also had caused her to get up every hour and vomit. Colleen and Frank took turns helping Grandma Helen, but with Frank still on crutches, most of the work had fallen on Colleen.

Colleen had nearly broken down. She hated seeing her beloved grandma so sick all the time.

This morning when Grandma had seemed weak and her skin paper thin, Colleen had insisted on going out to get some Pedialyte. Maybe the hydration would help. She'd sent a text to Jack to postpone their coffee date and made a quick trip to the store. When she'd returned, she had found her grandma once again in the bathroom, Frank on the floor beside her.

She'd needed reinforcements.

Praying someone was at home, she'd dialed her parents' number, almost weeping in relief when her mom had answered.

"Mom, I need you. Can you come to Grandma's?"

"Sure, Sweetie, I'll be there as soon as I can."

Colleen had just tucked Grandma Helen back into bed and

given her some more Pedialyte when her mom came in, her hair back in a bandana, ready for work.

"Thank you for coming. Can you help me get Frank settled?"

The two women worked together, helping Frank get to the recliner in the den to watch television. Her mom went to make Frank a sandwich and a hot drink.

"Thank you for helping us, Colleen," Frank said with a sigh. "I feel like an old fool, needing to be helped around like a baby."

"You're not an old fool," she protested. "Besides, everyone needs help sometimes." She smiled and kissed Frank on the top of his head.

As she flipped on an old western movie channel for him to watch, her phone pinged with a group text. Boone.

We need you at HQ stat. All hands on deck. We've got a situation, and I don't know what we're walking into.

She hustled into the kitchen where her mom was adding pickles to Frank's sandwich. "Mom, there's a situation for the Crisis Response Team." But how could she leave? What if Grandma Helen got sick again? "I'll tell Boone I can't come."

"No." Her mom's forceful answer gave her pause. "We'll be fine here. You go. Grandma just needs rest and fluids, and those are two things I can do. What I *can't* do is be helpful in the type of emergency that the Crisis Response Team is called for. You can. Go."

She jogged to her car intent on joining the team, but ran into the disaster before she reached HQ.

On the highway, just north of town, was a timber nightmare.

She spotted the red and blue lights flashing from the sheriff department's cruisers blocking the highway as she turned north and headed toward the accident. An ambulance was parked on the side of the road. Flares trailed away from the scene, warning drivers of the danger.

Beyond them, a logging truck canted sideways in the road, jackknifed around a light blue compact car. The chain holding the massive timbers must have snapped, and the huge logs had tumbled from the semi. Several pine timbers lay crushing the roof of the car wedged under it.

Farther up the road, other cars had piled up in an accident stretching almost a quarter mile, one car rear-ending the next. People milled everywhere. A murmur of sound rose from the masses, as though everyone was talking and shouting at once.

In the distance, she could hear a child wailing.

Oh. No.

Spotting Boone, she pulled over.

A few of the other team members were on scene, along with the Deep Haven Fire Department in turnout coats and Kyle and the rest of the sheriff's department. A few patrolmen were directing traffic.

The rain was still falling. A bitter breeze lashing her face told her that the rain would be turning to snow before this day was out. Though it was only noon, the sky was black.

Colleen saw Ronnie and Jack bent over someone on the ground and made her way toward them.

She dodged around a mother and daughter clutching each other, then wove her way through a mass of teenage boys. A fleeting thought of *Why aren't they in school?* was quickly discarded when she got close to Boone.

"Where can I help?" she shouted across to him. He motioned toward a log lying on the ground. Several people, including Ronnie, Jensen, and Jack, clustered around one end of it.

Drawing closer she saw why.

Sammy.

Trapped under the log.

His legs were completely obscured by the massive timber. The log, about a foot and a half in diameter, pitched sideways from the semi, one end resting on a smaller log, which, if they were lucky, was keeping some of the weight from Sammy's legs.

The situation was critical. Sammy needed help. Like right now, or he would lose both legs.

"He tried to pull the passenger out of the car, but the log fell on him," Jack murmured in her ear. Freezing rainwater trickled down her neck and made a path along her spine.

She fell to her knees beside Sammy. Took his hand. "Sammy, can you hear me? It's Colleen. We're here to help." She heard Boone on the radio calling for the chopper. Someone shouted instructions. The siren of one of the patrol cars suddenly fell silent.

Sammy opened his eyes. "Colleen, is that you?" She had to bend closer to hear his whisper. "Have I gone to heaven? Because I see an angel." She shot him a sharp look only to see him giving her a weak grin.

She smiled back at him. "Ha ha, funny man. You're still here in the real world, but you might be a little delusional."

He sobered. "I can't feel my legs. Am I going to die?"

She looked at his legs trapped under the log and then into his eyes. There was no way to assess the damage until the log was moved, but, "We're not going to let that happen."

Over Sammy's body, Jensen shot her a look. Let him. Emergency medicine was her thing. She wasn't going to let a friend die on her watch.

"What happened, Sammy?" Maybe he didn't need to relive this, but she wanted to keep him talking.

"I...I was hauling that load of timber—" He stopped and drew in a deep breath. Colleen put her hand on his wrist, checking for his pulse. "I came around the bend, and there was that little car..." His eyes drifted shut. Oh no. Had he lost control and hit the car?

Under her fingers, Sammy's pulse was thready. "Sammy? Stay with me, bud. What happened next?"

"Deer. A mama and her fawn. Jumped in front of the car. They braked. I couldn't stop fast enough." He drifted off again.

"We think the chain holding the load must have snapped when the semi jackknifed around the car. It doesn't look like Sammy hit them." Jack filled in the blanks. "He said he was pulling the passenger out when the last log slipped off the load. You can see the results." He gestured at Sammy, prone on the ground. Someone had strapped a neck collar around the lumberjack's neck, but the log still lay across his legs.

Colleen looked over at the car a few yards away. Ronnie had moved to the side of someone lying on the ground near the car's open front door.

She felt rather than saw the men and women from the sheriff's department keeping the crowd clear of the drama here in the center of the action as they worked to clear the traffic pileup beyond the logging rig. Occasionally headlights would flash over where she and Jack knelt by Sammy.

Boone hustled over to them. "The driver and passenger are going to go by ambulance. They're mostly okay, broken arm and possibly a foot. Colleen, have you got this under control? Ronnie and Jensen will have to take the others to Deep Haven's hospital in a few minutes."

"I'll need help, but yeah, I got this." Maybe if she spoke confidently, it would trickle down into her heart. She scrubbed the rain off her face. Again.

"Good. We need to send Sammy by helicopter to Duluth. Jensen, Jack, what do you think? Can we move this log off his legs?"

Jensen gave a terse nod. He and Jack called several other people over to help. Soon a small crowd had assembled around the log, ready to lift on Jensen's go ahead. Colleen tied a loose tourniquet around Sammy's upper thighs. When the log released, there was a danger of his lower legs filling with fluid. Compartment syndrome could cause him to lose both his legs. The tourniquet would slow the fluid from entering his tissue too quickly and causing it to die.

She grabbed his hand, held it between hers. When the log came off, she wanted him to lie still.

Jensen called out a count. "One. Two. Three." They heaved the log off Sammy and dumped it under the logging semi. Jack and some of the others checked to make sure the log wouldn't roll back.

Colleen couldn't see any obvious blood gushing from Sammy's legs. She cut away his pants. His lower legs were a strange purple color, but it was hard to see clearly in the darkness of the rainstorm and with the flashing lights of the emergency vehicles being the only illumination.

"I can't see anything." She squinted at the injured legs. Was the lurid red-blue from the ambulance lights or was there blood pooling?

"We need some light over here," Boone called out.

In the distance, Colleen heard a siren as the ambulance pulled away from the scene. And then another. The second ambulance must have arrived after she did.

Colleen knew there wasn't room for anyone to pass by them, so they must be sending tow trucks the long way around.

Someone had found a work lamp and now the area was flooded with light. The rays fractured and bounced off the raindrops.

"Can someone get a tarp?" she called out, hoping someone heard her. "We need to keep the rain off him or he's gonna go into shock."

Pastor Dan hurried over and stripped off his jacket. He held it over Sammy's legs. "Sorry, Colleen. Best we can do right now."

And then, suddenly, Jack was there. "How you doing, Colleen?" He knelt next to her and shrugged out of his jacket too. He placed it over Sammy's chest. "What do you need?"

"I have to check the back of his legs for any punctures. Can you lift, while I look?" She appreciated his quiet assistance as Jack lifted Sammy's leg. She slid her hand over Sammy's calf.

Sammy cried out in pain and attempted to pull away.

"I don't think I can complete my assessment if he's going to be moving like this." The rain ran into her eyes, frustrating her efforts to see anything.

"I'll take care of checking for protruding bones. You distract him." Jack's voice sounded hard. Battle ready. "Maybe you can sing 'Sweet Home Alabama.'"

She shot him a look. He winked at her. Then his face turned stony again as he refocused on the injured man in front of him.

"I still haven't felt for a pedal or femoral pulse yet. I don't see any obvious signs of compartment syndrome."

"I'll take care of it." Jack pulled Sammy's left boot off. Colleen shifted to sit at Sammy's head. She shucked off her soaking wet jacket and held it up in a canopy over his head.

"Hey, Sammy, stay with us, bud."

The man opened bleary eyes. Blinked slowly. "Colleen."

"Shh, don't try to talk. Hey, remember that time we had to make elephant toothpaste in chemistry class and decided to double the recipe?" Colleen forced a smile. "The look on your face when that goop began spreading all over the lab table was priceless. I still can't believe how long it took us to clean it up. I'm guessing Mr. Hanson never tried that experiment with high school seniors ever again."

An amused light flickered in Sammy's eyes, between the flashes of pain. "Your. Fault."

"What?" She feigned astonishment. "That was all you, bud. I would have measured correctly. You were the one who wanted to push it."

"You. Didn't. Stop. Me. Your. Fault." Sammy took a labored breath between each word. Had they missed a greater injury or was he just going into shock? She looked at his chest, counting the rise and fall of his breath—75 breaths per minute. Just a little high. She laid her hand along his neck, checking for a pulse. His artery fluttered under her fingertips. Concentrating on seeing her Fitbit in the rain, she counted again—110 bpm. Yep, a little high, but that was to be expected considering the circumstances.

She ran her hand around his ribs, double-checking that he didn't have a broken one.

"Not. How. I. Pictured. This." His mouth was crooked in a half smile.

"I still just want to be friends." But relief poured through her at his teasing. Plus, she didn't feel any swelling under his skin, a telltale sign of broken ribs. "Does your chest hurt?"

"Only the wound from…you rejecting me."

"Ha ha. I think you'll live."

She swiped at the rain still collecting on her face.

"Where is that chopper?" Jack muttered to himself so quietly Colleen barely heard him over the emergency crew activity and the sound of the rain.

At that moment, Seth Turnquist jogged up, followed closely by Aaron, his brother. The lumber company owners knelt down by Sammy. "Hey, Sammy. We're going to take care of this," Seth told him. Aaron nodded along.

A crew of men in an extended cab pickup marked Turnquist Lumber showed up. Aaron jumped up and went over to supervise as they began to discuss how to clear the semi and the fallen logs.

Several minutes later, a tow truck arrived to haul away the bent and broken car.

Just then the welcoming *thwap-thwap* of the helicopter drowned out any more muttering. Colleen took a full breath. The bird settled down a short distance away.

Boone, who had been pacing around the scene and alternating between lending a hand and giving orders, came over to them. "I need your help again."

Colleen watched for the back door of the helicopter to open.

When it didn't, she looked at Boone. "We need to go on the chopper again, don't we?"

"I'm afraid so. Rhino worked a double yesterday and last night, and he just got home. He's too tired to fly. And we couldn't get ahold of anyone else."

"I'm not certified yet. My test isn't until later this week." Yeah, Boone probably didn't need the reminder, but without that certification she didn't have the approval to treat a patient mid-air. She'd learned that flight nurse certification wasn't strictly necessary, but she sure would feel better with that paper in her hand.

Boone held up his hand. "Colleen, I understand your hesitation, but you're all we've got. This is what you've been training for."

She was not ready for this. What if something went wrong?

Next to her, Sammy groaned again.

She looked Jack in the eye. Hoping. Holding her breath. She couldn't do this alone.

"I'll get the stretcher." Jack hiked himself up and ducked over to the chopper, beneath the still spinning rotor.

A moment later, he pushed the Stryker litter toward them.

Lowering the bed to its lowest setting, then placing a hard, plastic backboard next to Sammy, he bent to talk to the injured man. "Sorry, man. This is going to hurt." He stood at Sammy's head and motioned Colleen to the other end. He waved Boone over. "We have to roll him on his side to get the backboard under Sammy. Seth, you hold the board in position. Boone, you take the middle. On my count."

Together they hefted Sammy to his side, tucking the backboard under, then repeated the gesture on the other side until he was fully on the sturdy board. All four of them grasped the hand holds on the backboard, then lifted Sammy the short distance up and onto the litter.

Sammy cried out, his voice echoing against the vehicles parked nearby.

As they loaded the litter onto the chopper, a burst of thunder ripped through the air. The spitting rain turned to sleet slapping its fingers against the front window of the helicopter. In the pilot's seat, Bill craned his neck around to look at them.

"Ready to get this bird in the air? Okay, let's light her up."

Colleen looked at Jack. He stood near the open door. After helping her secure the litter, he moved farther and farther away. He kept his gaze on the floor, fisted his hands, once. Twice. Then raised his gaze and met her eyes.

"Are you coming with us?" Her heart pounded. *Please, say yes.*

He looked away for a heartbeat. Two. Then he clenched his jaw and looked back into her eyes.

"Can't let you have all the fun." His weak attempt at a joke and a smile threaded through her. Jack was a good guy. Sure, he seemed a little reckless at times, but it wasn't recklessness if it worked. He saved lives. He was fighting his demons for her.

Colleen and Jack double-checked the litter fastenings as the chopper lifted off the ground. The helicopter wobbled a bit before settling into a smooth flight.

"He's lost consciousness." Wearing headphones, Colleen probably didn't need to shout, but with the rain pelting and the noise of the rotor she was having trouble concentrating.

"I see that. Let's get this blanket on him and an IV started. Who knows what we will need to do before the ride is out."

Through the gap into the cockpit, Colleen could see the sleet had now combined with snow. The sky remained a gunmetal gray, the clouds swallowing up all light. As the helicopter dipped into an air pocket, she grabbed onto the equipment locker to steady herself.

She looked at Jack. "It's going to be okay. We're going to save him, right?"

~

Here he was again, flying with that psycho pilot. Too bad Boone hadn't had time to act on his promise to look into hiring another one.

But Colleen was right—they had to save her friend.

Even if Jack had to shove the flashbacks into the deepest part of his brain.

Even if he had to ignore the strobes of lightning looking just like the blaze of a gun barrel.

The sharp, medicinal tang of alcohol and iodine filled the air, threatening to undo him. He hadn't asked for this. Had tried really hard to not be in this position ever again, thank you very much.

What could he do, though, when Colleen had looked so terrified? He'd received her unspoken plea loud and clear across the wet pavement that had separated them. Her last experience with that kid hadn't gone so well and she had to be afraid for her friend. There was no way he would let her do this alone again.

And there was no one else.

So he'd climbed into the belly of the bird and pretended that it didn't matter. That this storm raging around them didn't bother him in the least. After all, if Colleen could move past her fears and find something like peace, maybe he could too.

He managed not to flinch when one loud crack of thunder sounded just like a shoulder-fired missile. A glance toward the window revealed that Bill must be flying nearly blind.

The rain was mostly snow and sleet now, sheeting off the windscreen.

On the litter, Sammy had passed out. They had administered Ketamine and his pain was probably low, considering his legs looked like they'd been through a meat grinder. Both legs were swelling and angry red. Jack was reminded of the time he'd pulled a soldier out of a bombed building. That soldier's injuries from the blast looked eerily similar to Sammy's crushed limbs. Despite the obvious trauma to the legs, the skin was mainly intact. The damage must be internal.

He had to give the man credit. He'd heard his joking with Colleen. It seemed Sammy was a fighter. Good. He'd need that for the months of rehab he would likely face.

If he kept his legs at all.

With Colleen, Jack would just have to do what he could to ensure that Sammy did.

So, he inserted an IV in Sammy's left arm while Colleen started him on oxygen. Brushing past Colleen in the tight quarters, he slid a blood pressure cuff around Sammy's right bicep. Hit the button on the machine to inflate the cuff for a reading.

"BP 160 over 90," he said. A little high, but within an acceptable range, considering. Colleen jotted it down on a clipboard.

"I'll get a heart monitor started." Colleen eased open Sammy's shirt and attached the three leads. The machine started its blinking rhythm.

Finally, Jack was satisfied they'd stabilized Sammy the best they could with their limited equipment. There was still a danger of compartment syndrome with a crush injury. The blood filling the damaged muscles could cause the tissue to die and putrefy, but there was nothing they could do about that until they were sure he had that kind of damage.

Colleen started to shiver. The drop in adrenaline combined with her wet clothes could put her in danger of shock.

"Colleen, you are soaked through."

She pulled her hair into a messy knot on the top of her head and secured it with a rubber band from around her wrist. She sent him a tired smile. "Yeah, speak for yourself, tough guy."

Oh, he loved that bravery.

Opening a drawer in the equipment locker, Jack found two wool blankets. He draped one around Colleen and took the other himself. They checked Sammy's heart rate and breathing one more time. Colleen again jotted the numbers on the clipboard. The emergency staff would need the data when they arrived at the hospital.

A sudden change in pitch tossed Colleen against him. "Whoa. Are you okay?"

She nodded.

The helo gave another buck and they fell, rather than sat, into the jump seats located against the cockpit wall, one behind the pilot, and one behind the co-pilot's seat.

He fastened his seat belt, forced another flashback into the depths.

The tension in his shoulders relaxed a fraction. Sammy's injury was stabilized as best as possible. He'd coaxed a smile out of Colleen. Now they just needed to ride out the rest of this hour-long flight.

An updraft shot the chopper into the air.

Then it dropped in a sickening nosedive.

Colleen screamed.

The pilot swore over the intercom.

Turning to the right, Jack could see Bill fighting with the controls, trying to bring the bird under control. The nose came up a fraction.

Then they sheered left.

Outside, the ground rushed up at them. Below, he could see an old hayfield studded with the last row of dried and bent stalks. Here and there, snow was beginning to pile up. All around them, darkness and snow reigned. He didn't see the telltale signs of a homestead anywhere.

The field was growing bigger fast. Too fast.

They sheered right, then nosedived again.

In the cockpit, Bill swore again then shouted. "Brace yourself!"

Jack grabbed the strap dangling from the frame of the door. Across from him, Colleen did the same.

A moment later, the helicopter hit the ground, bouncing once then slamming into the ground and nearly tearing Jack's hand out of the strap. He looked over at Colleen. Her face was pale in the dim light.

They skidded a hundred feet across the dead field. A screeching, tearing sound came from below their feet.

The bird came to rest leaning on the left side.

Silence reigned for a moment, broken only by a ticking noise —the engine cooling perhaps.

Jack! Are you okay? Ryan's voice, pinging from the past. Jack spat once to rid his mouth of the sudden taste of desert dust.

No, not Ryan. Colleen. Calling his name.

He turned to her. She sat sideways, strapped into her seat, but she was working her buckles.

"Are you okay?" His question to Colleen came out hoarse.

"I...think so."

He pulled off his headset at the same time Colleen did. Now that the rotors were silent, they didn't need the amplification.

He unhooked his belts.

"Check Sammy," he told Colleen. Sammy's litter basket, though strapped in, was at an angle. "Bill, are you okay?" No answer. Jack swung through the doorway in the wall behind the cockpit. Bill lay at a strange angle in his seat, his seat belt harness holding him in place. Blood ran from a cut above his eye.

Jack gently probed for a pulse, careful not to disturb Bill's neck in case of whiplash, or worse. "Bill! " A thin pulse throbbed under Jack's fingers.

Outside, the wind howled. Something banged hard against the side of the chopper, and the helo went dark.

"Jack?" Colleen's voice was thin.

"I think a branch or something hit us. We've lost power, and the radio is dead," he called back to her.

He flipped a few switches, hoping—no, praying—that the radio would flicker back to life. No juice. He grabbed his cell phone and visually checked Bill's limbs, looking for any signs of obvious trauma. No blood there. His legs weren't trapped by anything in the cockpit. Beyond the bash to his head, he seemed okay. Breathing was normal, and pulse was okay. The angle of the helicopter would make it impossible to get him out the door on that side. They'd have to pull him out through the back. For now, Jack would bandage his head and leave him where he was. He was safe there for the time being.

He quickly strapped a neck collar on Bill, then applied a bandage to his head wound.

Jack made his way back to Colleen's side. "Bill is unconscious with a cut on his head. How's our boy Sammy?"

"No change. Breathing is steady, or at least close enough for his condition. BP stable." She thumbed one of the seat belt–like straps they'd fitted across Sammy to secure him on the gurney. The litter was leaning to the side, Sammy with it. "Do you think we should leave him like this? I'm concerned about this angle."

Outside the wind and rain lashed against them, a whistling howl echoing through the window where it had cracked on impact.

"We have to keep him in here. Lying at that angle is better than being outside in this storm. Let's try propping up his left side with some blankets."

Colleen found a few blankets and rolled them up. They worked together to place them under Sammy's body, loosening the straps holding him in place only when necessary. The man groaned once but didn't wake up.

Colleen rubbed her forehead with the back of her hand.

Suddenly he noticed blood trickling down her cheek. "Colleen, you're hurt."

"What?" She looked at her hand. "Oh. I'm sure it's nothing." She grabbed some gauze pads, pressed them on the cut, then scrubbed her hands before dabbing another stack to her forehead. She winced.

"Here, let me do that." Jack shuffled over to her side. He turned her face toward the light on his cell phone. "It doesn't look too deep. I'll clean it up and put on a few butterfly Steri-Strips." He took her hand and she winced again. "What is it?"

"My wrist. I think I sprained it when the helicopter came down. It twisted funny in the strap."

"Why didn't you say something before?"

"Sammy and Bill are our priority."

He carefully rotated her wrist. Died a little when she cut off a moan. "I don't think it's broken. I'll wrap it in a bandage."

"I saw some in the bottom drawer, on the right." Colleen pointed out the drawer with her good hand. He walked her over to the jump seat attached to the back of the copilot's seat. She perched on its edge as he wound the bandage around her wrist. Silence fell between them as he worked.

"Jack?" Her quiet voice interrupted his thoughts. "How are we going to get out of here?"

He checked his phone. No signal. "Does your phone have a signal?" He held his breath as she checked. Hoping.

Her face flashed in the brief illumination of her phone. "Full charge. No signal."

So much for hope. "Someone will have to go for help."

Colleen stared at him. "Jack, you have to go. You're the only one who can."

No. Absolutely not.

"I don't want to leave you behind." Ryan's face flashed into his mind. "You're hurt. And it's getting colder out there."

"I don't have any training for this sort of thing. You have a much better chance at making it out. We haven't done any orienteering yet. I don't know how to navigate out there."

A blast of icy wind punctuated her words.

He nodded. What she said made sense. This storm could be deadly for anyone who wandered too far off course.

"Please, Jack. You have to go. We'll be fine here." She softened her tone. "I don't have any of the survival skills you do. I can care for the men, but only you can save us."

She was right. "Colleen, we never got a chance to talk—"

"It doesn't matter. Whatever you have to talk to me about, it doesn't matter. Let's save these men and then we'll have plenty of time to talk."

He took her uninjured hand. "I'll be as quick as I can."

"Jack." She searched his eyes. "I...I love you."

He stilled a moment. Then cupped her cheek. "I love you too." Swiftly he kissed her. "I'll be back. I promise."

Then he let her go and turned to walk into the raging storm.

CHAPTER 14

*D*on't *panic.*

Colleen watched Jack run into the murky storm without calling him back.

That, right there, was a win.

Colleen checked the time on her Fitbit. It was only 2:00 p.m., but the storm made the sky twilight. A break in the clouds would bring much needed light to this tenuous situation.

Based on their flight time and the distance they estimated they'd been blown off course, she figured they had to be somewhere east of Brimson. He'd taken off in a westerly direction, heading toward the last position they'd glimpsed lights.

Don't cry.

It was up to her to keep Sammy and Bill alive.

And she refused to think about the crash. The helplessness of plummeting from the sky—

Nope.

Jack had taken his cell phone, and she needed more light than hers could provide. Colleen hunted in the cabinets and finally found a small, battery-operated lantern. She flicked the switch, and light broke through the darkness.

Outside, the wind howled.

Because of the odd angle of the helicopter, everything leaned. She moved her feet carefully as she made her way to the cockpit.

Bill was still out. The bandage Jack had applied to his head wound was beginning to soak through. She tracked down new supplies and cleaned the wound again, rebandaged it. Then she checked his blood pressure and heart rate, working in the cramped quarters of the cockpit.

Bill moaned once and then was silent. She slid a hand all around and under his harness, making sure that the fabric of the seat belt wasn't cutting into his skin or cutting off his breathing. Everything checked out fine. There wasn't much else she could do for him right now, and he was safest where he was.

In the back, Sammy began groaning, struggling on the gurney. She hurried back to him and put her hand to his forehead.

"Shh, try not to move." His skin was fiery.

"What's...happening?" In the dim light of the lantern, Sammy's skin looked pale and dry. His lips were white and cracked.

"The chopper went down in the storm. Jack is running for help." *Please, God, keep him safe.* She didn't know if she'd whispered the prayer or just groaned it. She refocused on Sammy and his fever. "I'm going to add some antibiotic to your IV. Try to stay still. The helicopter is leaning, so the bed you're on isn't flat."

She pushed the medicine through the IV Jack had inserted into his hand.

"Can I...drink?"

"A few sips should be fine." She found a fresh water bottle in the tiny fridge, cracked it open, and held it to Sammy's lips. A few drops dribbled into his mouth. He swallowed then opened his mouth again for more. She obliged, giving him a full swallow.

With a jerk, he started throwing up.

Colleen quickly turned his head so that he wouldn't choke on the vomit. She should have known better than to give him a drink. Rookie mistake.

The bile smell filled the chopper.

As she cleaned Sammy up, she noticed his breathing was growing shallow.

"Are you feeling okay?"

"Not so much." Sammy shifted on the gurney.

Colleen gently wiped his face. She laid her hand on his forehead again. "Your fever is getting better. I'll see what we have to get that pain under control. Are you allergic to anything?"

"Shellfish," he whispered. Tried a smile.

Always the funny guy.

The dim lantern light struggled to reach the back of the medicine drawer. Colleen squinted at the labels on the medicine. Nitroglycerin, Epinephrine, Haloperidol, Lorazepam —*Fentanyl.*

There! She snagged the vial, turned back to the gurney. The wind kicked up outside, rocking the helicopter. Colleen, off balance, reached out to steady herself. She whacked her injured hand against the metal cabinet.

The vial in her hand slipped. Fell. Shattered on the hard floor. Pieces flew everywhere, and the medicine drained between the cracks of the floor tiles.

No—*no!*

Sammy moaned. Then, "My legs!"

She stripped off the emergency blanket covering Sammy's legs. The lower half of the left one ballooned, swollen and purple. She touched the angry-looking skin. Pressed at the wound. Hard as a rock.

Compartment syndrome.

Sammy groaned, a deep impenetrable pain from the center of his core.

Think. *Think.*

There was a procedure for a situation like this—a fasciotomy. She needed to surgically release the pressure building up inside Sammy's muscles. She'd seen it done, even participated in the procedure a few times. But never in a totaled chopper, trapped in the middle of an October blizzard.

But he could lose his leg if she didn't do *something.*

What would Jack do? *Whatever it takes to save a life.*

Sammy cried out again.

Whatever hope of getting a certification could die if she attempted this. Even if Sammy lived…

He had to live.

Who had ever thought this was a good idea? She shouldn't be here.

Her hands shook as she found another vial of fentanyl.

Her stupid certificate didn't matter. Because she *was* here.

And Sammy had no one else.

Just get it done, Decker.

She prepared the shot and sent the medicine into his IV.

In a moment, he visibly relaxed, his breathing easier.

She positioned the lantern as close to the surgery site as possible, then rigged up her cell phone as a secondary source of light, praying the battery would hold. She tugged on a pair of latex gloves, the material snagging a bit over her wet palms.

"Sammy, hang in there. I'm going to relieve some of the pressure down here. Sometimes blood gets trapped in a wound and needs intervention." Maybe narrating her movements would keep the terror at bay. "I'm going to clean your leg. This might be a little chilly." A sharp alcohol scent rose in the air as she swabbed the area with a gauze pad soaked in cleanser.

Sammy's eyes were closed.

Here we go.

"Now I'm just going to cut through the skin." She imagined that day she'd assisted in this operation and the chapter in her medical textbook she'd read later. She needed to make an incision halfway between the fibula and tibia to expose the muscle compartments. Then she'd have to make four cuts into the muscle to release all four compartments.

She briefly closed her eyes and shot an arrow prayer skyward. She couldn't do this on her own. *God, I believe you gave me these skills. Help me use them wisely.*

Giving the scalpel firm pressure, she cut through the skin from the middle third of Sammy's leg down to his ankle. For such a long cut, almost two thirds of his lower leg, there was little bleeding. Just as she suspected, the tough fascia covering the muscle was trapping the blood.

Okay. She was really doing this. Next, she needed to incise the anterior fascia. She took a moment to reposition the light. She palpated the muscle to find the head and made a second cut.

Sammy screamed and passed out.

Working quickly, she held a stack of gauze pads to the wound, drawing the blood out and away from the injured muscle. She could feel the pressure loosen under her hand. She changed the stack of gauze and counted to ten. When the bleeding slowed, she again palpated the muscle to find and incise the lateral fascia. There. Sammy's muscle and the surrounding tissue were becoming flaccid and flat. Two more compartments left.

The third compartment turned out to be relatively easy. It was located a finger's length away from the first two. She dealt with it in under ten seconds.

Last, and most difficult, the deep compartment. She visualized the page from her textbook. If she retracted the tibialis anterior, she would have access to the interosseous membrane. With minute movements, she held back the anterior portion of the muscle and guided her scalpel down behind the already released muscle fibers.

The air filled with a coppery smell as she found and released the final compartment.

The dangerous pressure buildup was averted.

She rubbed the back of her hand across her forehead, being careful not to smear a swath of Sammy's blood over her skin. Then, keeping one hand on the wound, she stretched full length to grab the roll of bandages. Loosely wrapping the fasciotomy incision would help keep out infection. They would need to clean it thoroughly at the hospital, but at least it wouldn't send high levels of toxin straight to his heart.

She stripped off her gloves, threw them in the hazardous materials bin.

Her hands shook as she grabbed a bottle of water and twisted off the cap. She drank half of it in one long swig.

Colleen took his blood pressure manually and made a note of the results, then held the half-empty bottle to the side of her neck. Her wrist had begun to feel better. The sprain must not have been too bad.

Please, Jack, hurry.

Sammy grew restless again. She checked the vial of painkiller. Still some left. She drew it out with a clean syringe and pushed it through his IV. He settled again.

Her stomach unknotted.

So maybe this hadn't been such a bad idea.

She should start trusting her instincts, maybe.

~

He was their only hope.

Definitely no one knew he was racing through the woods looking for the road he had glimpsed minutes before the helicopter went into a free fall.

Jack blinked back the snow falling into his eyes, clouding his vision. His body shook with the cold, and it wouldn't be long before hypothermia set in.

He figured he'd gone at least five miles—maybe an hour out from the chopper.

And seemingly, no closer to rescue.

Falling.

He was falling through the air.

Jack shook himself. Now was not the time to be reliving the crash.

Pausing a moment at the tree line separating this field from the forest, Jack rested his hand on a tree trunk. The rough bark under his frozen fingers pulled him back into the present.

His mind warred between flashbacks to the dirt, heat, and gunshots of Iraq, and the very real possibility that he, and those on the helicopter, could die out in this Minnesota cold.

Which had him shivering to his bones.

Bill hadn't had a chance to send a Mayday, he was sure of it. Which meant that no one knew they were out there.

There was no rescue coming for them.

Focus.

After leaving the helicopter, he'd taken a moment to orient himself. The storm clouds obliterated much of the sun, but he had made out a dim glow in the west from where it descended. They had been flying southwest to Duluth, but the spinning crash left the helicopter pointed in another direction. Using the sun to guide him through the storm, he'd started off at a trot away from the fallen bird, and toward what he hoped was a road big enough to have houses.

Now, his tennis shoes were sopping wet, his feet frozen.

He pushed out again into the storm, leaving the relative safety of the trees.

Please let him find a farmer and a phone.

But the field was disorienting. The sameness of the dips, and the treachery of the lumps of dead hay still lining the dirt caused him to fall more than once. Each time, he had to take his bearings again.

His light jacket, thrown on this morning for a date with Colleen, did little to cut the frigid wind sheer. The wet fabric clung to his back.

It was very possible that he'd die of hypothermia out here. He flexed his fingers and found he could barely feel them.

The blizzard screamed at him through the trees, a shriek that raced through his mind with the echo of the sound of a shoulder-launched missile. The tree branches popped and cracked like the shadow of gunfire.

He couldn't take any more.

"I'm so sorry, Ryan." He wrapped his arms around himself, slipping, fighting for purchase on the slick ground. "I'm sorry I let you down." And now, if he didn't keep moving, the horrible reality would play out all over again. This time with the woman he loved.

And where was God? Absent, as usual.

Squinting into the wind, he stopped. Looked around. For all he knew, he could be walking in circles. Was the forest ahead a new one, or the same one he'd just passed?

At least it offered him shelter from the storm.

He took off at a lope, running through the field.

He tripped over a runnel of soil, or maybe hay ruff, and went flying.

He landed with a shoulder-jarring explosion, hard in the sopping, near-frozen ground.

Nearby, a wrenching, grinding crash split the air.

And, just like that, he was back on the helicopter. Instinct had him covering his head with his arms.

Get it together, Stewart!

After a moment, he looked for the explosion and spotted a huge tree limb, fallen right into the path he would have taken.

If he hadn't tripped...

Get up, Jack, Ryan said. *You have to get up.*

For Colleen. He rolled over, pushed up.

C'mon, man. His voice, or maybe Ryan's. He found his feet.

The wind had whipped his tracks away.

The dim gleam of the sun had vanished.

Shoot. Every pine tree looked identical. Had he passed that thicket of buckthorn on his way in, or was he headed toward it?

The sky was white, closing in with a blinding fog. Oh, he didn't have a hope of finding help.

He was going to wander around until he froze to death.

"God, help me." A groan, or cry, Jack wasn't sure which.

He surely didn't expect an answer.

In the distance, a shaft of light cut through the trees. Jack stared at it, frozen, afraid to move his gaze away. The light materialized into a form—a four-wheeler. A man at the wheel.

An angel in a tan jumpsuit, work boots, and a black wool hat, driving a magnificent Polaris ATV.

He sorta wanted to say hallelujah.

The older man drove right up to him. "Are you one of the guys from the Deep Haven rescue chopper?"

Jack just nodded.

"I heard over my ham radio that they were missing a helicopter. Said you'd gone off the radar a few miles from my place, so I figured I'd ride out and see if I could track you down."

Jack wanted to fall to his knees.

"You okay?"

Not in the least. "Yeah. I think the chopper is three, maybe five miles from here. I don't know."

"C'mon, son," said the man. He opened up a back accessory compartment and pulled out a camping blanket. Tossed it to Jack.

"I'm going to call this in." The man produced a walkie-talkie from a pocket in his jumpsuit and thumbed it on. "This is Spud Johansen. I found one of the team. Over."

A voice on the other end confirmed. Asked about his location. Spud looked up at Jack with a glance. "Can you take me to the helicopter?"

Oh, he hoped so. Jack gave a terse nod.

Spud spoke into the walkie again. "I'll call in a location when I have it. Over." The walkie squawked in the affirmative.

"You have no idea how glad I am to see you," Jack said as he got on behind Spud. "Thank you for looking for us."

"Ain't nothing. Where to?"

Jack hunched behind him, pulling the blanket around him. "I think I came through the woods over there."

Spud gunned the throttle and they took off in the direction Jack indicated. They ducked under tree branches, and Jack held tight over a few deep pockets in the ground. The GPS mounted on the dash blinked their progress through the forest, then out into the open field, and finally through another forest.

No wonder it had all merged together. But Spud seemed to know where he was going.

The white had descended, and Jack would have walked right by the chopper had he been on foot. But the ATV's lights illuminated the wreckage in the middle of a field.

How they'd lived, Jack couldn't guess. Both skids lay several feet from the machine. The undercarriage was scraped, holes gaping in the skin.

A long piece of metal protruded from the area near the helo's fuel tank. They had been inches from dying in an explosion.

Jack clenched his hands into fists to stop the shaking.

He got off and stalked over to the chopper. Spud called in the coordinates from his GPS to the voice on the other end of the radio.

Jack heaved open the helicopter door.

What had happened here?

Blood pooled on the floor of the chopper, bloody bandages wrapped around Sammy's lower leg. He was attached to oxygen and a faint metallic odor filled the air.

Colleen sat next to him, her hand on his chest, her eyes puffy.

"Colleen?"

"He nearly died on me, Jack. I was so scared." She seemed in shock.

"What happened?"

"Compartment syndrome."

Oh no. "Colleen."

She looked at him. "I did an emergency fasciotomy. I think... I think God saved him."

She was calm for such a traumatic experience. He climbed inside. "I brought help."

Then she covered her face with her hands.

Jack crawled over to her, pulled her against him. "Shh, Colleen, it's all right. I'm here. We'll figure this out together."

She nodded, but he heard sobs. He rubbed a hand along her back until she stopped shaking.

"I'm okay. I'm okay." She pulled back. Scrubbed a hand over her face. Looked up at him. "You're shaking. Are you okay?"

"Cold. Fine." He met her eyes, then turned to the front of the chopper. "How's Bill?"

He remained unconscious, his neck in the brace. Jack touched his wrist. Still a steady pulse.

"I'm worried that Bill hasn't woken," Colleen said.

Him too.

Spud opened the door and poked his head in. "Help is on the way from Beaver Bay. They think they can get an ambulance back here. We'll have you tucked in and on your way soon."

He leaned over and held out his hand to Colleen. "Spud," he said.

She met his hand. "Thanks, Spud."

Jack turned to him. "I still can't believe you found me. It's a whiteout—"

"I heard your gunshot."

Gunshot?

Oh. The branch? Really?

"I was just in the right place, at the right time," Spud said.

Jack gave him a wan smile. Yep.

Or maybe it was God who'd showed up after all.

CHAPTER 15

*I*f there was ever a happy ending, it was this one.

Sammy was still breathing by the time the Beaver Bay ambulance rolled into the Duluth hospital ER.

Colleen and Jack had squeezed into a second ambulance, sent by Two Harbors. Bill, still unconscious, lay on the stretcher while the EMTs worked on him. Colleen's wrist was fine, and the EMTs reapplied a bandage to the cut on her forehead. Jack had suffered a bit of frostbite on his fingers, but he'd heated up fast when help arrived.

In fact, to Colleen, something about him seemed different.

Or maybe this was just the hero in him. Not talking about how he could have died out in the storm, but focusing on Sammy.

On her.

He'd pulled his blanket around her on the drive to Duluth, his body radiating warmth in the silence of the drive. The storm was starting to break, and by tomorrow, the snow would turn to slush, making the whole storm into an incredible Minnesota fluke.

Now Jack sat next to her in a small alcove next to the nurses' station on the surgical floor as they waited to hear how Sammy was doing. They'd both changed clothes—courtesy of the ER nurse who had checked them over for hypothermia. Jack's pair of blue scrubs and hospital socks made him seem very human.

Except, frankly, he wasn't. "Thank you for your bravery today. You keep showing up for me. You're my hero."

Jack looked at her. "I think you're the hero."

"Yeah, well, tell that to the AMA. I barely squeaked by on that intubation of Elijah. If Boone and the others hadn't vouched for me...well... But now, any hope of me getting certified is probably dead after the emergency fasciotomy. I just hope Sammy doesn't lose his leg."

"Don't let those stupid EMTs get in your head. You did what you had to."

Yeah. It hadn't helped that the EMTs from Beaver Bay had completely freaked out over Sammy's wounds.

Or that one of them knew Sammy. *If he's an amputee, it'll be your fault.*

She wasn't going to forget that anytime soon.

"Yeah, well, things that happen in a panic situation often play out poorly in the light of day."

Probably—and this was most likely the best idea—she should surrender the job to Jack and head back to Minneapolis.

If she was able to keep her medical license at all.

Shoot—*shoot!*

Jack got up. Began pacing. Finally, he turned to her. "There's something I need to tell you."

Whatever else he was going to say was interrupted by a voice she knew. Meredith Johnson had barged into the nursing area. "Is my son here?"

Colleen stood and went over to her. Jack retook his seat at the edge of the room.

"Mrs. Johnson." She touched the older woman on the shoulder.

Meredith swung around. "Colleen! Thank you. Thank you!" She swept Colleen into a tight hug.

"It was a joint effort." She started to pull back, to acknowledge Jack, but Meredith didn't let go. Looking over Meredith's shoulder, she realized a few others had crowded around as well. Pastor Dan, his wife Ellie, and her own mom circled them. She met her mother's eye.

"When we heard about the accident, we volunteered to drive down with Meredith," her mom said. "Dad came over to stay with Grandma Helen."

Meredith let Colleen go, but then her mom grabbed her for a hug too. "I'm so proud of you," she whispered into Colleen's ear before pulling away.

A doctor approached the group. "Which one of you is Sammy Johnson's family member?"

"That's me." Meredith stepped forward and Ellie took her hand. "I'm Sammy's mother. Do you have any updates for me?"

"I can share that with you in private if you'd like."

"That's okay. I want my friends with me."

"Sammy is stable. The emergency fasciotomy has been cleaned up, and my team and I set the bones that were broken in his other leg. We will monitor him for a day or two to see if he needs further surgery. He's in a recovery room now, but you can go see him in ten minutes or so. I'll send a nurse out when he is ready."

Meredith let go of Ellie's hand and grabbed both of the doctor's hands. "Thank you! Will you be able to save his leg? Will he walk again?"

"I'd say his chances are very good. If we can keep infection at bay, he will recover fully. Whoever did that emergency surgery probably saved his leg as well as his life. Risky, but the right call."

As the doctor made his way back down the hall, Colleen allowed his words to sink in. *Risky, but the right call.*

I suspect He put that love of a challenge and adventure in your heart for a reason.

What had Spud said—right place, right time?

Maybe this *was* what God was calling her to.

Which meant—what? Maybe she shouldn't walk away from her flight nurse certification quite so soon. Maybe she'd keep that appointment on Thursday after all.

A woman wearing a suit and carrying a clipboard and cell phone pushed through the doors at the end of the hall. When she was close enough, Colleen could see that her nametag labeled her as Marge Qualley, Hospital Administrator.

"Is one of you Colleen Decker?" The woman scanned the group.

What in the world? Was she going to be disciplined by the medical board? Clearly, she'd hoped too soon. "I'm Colleen." She stepped toward her.

"I've been asked to see if you would be willing to hold a short press conference."

What? "Um. I'm sorry, what? Me?"

"There are several reporters downstairs who would like to speak to you about saving those people. They were covering the accident and heard about the helicopter crash."

"It wasn't just me. We were a team."

"Well, bring the team." The woman typed something into her phone. Then she wrote a note on her clipboard, tore it off and handed it to Colleen. "Room 118. Downstairs, next to the gift shop. I told them you would be there in ten minutes."

Without giving Colleen a chance to reply, she walked back the way she had come.

"Mrs. Johnson?" a nurse called from the swinging door to the patient rooms. "Your son is awake. You can visit him briefly now."

"Annalise?" Meredith reached out for her hand. "Will you go with me?"

Colleen's mom put her arm around the other woman's shoulders, and they walked together down the hall and out of sight.

Pastor Dan and Ellie each took a seat in the plastic chairs.

"If you need a coffee, there is a machine in the bigger waiting room down the hall," Colleen said. She had discovered the coffee setup earlier when her pacing had taken her out of the range of this smaller room.

"Thanks. I know where it is." Pastor Dan shrugged ruefully. "I'll head down to the coffee shop. The joe is a little more palatable from there."

"I suppose you've been here before." She knew he was dedicated to his congregation. He'd probably sat in those terrible chairs many times over the past ten years.

Jack cleared his throat and for the first time since Meredith had come in, she noticed him standing away from her, his hands behind his back. He'd stopped pacing, but hadn't joined the group.

His blue eyes were hooded under his messy hair and five o'clock shadow. She couldn't read the expression that lingered there. "I think you're stalling."

"I don't know what you're talking about." Maybe she could play dumb and this media interview would blow over.

"Are you scared?"

"What? No. *Of course not.* I just don't think it's right to go down there and take all the credit for something that was a team effort."

"You could go down there and tell them that."

His logic was infuriating. "I will if you come with me." There. Maybe a dare would shake him out of whatever funk he was in.

At her words, he paled a little. Now who was scared? He swallowed. "No thanks. I'm not interested in speaking to the media. Besides, they only want to see you. You're the hero."

He still thought she was a hero? "Well, I don't think so. I was just doing my job." She crossed her arms.

"Doing your job after a helicopter crash nearly killed you. I think you are very brave and don't give yourself enough credit. C'mon, Colleen. It won't be that bad. I really think you should do it."

"Fine." She uncrossed her arms. Let the dare shine in her eyes. "I will if you come down with me. I'll need moral support."

He let out a breath. "Fine. But I'm standing in the back."

The ride down the elevator lasted a year, at least. Colleen reached for Jack's hand. His warm grip settled her nerves. Gave her courage.

I think you are very brave.

"Listen, Colleen, we never got to have that talk." Jack turned her to face him. "After we get home, can we—"

The elevator doors opened.

Lightbulbs flashed and voices chorused. Jack dropped her hand and stepped back and halfway behind her.

One voice rang louder than the others. "Ms. Decker, is it true that Turnquist Lumber caused the deaths of four people today?"

What? "I don't know where you are getting that information, but it is false." Colleen walked out of the elevator and was swept along by the crush of reporters. She lost track of Jack. "No one lost their life today."

"What about the report of negligence regarding the tie-downs on the lumber truck?"

"I really can't speak to that. Those types of questions aren't for me to answer. I do know that the driver of the lumber truck was injured when he was helping the passengers of another car." There was no way she was going to let them besmirch the name of a good man. Sammy Johnson almost lost his life saving those people. "He is a hero. In fact, all the people on the team out there today were heroes."

"We heard you saved the life of a child last week too." Another reporter shoved his recorder near her face. She flinched hard and raised her hand to block her face and suddenly, there was Jack.

"Everyone stand back." He stepped in front of her. "We'll meet you in the press room."

"Win Stewart?" The reporter's eyes widened. "Are you a member of the rescue team?"

Win? She looked at Jack.

He had held up his hand, but seemed suddenly flummoxed by the reporter's question.

"What have you been doing since you were released from prison?"

Prison?

"No comment." Jack began pushing his way through the crowd.

The other reporters noticed him now. "Win! Winston Stewart! Were you part of that accident today?"

The crowd followed him like metal shavings to a magnet.

"How long have you been out of prison?"

Across the long hall, Jack reached a door and ducked into it, the reporters trailing after him, still shouting questions.

Colleen just stood there. What had just happened?

A lone reporter stood inside the door, texting. Colleen walked up to her. "Why are you calling him Win?"

The woman—in her mid-thirties, maybe, dark hair pulled back in a ponytail, the local Fox News station emblem on her jacket—looked up.

"That's Winston Stewart, son of Christopher Stewart, the congressman."

Jack was the son of a congressman?

The reporter reached for the door. "I can't believe we finally found him."

"Found him?"

"He was recently released from prison for attempted murder."

~

Jack felt like a coward. No. He *was* a coward. He'd just left Colleen there in the hospital hallway with those reporters crowded around her. Her stricken face should have convinced him to stay, to protect.

Instead, he couldn't look her in the eye. He'd offered a few loud *No comments* to the reporters, desperate to get away from their questions. And then, he'd spotted a way out. The men's room. He'd pushed through the crowd, practically daring someone to follow him. Running.

And now hiding.

He stood at the sink on the far end, splashed water on his face. Rubbed it dry with a rough paper towel.

He should have known better than to be in the same room as the press. Of course there would be someone there who knew who he was. His dad was too prominent for them to be ignorant of his face and name.

He looked at himself in the mirror. A few drops of water still clung to the hair at his forehead. A hint of a beard roughened his chin. His eyes were sunken pits in his pale face.

The door to the bathroom opened and he whirled.

"Someone pointed me in this direction." Pastor Dan stood in the doorway and left one hand on the door. "Do you mind if I come in?"

"It's a free country."

Dan let the door close behind him, a coffee cup in his hand. "I caught the tail end of that circus out there."

"How's Colleen?"

"She's holding her own. She's refusing to talk about you and instead is focusing on Sammy and the heroics of the team."

"Some hero I am."

Dan wiped the edges of one of the sinks before leaning a hip against it. "The way I hear it, your actions today saved the lives of three people. That's pretty heroic."

"Tell that to the rabid mob outside. They only see me as a felon."

"Is that true? Or is it that *you* only see yourself as a felon?"

"I am a felon."

"It's true that you were convicted of a felony, but that doesn't define you. Your relationship with God is what defines you."

Nathan's words from that morning rang in his ears. *God knew David's heart, and He knows yours too. What's on the inside of a man is more important than his circumstances.*

"I don't know if I can believe that."

"Look, I know some things feel irredeemable, but God promises if we confess our sins He is faithful to forgive us and washes away all our unrighteousness." Dan pushed away from the sink. "I'll leave you be now. I'd hate for this bathroom chat to get more awkward."

After Dan left, Jack washed his hands, scrubbing them red. He should drive back to Kellogg. Or maybe just leave and go...anywhere.

Except.

Colleen.

She deserved better. An explanation at least.

Even if she would never forgive him.

He opened the bathroom door, poked his head out.

The hallway was clear so he walked out, head on a swivel looking for Colleen. He spotted her strawberry-blonde ponytail as she stepped into the elevator.

"Wait!" he called.

She shoved a hand in the doors to keep them from shutting, but then her face clouded over when she saw it was him. She put her hand down and the doors responded immediately, sliding shut. He sprinted the last few steps and squeezed in before the elevator closed.

Colleen punched floor number five. Then crossed her arms. Stared at the floor.

"Colleen, look at me."

A muscle in her jaw jumped, her breath hitching, as if she might be trying not to cry.

"Colleen, please. I'm sorry for just leaving like that. I should've stayed and answered their questions. Answered *your* questions."

The elevator dinged at the second floor.

He waited.

It dinged for the third floor.

The fourth.

"Colleen?"

"I just can't believe you have been lying to me all this time." She looked up, her eyes filmed with tears.

Aw. "I'm sorry about that, I truly am. I was trying to start a new life for myself." His words sounded lame, even to him. Because she was *right*.

Lies by omission were still lies.

"A life built on deception. How many others know about this?"

The elevator dinged again. They'd reached Sammy's floor. He hit the button to keep the doors closed. "Well, Boone and Adrian, probably a few others on the team. I told your dad too."

"Oh, great, so now I'm the laughingstock of the team for not knowing. Everyone else was probably pitying poor little Colleen, always falling for the bad guy." Colleen's voice shook, even as she gasped. "Wait. Adrian? Is that what that whole scene in the Sunday school room was about?"

Jack nodded, hating that he'd let that lie sit too. "I guess the guy I hurt was a cousin of Adrian's or something. We knew of each other back in Kellogg. Adrian's parents and my dad move in the same social circles."

The elevator dinged again. She hit the button to keep the doors shut. "Right. You're not just a convict, you're a *high society* convict." Tears dripped off her chin and she angrily wiped them away and turned from him. "Adrian was right—you don't belong here. You should leave."

And there it was.

"Colleen, please. Don't say that. Give me a chance to explain."

She rounded on him, her eyes suddenly fierce. "Stop. You had your chance. It's over, Jack—or whoever you are. I clearly don't know you at all."

And that just wasn't fair.

She reached for the door open button but he got to the other one first.

"I've shown you who I am. Every moment we've spent together, I've been who I truly am."

She looked at him, her eyes freshly filling.

Oh, Colleen, please—

"There was a lie beneath everything you said or did."

Yes, but, "Never an *outright* lie. Just not the story about the one thing that I wanted to forget ever happened. I wanted to prove myself." He caught her arm.

She shook off his hand. "The only thing you proved to me was that I was super gullible to have believed in you. Another stupid mistake I made. Add it to the list of bad decisions. Falling in love with a felon."

Her words sunk deep.

Her next words cut even deeper. "Too bad you didn't care enough about the truth to tell me who you really are. Whatever it takes, right? I guess for you that means bending the truth when it suits you." Her gaze bore into his, unmoving.

So, then, this was it. "Okay, Colleen. Have it your way. Yes, you were gullible to fall in love with me. I'm sorry I lied. But most of all, I'm sorry I can't be the perfect man you're looking for."

The elevator doors slid open. Outside stood Peter and Ronnie.

"There you are." Ronnie still wore her EMT uniform. "We were about to go downstairs to look for you. We wondered if you needed a ride home. Peter drove down to..." She broke off as she looked from Colleen to Jack and back again. "Hey, is everything okay?"

Colleen said nothing, just pushed out of the elevator stalking between Ronnie and Peter. "I'll catch a ride home with my mom."

Peter swiveled to face Jack. "Everything okay?" He repeated Ronnie's question. "You don't look so good, man."

Jack shook his head, looked away.

But what did he expect? That she would ignore it all, throw her arms around him, and welcome him into her life? Maybe. Kinda.

What an idiot. Once a criminal, always a criminal. Colleen wasn't going to forgive him. And she was right—he didn't belong here.

Maybe he'd never left prison after all.

CHAPTER 16

*C*olleen was right. He needed to leave.

It was bad enough that their fight had happened in front of Ronnie and Peter, but the words she had hurled met their mark.

Another stupid mistake I made. Add it to the list of bad decisions. Falling in love with a felon. Reeling, he had driven aimlessly around town for an hour or possibly two before ending up back here, the place where he'd tried to hide.

Jack looked around his apartment. Pulled out his duffel. He dumped the contents of the bureau into the duffel bag. He laid the photo of his father, stepmother, and half brother on top and zipped it shut.

There was a lie beneath everything you said or did. She was right. He never should have tried to hide what he'd done. He'd thought it was for the best of reasons, but really, it had been only to protect himself. To keep from being hurt and rejected. Again.

He'd thought if he could just stay out of everyone's way and not let people get to know him, he would be able to wall himself off from pain forever.

What a joke that had turned out to be.

He hunted in the closet for a broom and carefully swept the apartment. Then, finding a rag, he wiped down the few surfaces the tiny place offered. He rinsed and wrung out the rag and hung it on the sink to dry.

It would be better if he just left, found a place where he couldn't get involved. Couldn't let himself care.

He took one last look around. Stared at the island in the picture on his wall, once more willing himself there. When a hole in time and space didn't open up and swallow him onto the sunny beach, he shrugged into his jacket, slung his duffel over his shoulder, and headed downstairs.

Stepping into the coffee shop felt like relaxing into a warm embrace. The warmth and enticing coffee aroma begged for him to sit and stay awhile. But he was done staying. It was time to go.

At the counter, Kathy was retying her apron over her sweat-shirt and jeans.

"Oh, hi, Jack. I was in the back taking a short break. When I heard the door, I was afraid I'd miss a customer."

"Just me, I'm afraid."

"Aw, there's nothing 'just' about you. You're a bona fide hero. At least that's what they tell me."

Jack didn't like being called a hero, but somehow hearing it from Kathy today didn't bother him as much. "I've come to return your key. I'll be leaving today. I'm sorry for the short notice."

"I can't believe you're leaving. I thought you'd come here to stay. Did you find another place to live?"

The rapid-fire sentiments left Jack no time to answer. He put his hand up to slow her down. "Everything is fine." *Liar.* Maybe Colleen had a point… "I'd hoped to stay, but I don't think I'm cut out for this town."

Before she could say anything more, he placed the key on the counter, turned, and walked out the door.

His truck was parked a few steps away. He tossed his duffel into the back end. Across the street, the gray-blue sparkle of Lake Superior drew his eye. The snow and cold from the day before had been chased away by the late fall sunshine. According to the weatherman on the news that morning, yesterday's snowstorm had been a fluke and they were in for a stretch of warm, dry weather.

Near the water, a family was tossing a football around the beach and laughing. An older couple walked along the shoreline, holding hands, heads bent toward each other. Another group clustered nearer the road.

Jack rubbed at his chest and turned away from the carefree scene.

He dug in his pocket for his truck keys and headed back to the front of the vehicle. Startled. Standing around the front fender stood Kyle, Boone, Peter, Ronnie, Cole—and was that Adrian?

Maybe they'd come to make sure he left town.

Peter stepped forward. "Hey, man. After what happened yesterday, we thought we'd better come check on you."

"Actually, I said I'd check on you, but then these guys all wanted to tag along." Ronnie propped her hands on her hips. "Sounded like Colleen was really raking you over the coals."

Yes, well. "Actually, I deserved all of that. Most of it anyway." He shoved his hands in his pockets. "Look, what Adrian said that day at church...he was right. I was in prison for third-degree aggravated assault for a year. I'd just been released when Boone brought me up here." Jack couldn't look at them. "I asked Boone to keep it quiet because I didn't think I was going to get involved around here, but then...it felt nice to be part of a team again."

Before anyone could say anything, he plowed on. "I want

you to know that I'm leaving. I don't want my prison time to tarnish the reputation of the team. People need to be able to trust their leaders in a crisis, and the people of Deep Haven need to be able to trust your team. My reputation will follow me everywhere, but it doesn't have to affect the good work you're doing."

"Jack, I told them the full truth about that day," Boone said.

Ronnie nodded. "Yeah, he told us how you were protecting that woman and how you didn't want to fight. How he saw the whole thing at the restaurant and had been trying to decide how to intervene with that lady but you beat him to the punch." She gave a chagrined look. "I didn't mean that literally."

Jack offered a wry smile. Some of the tension dissipated.

"Anyway, we've seen how you are around people. That you are quick to help and are brave and compassionate. We believe Boone." Ronnie smiled at him. "For a guy trying to hide out, you sure didn't do a good job."

He looked them each in the eye.

No one returned a look of judgment. Still... "That doesn't change the fact that I should leave." He headed toward his truck door.

Adrian stepped forward.

"Wait, Jack. I need to apologize. I shouldn't have believed all the gossip about your conviction. After our, er, conversation on Sunday, I went back and read through some of the court reports. You got a raw deal, man. That fight was never your fault. I'm sorry for accusing you. I called and talked to my mom too. She said that Dad never really liked his cousin because he was such a womanizer but he just had to stand by him to save face in public. I totally misunderstood the whole thing." He gestured to the others. "The team here says that you are a good guy, and I trust them. I'd like a chance to get to know you myself. I'd like you to stay."

"We'd all like you to stay," Ronnie put in.

Her words settled inside him, took hold. He hadn't felt this way since...well, he wasn't sure when.

He looked at Cole and remembered his words from the gym. Had it really been just a few weeks ago? *You've got to understand the MO of everyone in this town. Once you're here, you're family. We watch out for our own.*

Cole must have been remembering the same conversation because he nodded and added, "Sorry, buddy. Like it or not, you're family now."

This was all well and good, but how could he stay when every moment he spent in this town would remind him of Colleen and the lost chance between them? He couldn't very well be on the same team as her. Having to stand by and watch her fall for someone else, maybe Sammy Johnson, would tear him to pieces.

"Thanks, guys. You have no idea how much that means to me." He put his hand on the door handle of his truck. "But, no. I can't stay here."

He swung into his truck and backed out of his parking spot, leaving them behind.

~

Colleen scrubbed at the dish in her hands. But as hard as she washed, she still couldn't get the stubborn bits off. Much like trying to rub the memory of the argument with Jack out of her brain.

After leaving Jack behind, she had spent a sleepless night wrestling with her blankets. Then today she had come over to help Grandma Helen with some cleaning. Her grandma apologized that she and Frank hadn't washed the dishes from dinner the night before. They'd been too tired and had gone to bed early. Colleen didn't mind. Scrubbing at the dried-on bits was a good use of her angry energy.

Her grandma's kitchen smelled of apple pie. Colleen suspected that Grandma Helen used an apple air freshener as she hadn't felt well enough to do any baking for quite a while now. Grandma Helen sat at the kitchen table, keeping Colleen company as she worked.

"What did that casserole dish ever do to you?" Her grandma's gentle tease brought tears to Colleen's eyes.

"Ha ha." Colleen paused, hands in the sudsy water, and wiped her eye on her shoulder.

"Oh, honey. Is something wrong? You seemed quiet when you came in. Not like yourself." Grandma Helen stood and touched Colleen's shoulder.

A tear dripped into the sink. "It's Jack."

Grandma Helen handed her a dry towel. "Here. The dishes can wait. Sit down at the table and tell me what's up."

"I must be the most stupid and gullible person on the planet. Everyone is laughing at me."

"Oh, honey, surely it isn't that bad."

"Jack has been lying to me since the first time we met."

Her grandmother stood and went to the stove. She filled the teapot, waving Colleen off when she rose to help. "This sounds like we need a fortifying cup. Tea or hot chocolate?"

"Hot chocolate, please." Colleen sat back down as Grandma Helen pulled a tea bag out of the cupboard along with a hot chocolate packet.

"I don't know Jack, but calling him a liar is a serious accusation." She shook the hot chocolate packet before tearing it open and dumping the contents into a mug. When the teakettle started screaming, she picked it up and poured steaming water into both of their mugs.

"Here, Grandma, let me help you." Colleen half rose out of her chair again.

"Nonsense. I may be an old woman with cancer, but I can still wield a spoon now and then." She gave each of their drinks a quick stir then carried them to the table and set them on the cheerful, apple-studded tablecloth. "Sip carefully, it's hot."

Wrapping her hands around the mug, Colleen allowed its warmth to run through her fingers and up her arms. She studied the swirling chocolate for a moment before speaking. "Jack went to prison for putting a guy in a coma." She expected her grandmother to gasp or express surprise, but when she glanced at her, Grandma Helen was just coolly regarding her from across the table. "Well? He went to prison, Grandma, and he didn't tell me."

"Is it the prison you are mad about or that he didn't tell you?"

"Both!" But, was it really? And, also, was Grandma about to defend him? "You don't even know what he did!"

"Okay, why don't you tell me?"

Seriously, her calm demeanor was getting irritating.

"He beat up a guy and then spent time in prison for it. The man could have died. I fell for a criminal."

She heard the front door open and close. A few moments later, her dad walked into the kitchen. "Hello, ladies." He bent and pressed a kiss to his mother's cheek. "I thought I'd drop in and see how you both were doing. Colleen, you left in a hurry today."

"Would you like some hot chocolate, Nathan?" Grandma Helen lifted her cup and gestured toward the stove. "All I have is instant, but the water in the kettle should still be hot. Otherwise there's lemon tea in that box there."

He pulled a mug out of the cupboard. "Hot chocolate will be great." He fixed his cup and then sat with them at the table. "So, what are we talking about?"

"Colleen has been telling me about Jack." Grandma Helen took a sip of her tea while shooting a significant look at Colleen.

Fine.

"I found out that Jack did time, Dad." The sip of hot chocolate soured in her stomach.

"Oh, good, he told you. I wasn't sure he'd get a chance with all the excitement yesterday."

"Oh yeah, he told me. How long were you going to sit on that info?"

"He told me before Sammy's accident. I haven't had a chance to talk to you since then."

"Perfect. What—the entire town knew before I did? I guess I really am living up to the town's expectations. There goes Colleen, falling for the bad boy, again."

Her dad set down his cup with a thunk. A slosh of chocolate landed in the middle of an apple. "What? That's not true."

"He's a criminal, a liar, and he takes chances with people's lives, Dad. Everyone knew about it and no one told me."

"What exactly did Jack tell you?"

She gestured with her hands. It was unbelievable that her dad would take Jack's side on this. "He didn't have to tell me anything. I found out yesterday from the reporters that Jack did time in the Stillwater prison for assaulting a man." After the initial statement that Jack had murdered someone, one of the other reporters amended it to putting the man in a coma for a month. "He confirmed it himself."

Her dad leaned forward. "What else did he tell you?"

She crossed her arms, in that moment closer to her teenage self than ever. "Does it matter?"

"Yes, it matters."

"He didn't really say anything else. Just that the reporters were right—he had been convicted. Some relative of Adrian Vassos, if you can believe that."

"Colleen, sometimes things aren't what they seem. Love and trust need to go hand in hand. I wish you had heard him out."

"I can't believe you're *defending* him. After what happened with Mom, I would think you wouldn't trust people with criminal pasts either." Okay, that was a low blow because technically her mom had a criminal past too. Just not something as dramatic as going to prison for beating a guy half to death.

"It's because of what happened with your mom that I know love is precious and that we should trust those we care about. And that we should talk to them and be willing to listen in return."

"But he isn't who he said he was."

"He's exactly the man he showed himself to be. Last night I talked to Boone about it. He confirmed to me that the incident happened when Jack was defending a woman the man was harassing. He didn't do anything to Mr. Barelli, but when the guy took a swing at him, Jack shoved him out of the way while sidestepping. This caused the drunk man to stumble and hit his head. Later, the DA claimed it was intentional. Boone testified on his behalf, trying to get the judge to drop the charges. He got the lightest sentence possible, but Boone says he didn't even deserve that much."

Oh. "He was defending a woman?" Colleen's voice sounded small in her own ears.

"Yep."

"Why didn't he tell me that?"

"Did you give him a chance?"

"I guess not. But he *said* he was guilty."

"Boone told me that Jack had a hard time forgiving himself for that incident. The whole thing was a big mistake. He regrets going out when he was just back from Iraq. He felt that maybe he was to blame, but Boone never believed that. He was there when it happened. He said that the other guy would have beaten Jack and then probably turned on the woman too."

Her grandma took her hand. "Honey, all relationships start with trust. You obviously know how Frank and I met. He was hiding something from me too. But, when I opened up my heart to love and learned to trust him, God used that story for good. I learned that the Frank I knew and fell in love with was the same man, no matter his past."

The doorbell pealed through the air in the quiet kitchen. Needing a moment to think, Colleen stood. "I'll get it."

She went to the door, opening it to find a delivery man in a brown uniform. He held out a pink box wrapped with a teal ribbon. "Helen Harrison?"

"Yes, this is her house."

"Special delivery." He handed her the box and then went whistling down the driveway.

Hart's Bakery in gold letters scrolled across the top of the box.

Colleen checked the packing slip tucked under the ribbon. Two dozen ginger cookies, ordered by Jack on Sunday afternoon for two-day delivery.

Oh.

My.

She walked back into the kitchen. "They're from Jack."

Her grandmother took the package. "Oh, what a sweet man."

Yes. Painfully sweet.

Worse, her dad was right. The Jack she knew didn't fit her picture of a criminal. Or maybe he was what a redeemed criminal looked like. And weren't they all in some way redeemed lawbreakers? Yes, Jack was exactly the man she'd thought he was all along. The brave, smart, thoughtful man she'd fallen in love with.

Her eyes filled. "I made a mistake." She looked up at her dad.

Her dad wore a grim look.

"What?"

"I was just told by Kathy at the Java Cup that Jack's apartment was available for listing. He's leaving town—if he hasn't already left."

Her eyes widened.

"Well, what are you waiting for?"

Nothing. Not a thing.

She headed for the door. Pointed her car down the hill toward town.

In the sparkling waters of Lake Superior, a few boats bobbed on the waves.

As she pulled into the parking lot outside the Java Cup, she already could see that Jack's truck was not there. Inside, Kathy confirmed that Jack had turned in his key that morning.

"I don't know where he went, Hun." Kathy's sympathetic gaze conveyed understanding.

Colleen's heart sank so fast it could have been an anchor for one of the boats in the harbor.

She was too late.

CHAPTER 17

*C*olleen should have known she could never do this.

She felt like all she'd done was study in the two days since Sammy's accident, but the questions on the certified flight nurse exam were...off the hook. She'd nearly memorized her manual, reviewed all the lessons Jack had given her, and she still didn't have a clue how to answer the scenario in front of her.

Boone had explained the test when he'd set her up in his office. "You'll have three hours to complete up to one hundred and seventy-five questions. The exam is pass/fail." He clicked on a website in his internet browser. "Do you have your login info?"

She gave it to him and the exam popped up. She had registered for the remote exam with an online proctor—a woman who lived in Edina who had logged on to monitor her progress. They required that she be in a room without distractions.

Boone stood up and motioned her into the seat. "If you reach seventy-five percent correct answers, you pass and you won't need to take the rest of the test. If you answer too many wrong, same thing. If you run out of time, you'll fail and will need to reschedule for a new exam."

Great. No pressure.

Boone had wished her luck and left her with the online proctor who explained the rules again. Using the webcam, she proved to the proctor that she didn't have any study guides or any other forbidden materials on or near the desk.

The online proctor had approved her eligibility to start over an hour ago.

So far, she'd answered six questions.

Out of one hundred and seventy-five.

She rubbed her slick hand across her jeans. Willed her leg to stop bouncing. She reached up and adjusted her ponytail, tightening it against her head.

Each tick from the clock on the wall told her she was in over her head.

She knew the test was comprised of questions taken from thousands of real life emergencies that nurses, medics, and rescue teams from all over the world faced every day. She couldn't imagine being in some of these positions. "A friend has sudden difficulty breathing with fast respirations and chest pain during lunch. She passes out and you notice tracheal deviation. What are you looking for to help her breathe?"

Or the next one. "An aircraft has completed a hard landing after mechanical failure. What is the procedure for exiting?" Okay, that one hit close to home.

She clicked to the next question. "You have found a victim of a bear attack. His right arm is severed from his body. What do you do first?"

Um, besides panic?

Wait. No.

She slowed her breathing and then she could hear Jack's voice in her head. *Stick to the basics and go from there.*

And then her heart slowed. Her jumpy leg planted itself

firmly on the floor. She could do this. God had given her these talents, and He would help her use them.

Stick to the basics. She reread the options. All the answers on the question in front of her looked correct, but only one started with the ABCs of emergency medicine. Airway, Breathing, and Circulation. She clicked answer B.

She moved on to the next question. Remembered Jack's words about in-flight procedures. Answered it correctly.

The sound of clicking keys grew faster as she answered each question moments after reading it.

As she entered the next question, she glanced at the clock. Another hour had passed, but she still had plenty of time.

The computer gave a jubilant chime. She stared at the results on the screen.

She'd *passed.*

Yes. "Yes!"

On the screen, the proctor laughed. "Your certificate will be in the mail, but for now, I'll certify your results and you can print them off for confirmation."

"Thank you again." With a huge grin, she logged off the testing site. Then she sobered. She wished she could tell Jack. Thank him for his help. She would never have passed without his guidance and his quiet reminders. It almost felt like he had been there leading her through the test.

Too bad she had no idea how to find him.

She'd driven past the Java Cup and the VFW a few times over the past 48 hours, but the parking lots stayed stubbornly empty of Jack's black Silverado.

Thank you, Jack.

"I heard you cheering." Boone stuck his head in at the doorway of his office. "Does that mean you passed?"

She couldn't stop the grin from reappearing. "Yep. I'm fully certified. We should get the official paperwork in the mail in the next few weeks. Still want a flight nurse?"

"You bet I do. Congratulations, Colleen. I'm happy for you."

She came around from behind the desk. "I have another favor to ask."

He folded his arms across his chest. "Okay, what—"

"I totally messed up. I said all kinds of horrible things to Jack, things he didn't deserve. I want the chance to apologize, but he's left town. I want to give him something to thank him for his help. Any chance you can give me his address in Kellogg?"

Boone looked like a deer caught in headlights. "Uh, Colleen..."

"No." She stopped him. "You're right. I don't deserve a second chance. I blew it with Jack. A great guy like him needs a woman who can believe in him right from the start."

"Colleen." Boone held up a hand.

"Forget I even asked. You're right to stand up for him. I'm sorry I asked you to get involved. You're his friend and you should be loyal to him. I'll track him down another way."

"Colleen." Boone's strained voice finally broke through her monologue. She looked at him standing in the doorway. "Jack is out on the climbing wall. He's been staying with me."

Oh.

Oh!

Colleen pushed past him through the door and raced to the two-story bay. On the toughest part of the rock wall, Jack hung from a single handhold, his muscles straining against his shirt. She watched as he gracefully reached out with his right foot and took hold of a grip, then spider walked the rest of the way to the top.

She had to stop herself from swooning.

Jack didn't seem to notice the others in the room as he rappelled back down the wall, landing at the bottom with a soft thump.

She swallowed hard and walked over to where he was releasing himself from the rope.

He turned. Stopped dead.

"Colleen."

～

Colleen.

He caught his breath. Yes, he knew she was in the office taking the test, but she'd apparently finished before the allotted time and...

Oh, who was he kidding? He'd been dying to see her. Had even driven by her house a couple times. But she had been pretty clear about wanting him out of her life.

So he'd created a wide circle, avoiding her. Sleeping at Boone's house. Working late at the VFW.

He'd even perfected his chicken recipe. Last night he'd cooked it for the team. After eating his Mama Creole's chicken, they'd asked him to stay on permanently as volunteer crew chef, maybe someday something more. He looked forward to putting a new spin on a chili recipe for the next training day. Someone once mentioned they used star anise. That would be interesting.

In front of him, Colleen moved forward a half step.

Jack swallowed hard. "I'm sor—"

"I'm sorry." She gave him a half smile. "I passed the test."

He pulled off his gloves, one at a time. "That's great. I knew you could do it." He held himself back from reaching for her. She moved forward again until she was only an arm's length away.

He managed not to apologize again, but it was right there.

Oh, he was sorry for so many things.

"I should have let you explain." Her eyes roved over his face. "But more, I should have believed you. My dad reminded me that love is rooted in trust."

The whole bay went quiet. For the first time, she seemed to notice the other members of the team had stopped what they were doing and were now standing around. Staring at them.

Ronnie cleared her throat. "Uh. Do you guys need a minute?"

"Most of our relationship happened in front of you, so I think this part can too." Colleen shot a dimpled grin at Ronnie. "Also, someone once told me that if you have a public argument, the apology should be public too. So, here goes."

She reached his side and put her hand on his forearm. "Jack, when I came back home, I was...I was trapped. Trapped inside my stupid regrets and panic attacks and the fear that I'd never be the person I was before I was kidnapped so many years ago. That Colleen was brave and strong and I think I've been sort of faking it for years. Trapped maybe in my own prison. And then...and then you taught me how to climb and rappel and save lives in the sky and most of all...trust myself. You helped set me free. And I want to do the same for you." She stepped forward, put her hands on his chest.

He drew in a breath.

"I forgive you, Jack Stewart. You're not a criminal in my eyes. You are a man worth trusting, worth believing in. Worth loving." She smiled. "And I do love you."

I love you too.

"Can you forgive me for hurting you? I should never have said those things to you. You did show me your true self, and I should have trusted you."

He swallowed. Then smiled, aware that his eyes had heated. "I definitely forgive you." He touched her face. "You helped me step back into life, even if I did it with secrets."

"No more secrets," she whispered. And then, she kissed him.

Right in front of his team.

Their team.

And he couldn't care less.

He pulled her closer and she wound her arms around his

neck. And then it was just them, hanging by a moment—this perfect, wonderful, free moment.

This. This was what it felt like to belong. To be loved.

To be free.

He was about to deepen the kiss when he heard clapping and whistling. Breaking off the embrace, he looked sheepishly at Colleen and then at the group of people clustered on the other side of the room.

Boone was grinning, his arm slung around Vivien's waist. "Forgot you had an audience, didn't you?"

"Maybe a little."

"C'mon, guys. It's obvious we aren't needed here anymore." Vivie made shooing motions and then started to drag Boone away by the hand. "The good part is over anyway."

The group made their way up the stairs and into the break room, taking their chatter with them.

Jack rested his forehead on hers. "I love you, Colleen. Every brave, spunky, beautiful bit of you."

"I love you too, Jack."

"Call me Win."

She shook her head. Smiled. "Sorry. You'll always be Jack to me."

EPILOGUE

The crowd in the gym rang out with a shout as Colleen missed a spike. Jack and the rest of the team had squared off for another game of volleyball on Saturday afternoon. It seemed like the whole town had gathered here at the high school for the Deep Haven Community Church's annual Fall Festival. He could hear laughter drifting in from the central commons area. Outside, the late October air had warmed and melted all the snow from Monday's storm.

Around them, the school had been transformed. Jack and Colleen had helped Pastor Dan and Ellie and a few others set up for the Fall Festival. Groupings of pumpkins, corn stalks, and hay bales decorated the spaces between the game booths in the school commons. Twinkle lights hung over the tables set for dinner, making the whole place look like a pumpkin patch under the stars. Now the group was taking a break while others ran the booths and were blowing off some steam on the volleyball court in the gym.

Jack snuck a quick glance at the clock. He'd need to check the turkeys he was smoking on a pellet grill outside the gym doors in a few minutes. He'd modified his Creole recipe for the larger birds. Bigger crowd, bigger appetites.

"C'mon, Jack. Let's see if your serve is as good as your cooking," Cole called from the other side of the court.

Jack tossed the ball in the air before hitting it with the heel of his hand. It lopped over the net. Megan, Cole's wife, got under it and hit it back to Jack's team.

Both sides volleyed back and forth, vying for dominance. The good-natured taunts flew almost as often.

On his side of the net, Jack joined forces with Peter, Ronnie, and Colleen. Cole, Megan, Kyle, and Dan filled out the other team. A few others, including Vivien and Josh, Megan's son, sat on the sidelines.

"I talked to Meredith Johnson this morning," Dan said during a lull. "She said Sammy's doing well. The doctors think that with time and therapy, he'll walk again. Also, Bill Hooper should make a full recovery, but it looks like the CRT will need a new pilot. He says his flying days are over."

"Game point," Kyle called, then served the ball.

It came straight for Jack in the middle blocker position. He squared up under it as the door to the gym thumped open, a waft of smoke billowing in. A man with silvery hair and an expensive suit stood in the doorway next to a slim brunette in a navy pantsuit. A gangly teen, curly dark hair peeking out from under a green hoodie, hung back behind them.

The ball smacked the side of Jack's head before landing in bounds.

Jack barely noticed as Kyle's teammates began jumping and cheering. "Dad?"

His dad shut the door and started walking through the gym, skirting the game players.

Jack jogged over to meet him halfway.

"Someone told me we could find you here." Christopher

Stewart pulled off his sunglasses and tucked them into his front jacket pocket.

"I thought you were headed to London." Jack stopped short of his dad. He shoved his hands in his pockets.

"I canceled my trip. I wanted to come and see where my son is making a home for himself." His dad gestured toward the door. "I hope you don't mind, but I brought Melissa and Ethan too."

Melissa, a slight smile on her face, walked over to them. She motioned for the teen to join them.

"When you said you'd come up, I didn't think you meant it." Jack ran a hand through his hair.

Melissa and Ethan reached them. "Hey, Win," Ethan said.

Jack didn't correct him, just gave a little wave. "Hey, kid."

"We wanted to get to know Deep Haven, maybe meet your teammates." Melissa's pause and glance at his father told Jack the full story. They weren't sure how he would receive them.

Yeah, well, those days were past. Jack crossed the few remaining feet and hugged his father. Turning to Melissa and Ethan, he gave them each a side hug.

He cleared his throat, its sudden thickening taking him by surprise. "I'm glad you came up. Was it a good drive?"

"Perfect weather for it," his dad said.

"Well, you're in luck. I hope you can stay for supper because I fired up the pellet grill. I adapted a recipe for Mama Creole's chicken, except I'm using turkeys. There should be plenty."

His dad met Melissa's gaze. She nodded. "Looks like we're staying."

"And I'm hungry," Ethan said. They all laughed.

The congressman reached over and tousled his hair. "You, my football player, are always hungry."

"What can I say?" Ethan smoothed down his dark curls. "A man's gotta eat."

Out of the corner of his eye, Jack saw Colleen coming over.

He held out his hand to her. When she took it, he said, "Dad, I'd like you to meet Colleen, my girlfriend. Colleen, my dad, Christopher Stewart."

"Hello, sir." Colleen dropped Jack's hand and shook Christopher's.

"It's great to finally meet you, Colleen. My son has told us a lot of good things about you." He put his arm around Melissa. "This is my wife, Melissa, and my other son, Ethan. Jack, can I speak to you alone for a few minutes?"

Jack shot Colleen a look. She smiled, nodded and took Melissa by the arm. "I'd love to hear a few stories about when Jack was younger." As she walked away with Melissa and Ethan in tow, she gave him a wink over his shoulder. Whatever his dad had to say couldn't erase the joy bubbling up in him.

Christopher and Jack stepped into the hallway. "Listen, Jack. I've done a lot of thinking over the past few weeks. I had a call from Thomas Silver, and some of the things he said about having the opportunity to reconnect with his children were a real wakeup call."

"Dad, you don't have to—"

"No, son, I do." His dad cut him off. "My actions over the years were full of mistakes. I wanted to give you a good upbringing and allow you to grow without being under my shadow all the time. But instead, I made you feel like I didn't want you around—like I was ashamed of you." Christopher laid his hand on Jack's shoulder. "The truth is, I am proud of you."

Jack's breath whooshed out. His dad wasn't ashamed?

"During your trial, I stayed away because I didn't want my notoriety to influence the judge to give you a harsher sentence. But that was wrong of me. I should have been standing up for you on every platform I had. Can you forgive me?"

"Yes." He couldn't manage any more than that thanks to the lump in his throat. His dad seemed to understand as he tugged him into an embrace.

"There's something else." His dad pulled back, scrubbed a hand over his face. "Thomas and I are working to get your criminal record expunged. You shouldn't have to live with that hanging over you."

Jack took a deep breath then blew it out slowly. "Thanks, Dad. I appreciate that."

"Now, I don't want to keep you from your friends. Let's get back in there." His dad walked next to him back into the gym, keeping his arm slung across Jack's shoulders.

Jack introduced his dad and Melissa to a few people as the teams re-formed on the volleyball court. They convinced Ethan and Josh to join a team. When the game started, Jack found himself facing Colleen on the other side.

His dad and Melissa sat with Dan on the bleachers nearby.

During breaks in the noise of the game, Jack heard flashes of the conversation between his dad and Dan.

"You've got a great son there. We're glad to have Jack on our team," Dan said.

"I've always been proud of Win—I mean Jack," his father replied. "We had a rough go of it after his mother died, but I think we figured it out."

Jack volleyed the ball back to the other side. Colleen flashed him a thumbs-up.

"Hey, no cheering for the other team," Megan teased her.

On the bleachers, Dan was saying, "It couldn't have been easy."

"It wasn't, but W—Jack is a man of integrity, and I appreciate that. Even this past year and during his trial, I admired him for standing up for what is right."

New warmth bloomed inside him. Jack forced himself to focus on the game. He had plenty of time to sort out these things with his dad later.

He hit the ball over the net.

Colleen spiked it back, the ball hitting the floor in front of him before he'd even registered that it was already on his side.

Colleen did a funny little jig and high-fived her teammates. She squared up at the net and put her hands on her hips, quirked an eyebrow at him. "That's right. That's how it's done here. Didn't you know that I'm the queen of volleyball in Deep Haven?"

That wasn't all she was the queen of.

They'd lost the serve so he rotated and found himself opposite her. He grinned and met her beautiful eyes through the net.

Right place, right time. "Bring it."

CONNECT WITH SUNRISE

Thank you so much for reading *Hangin' By a Moment*. We hope you enjoyed the story. If you did, would you be willing to do us a favor and leave a review? It doesn't have to be long—just a few words to help other readers know what they're getting. (But no spoilers! We don't want to wreck the fun!) Thank you again for reading!

We'd love to hear from you—not only about this story, but about any characters or stories you'd like to read in the future. Contact us at www.sunrisepublishing.com/contact.

We also have a monthly update that contains sneak peeks, reviews, upcoming releases, and fun stuff for our reader friends.

As a treat for signing up, we'll send you a free novella written by Susan May Warren that kicks off the new Deep Haven Collection! Sign up at www.sunrisepublishing.com/free-prequel.

OTHER DEEP HAVEN NOVELS

Deep Haven Collection

Only You

Still the One

Can't Buy Me Love

Crazy for You

Then Came You

Hangin' by a Moment

Right Here Waiting

Deep Haven Series

Happily Ever After

Tying the Knot

The Perfect Match

My Foolish Heart

Hook, Line, & Sinker

You Don't Know Me

The Shadow of Your Smile

Christiansen Family Series

Evergreen

Take a Chance on Me

It Had to Be You

When I Fall in Love

Always on My Mind

The Wonder of You

You're the One That I Want

For other books by Susan May Warren, visit her website at
http://www.susanmaywarren.com.

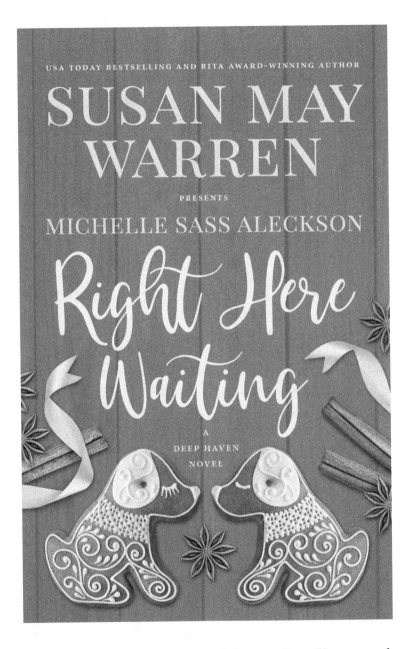

Turn the page for a sneak peek of the next Deep Haven novel,
Right Here Waiting ...

SNEAK PEEK

RIGHT HERE WAITING

Deep Haven in November was like a sad old man fighting for his life and losing. Nick Dahlquist might not be an old man at the ripe old age of thirty, but it was hard not to feel like one with his throbbing leg. He looked up at the bleak sky. Sunlight was hemorrhaging fast. What was left spilled over the ridge onto his hometown and the bay below. Soon darkness would swallow it too. The wind off Lake Superior bit at Nick's exposed ears. His thermal shirt and down vest did little to fight it off.

If November was going to be this cold, it could at least have the decency to throw a little snow down.

Because without snow, his sled team was stuck.

Kinda like his life.

And if he wanted to get out of this rut, he'd need a good foot or two of the white stuff soon. Then he could start training in earnest for the Mush Puppies dogsled race. Thanksgiving weekend would be here in just under four weeks and he and his dogs needed to be ready. Sponsors would be watching the first race of the season and if he had any hope of going back to the

Iditarod come March, Nick and his team had some convincing to do.

He released a long breath before yanking open the VFW door. The cheers and the smell of onion rings that used to beckon good times hit him in the face as he walked in.

These days he'd be okay if he never ate another VFW burger again. The flavor carried too many memories.

So why did he agree to meet Darek Christiansen here?

He walked farther in, and aside from the people seated at the bar, he counted five long tables arranged in two rows, each with a bell in the middle all set for Trivia Night. The seats were filled with familiar faces, familiar teams with names like The Facts & The Curious, Nerd Herd, the Smartinis, Les Quizerables, and his old team, which split off the Fellowship of the Quiz group when they grew too big to fit around one table. They were now the Huskaloosas named after their high school mascot. Chatter and laughter he once joined in grated on his nerves.

The Huskaloosas were missing a few players, but his cousin Peter was still there with his girlfriend Ronnie and her little brother, Tiago Morales. Beth Strauss and Lena Larson were at the table, Ree Zimmerman and Seth Turnquist had their heads together, but no one was scribbling names down. And of course, *they* were there. Also, together.

Nick watched Vivien Calhoun. Tall, willowy, brunette, blue eyes that dazzled on stage and a smile that turned him inside out. She looped her arm around Boone and tossed her hair back over her shoulder. Nick could practically smell her perfume. She turned her head toward him. He looked away before she caught him staring.

Nick should've insisted on meeting somewhere else. Or he could've ignored the resort owner entirely.

Well, not really. He could only ignore so many messages from a guy like Darek Christiansen. Especially with the news yesterday from Licks and Stuff saying they were pulling their sponsorship due to budget cuts. Nick couldn't afford to lose any more support. Not with the foreclosure notice he received today.

His eyes adjusted to the dim lighting and made out Darek's tall form and dark hair at a table in the back. The man wearing an Evergreen Resort hoodie dwarfed the blue plastic chair he sat in as he nursed a bottle of root beer. At least he sat as far as he could from the Trivia Night event. Nick tucked his head and scooched past his old team without anyone noticing.

Now it was show time. Nick plastered on a big grin. "Hey, Darek. You folks staying warm enough out there at the Evergreen?"

Darek set down his bottle. "Yeah, but can you believe this cold snap? Sure could use some snow cover before our septic systems freeze."

Nick nodded. "No kidding."

As soon as he sat down, their usual server, Melissa Ogden, approached in her typical tight jeans, short dark hair and a lot of makeup. He had played basketball with her older brother Anthony. But she must've been five or six years behind him in school.

"Hey, Nick. It's been a while. What can I get ya?"

"Just coffee."

Darek balked. "Coffee? Aren't you gonna eat?"

"Na, not hungry."

"Suit yourself." Darek turned to Melissa. "I'll take a double cheeseburger and fries. And another root beer." After she left, his attention swung back to Nick. "I suppose growing up in the restaurant biz, a simple burger doesn't cut it anymore, huh?"

That wasn't the case, but no need to get into it. Unlike Darek, Nick had no desire or skill to take over the family business. The thought of being stuck inside the hot kitchen of his parents' restaurant all day long almost suffocated him. "I'm not too picky most of the time. Just full tonight."

Darek stared for a beat. "You okay, Nick?"

Nick's smile must've slipped. He shored it back up. "I'm great."

"So what's up with the hair and beard? You trying to grow them out like Peter?"

"Which NFL Viking running back rushed two hundred and ninety-six yards in a single game his rookie season?" Mayor Seb Brewster asked the trivia players from the band stage on the other side of the room.

"Adrian Peterson. 2007," Nick mumbled into the mug of coffee Melissa set before him. He took a small sip of the steaming hot coffee. "I'm fine, Darek. Don't worry about me. So, what did you need to meet me about? You said it was urgent."

The big guy looked him in the eye with unwavering concern. "It is urgent. I'm worried about you. Wanted to see you for myself."

Nick forced out a chuckle. "I told you, I'm fine. You really called me down here to talk about my hair and my eating habits? What are we? A bunch of girls?"

But Darek's intense stare held no humor. "I don't think you are fine. Regardless of your hair, this time last year you had dogsledding adventures booked for every weekend in December, January, and February. This year you have one. One time slot. I've had guests call because they can't get a hold of you to schedule and your website needs to be updated with the new online booking program. That's not like you, Nick. Usually you're great with the guests. I mean you have like a million followers on Instagram. So, what's going on?"

Seb cut in with another trivia question. "Which character in the *Star Wars* movies is partially named after George Lucas's son?"

Duh. "Dexter Jettster."

"What?" Darek asked.

"Nothing." Nick sneaked a peek at his old team. Peter

shrugged. Ronnie wasn't even paying attention, and Seth and Ree were making puppy dog eyes at each other. They were clueless.

He faced Darek. "Hey, man, don't worry about me. I've just had a lot going on. I'm training hard and trying to get ready for the season." Everyone might think he was the joke of the town the way they plastered his failed attempts on the wall, every newspaper article a reminder of coming close and not quite making it, but he would show them. And, yes, he was a Dahlquist without a culinary degree or restaurant to run. But this was the year. He'd make his *own* legacy, grow his kennel into something impressive. And running the Iditarod was his ticket in.

"That's what you're doing hiding out in the woods? How do you train for dogsledding when there's no snow?"

One glance out the window showed the wind whipping a tattered flag out on Main Street and not a soul on the sidewalk. "You improvise. I have a wheeled cart I designed that I hook the dogs up to. It's not quite the same, but it helps. Sometimes I run them with the ATV."

"I understand you need to train, but you better find time to update your website and talk to your customers too. We have a deal. We sponsor you and you offer our guests their winter dogsled adventures. We both benefit from the advertising, right?"

Nick set down his mug. "I know our deal. I'll get the website updated. You can count on me."

"You turn in your Iditarod registration yet?" Darek waved to someone behind Nick.

"No. But I will."

If he could get the bank off his back *and* come up with the four-thousand-dollar registration fee. Although if he didn't run the Mush Puppies race at the end of the month it wouldn't matter because he wouldn't have his third qualifying race done.

And there would go his dream of actually finishing the Iditarod and being taken seriously as a full-time musher, the one dream he had left.

"In which film did James Bond drive a Ford Mustang?" Seb asked.

Nick whispered under his breath at the same time Daniel "Boone" Buckam shouted, "*Diamonds Are Forever.*"

Nick glanced at him. How was it the man was tan even in November? His dark blond hair was perfectly styled. His fleece pullover a shade of forest green Vivien always loved. She probably picked it out for him.

The team finally put some points on the board and cheered. Nick tried not to cringe as Boone swooped in for a victory kiss from Vivien.

He looked away. Nope, he never should've come here.

Nick gulped one last swallow of the bitter coffee and stood. "Look, Dare, I appreciate the concern, but it's not necessary. I'm just busy. I'll update the website and get caught up. Promise." He'd probably sell this whole charade and get the guy off his back if he sounded more like his old self, so he dug deep to find what he hoped was a lighthearted smirk. "I'll even shave and get my hair cut if it makes you feel better."

Nick turned to leave the table but only made it a step. He ran right into the woman haunting his dreams instead.

Vivien.

His radar must be off because usually he knew exactly where Vivie was in a room. Her wide blue eyes captured him. Her jasmine scent wrapped around him, almost strangling his breath. And, yes he smelled every perfume in the mall once to find which one she wore just so he could identify the scent.

But that was a long time ago. Back in the day when they would skip their last class and go ice-skating or play video games or make late-night burger runs when her cravings hit.

Yeah, he could admit it—he was a fool for whatever Vivie wanted.

Mostly because she was always up for his crazy ideas. She was the only one who didn't call him by that humiliating nickname after the fire. But also because she was the prettiest girl in the class.

Deep in the back of his mind, he'd always believed they were made for each other.

Apparently not.

Nick backed up and hit his shin on his chair. Pain shot up his leg. Darek chuckled, still sitting at the table, watching them.

Vivien laid a perfectly manicured hand on Nick's arm. A sparkling diamond ring on her delicate finger sent a shock wave straight to his heart.

"Nick, why aren't you sitting with the team? We haven't seen you in weeks. What happened to our Mr. Life of the Party?" Her gaze turned concerned.

There were a lot of things from Vivie he wanted. Her pity was not one of them.

He cleared his throat. "Sorry, Viv. I was just heading out. I've got some work to get caught up on. Gotta update the website and all." He bent down and rubbed his shin." Besides, I don't do trivia anymore."

She shook her head. "Don't do trivia—what are you talking about? You've done trivia every Monday night for the last fifteen years."

Darek speared him with a pointed look. "Yeah, and he knows all the answers too."

"And since when did you start growing a beard?" Vivie asked.

Nick shrugged. "Things change. No more trivia, and I don't shave anymore. I'm getting ready for the Iditarod."

Before Vivie could respond, the most unwanted change of all walked up to them. Boone slid an arm around her waist. "Do you want me to order you some more fries since you ate all mine?"

She shot him an almost believable expression of innocence. "I don't know what you're talking about. But you look like you want some onion rings. And a burger too. With extra pickles." She sent him off with a flirty wink and the unmistakable look of longing.

A longing Nick understood all too well.

This summer when Boone showed up, Nick kept hoping he would join Vivien's long list of two-week boyfriends. The few guys that stuck around more than two weeks were the relationships Nick had worried about over the years as he waited for her to leave New York City and come back home. When she finally did return to Deep Haven this summer, he took a cue from his cousin Peter. Watching what he and his girlfriend, Ronnie, had gave him the courage to take a chance and ask Vivie out.

And Vivien thought he was joking.

So he laughed it off too. Then Boone swept in and took the spotlight. The ring on her left hand and the sinking feeling in his gut said Nick had missed his chance forever. She obviously found her leading guy.

And it was time for Nick to bow out. Now.

He left with a wave and burst out the glass doors into the cold night. He jabbed his fingers through his unruly mop. The coffee roiled in his stomach and burned his throat.

What was he doing here?

Maybe he should leave. For good. Start over somewhere else.

And where might that be?

Hopping into his truck, he drove out of town and up the ridge to his cabin in the woods.

Sure, it was just a two-bedroom log cabin he built with his own hands. Nothing fancy, but he placed every rock on that stone chimney and fireplace. He designed and constructed both the custom-built Quonset dog kennel out back and another large shed off to the side. And it was all surrounded by a yard of towering pines, spruce, and other evergreens with a mix of birch and oak.

No. He couldn't leave this. He had miles of trail right outside his back door, perfect for training and outdoor adventure. He just needed to get over Vivien Calhoun and get on with his life. This was never the kind of life she wanted anyway. Deep down inside, he knew that.

He did one last check on the dogs and went inside. Kasha, his lead Alaskan husky met him at the door. She was a mix of gray and tan fur and had a drive to win that matched his own. Now that her leg was healed, she was anxious to be with the other dogs outside. He should probably board her with the rest of the pack now, but her presence helped fill a little of the hollowness that invaded his cabin this fall.

Nick called for Kasha to follow him to the brown leather couch by the fireplace. He stoked the fire and grabbed the jar of his special recipe salve off the mantel. The yellow ointment released an earthy resinous scent as he rubbed it on Kasha's leg. It had already helped heal the wound on her skin better than the stuff his previous vet gave him. The vitamin E and coconut oil mixed with shea butter and some frankincense and tea tree oils did wonders. And he needed Kasha in top form.

He scratched the dog behind her ear.

"We just need a little snow, huh, girl? Then we can get back on the trail. Shake this funk off."

She licked his hand and lay on her rug by the door, not convinced of anything he had to say.

That was it though, right? He'd get over Vivien and find a reason to laugh again eventually. He just needed some fresh powder, and the trail would bring him back to life like it always had.

But Darek was right. At this point he couldn't afford to keep ignoring his emptying bank account. He needed to fill those winter bookings if he was going to have the money to pay back his loan in time. And feeding almost thirty dogs was not cheap, even if eight of them were puppies.

Nick walked over to his kitchen counter. The bank notice lay on the counter. He picked it up and scanned it once more. Sixty days. He had two months to come up with the loan amount or they were taking the house. The kennels. The property. Everything. He threw it back down on the kitchen counter and picked up his laptop from the coffee table.

Tonight, he had to get that program updated. Darek sent him the instructions that would update the scheduling program and connect it with the Evergreen Resort website. He opened the link he needed, but the single-spaced instructions read like a foreign language. After he read the same line five times and still didn't understand it, he released a grunt and fisted the hair at his temple. It wasn't the program that was the problem.

He couldn't get that diamond ring on Vivie's hand out of his head. It winked at him, mocked him. He should just toss the laptop into the fire along with the Iditarod registration now and save himself the heartache.

A ping alerted him to a private message. He opened up the app and read.

LadyJHawk: *Hey, loyal fans are beginning to wonder if you're lost on the planet Hoth. Should we send Luke and Han out on the tauntauns to find you? ;)*

The *Star Wars* reference about the furry snow creatures brought a smile to his lips. A real one he didn't have to manufacture for appearances. His fingers typed out a response.

NixDogQuest: *Nah. Don't want the Empire to find my hideout.*

LadyJHawk: *For real, you okay? Haven't heard from you in a while.*

For some reason when JHawk asked, the question didn't wrangle so much. Chatting with her over the last couple of years they'd developed an online friendship. It was easier to open up to someone he was never going to see. Not in real life anyway. And she probably deserved something after a few days of silence.

NixDogQuest: *Just busy. Thanks for checking. How is C doing?*

Kasha barked, needing to go out one more time.

"Oh sure. Now you need to go outside? Just when I have a woman who actually wants to talk to me?"

Kasha barked again.

"Okay, okay. I'm coming." He would come back to the chat later. He closed the laptop and stepped out onto his front porch in his thermal shirt and jeans. Kasha sniffed around and didn't go far to do her business.

Nick stuffed more logs in the outdoor wood boiler and trudged back to the deck with Kasha on his heels. The darkness of the night closed in around them. A sharp gust of wind kicked up, rattling the branches of the bare oak tree next to the deck and carrying the howl of a distant wolf. Leaning on the railing Nick released a long breath.

I could really use some snow, Lord.

He looked up at the moonless sky.

Stars.

No clouds. No precipitation. No snow. Just dim stars resembling diamonds all looking down and laughing at him.

ACKNOWLEDGMENTS

What a wild ride writing this book has been! Sometimes going full tilt, and sometimes hanging moment by moment. I'm filled with gratitude for all the people who came along for the journey.

Susie, Lindsay, Rel, and the rest of the Sunrise team were their usual impressive selves. Seriously, gals, you're the best. Encouraging, supportive, approachable, and all-around amazing. I love working with you. Let's do this again!

A shoutout to Rachel and Michelle, my intrepid fellow Deep Haven Authors. Without the two of you, I would have been hopelessly lost. Thank you for cheering me on every time I needed it, which was always. Just keep swimming!

A thousand thanks to Nikki Christenson, my sister-in-law. She read through many of the nursing pieces and cleaned up my language and descriptions of the procedures. Any mistakes or misrepresentations are all my own. Thanks for your help, Nikki!

Eric, Macy, and Anna, thanks for being my brainstorming partners, my naming helpers, and my chocolate fetchers. This book wouldn't exist without your support and I am grateful for that support every day. You three are awesome and I'm glad you are my family.

ABOUT THE AUTHORS

 USA Today bestselling, RITA, Christy and Carol award-winning novelist **Susan May Warren** is the author of over 80 novels, most of them contemporary romance with a touch of suspense. One of her strongest selling series has been the Deep Haven series, a collection of books set in Northern Minnesota, off the shore of Lake Superior. Visit her at www.susanmaywarren.com.

 **Andrea Christenson** lives in Western Wisconsin with her husband and two daughters. When she is not busy homeschooling her girls, she loves to read anything she can get her hands on, bake bread, eat cheese, and watch Netflix—though not usually all at the same time. Andrea's prayer is to write stories revealing God's love. Visit her at www.andreachristenson.com.

Hangin' By a Moment: A Deep Haven Novel

Published by Sunrise Media Group LLC

Copyright © 2021 by Susan May Warren and Andrea Christenson

All rights reserved. No part of this publication may be reproduced or transmitted in any form or by any means without written permission of the publisher.

This book is a work of fiction. Names, characters, places, and incidents are either products of the author's imagination or used fictitiously. Any similarity to actual people, organizations, and/or events is purely coincidental.

Scripture quotations are taken from the Holy Bible, New Living Translation, copyright ©1996, 2004, 2015 by Tyndale House Foundation. Used by permission of Tyndale House Publishers, Carol Stream, Illinois 60188. All rights reserved.

Scripture quotations are also from The ESV® Bible (The Holy Bible, English Standard Version®), copyright © 2001 by Crossway, a publishing ministry of Good News Publishers. Used by permission. All rights reserved.

For more information about Andrea Christenson and Susan May Warren, please access the authors' websites at the following respective addresses: www.andreachristenson.com and www.susanmaywarren.com.

Published in the United States of America.

Cover Design: Jenny at Seedlings Designs

Editing: Barbara Curtis

CPSIA information can be obtained
at www.ICGtesting.com
Printed in the USA
BVHW031723180222
629490BV00003B/19

9 781953 783103